MOST PERFECT THINGS ABOUT PEOPLE

Beally Family tree

Dustin — Audrey

Trigger — Sherri

Carver | Quinlynn Minster | Birdie

Me

Hermia

Tony — Jane

Kirby ???
no name yet
its a feetus

By: Soccer Beally
1991

1

Our family used to live in the basement apartment of a four-story semi-detached in Port Woodlot, Ontario. Soccer and me shared a room close to the back. It had four walls with old pinkish wallpaper peeling off, and a long, narrow window close to the ceiling. There was also a queen-sized mattress Soccer and me shared, and a small cabinet where we kept things like clothes, or random junk, like marbles and the pocketknife.

Soccer was my little brother. He was two years younger than me, but looked even younger than that. I mean the kid had the chubbiest baby cheeks you'd ever seen in your life, all rosy and round, like fleshy jell-o blobs stuck to the sides of his face. He was a scrappy kid too. Little hands constantly clenched into little fists. Soccer loved punching things, particularly people. I remember this one time he socked our sister Quinlynn in the cheekbone for no good reason, gave her a purple eye. So Dad dragged Soccer into the furnace room after that and beat the piss out of him for a good five minutes, the sound of the belt slapping Soccer's ass like a hardcover book slamming shut. Soccer came back to the bedroom after with his eyes and cheeks all shiny, and he was wiping snot off his lips with the back of his wrist. You okay? I asked him. He nodded, then walked right up to me and punched me square in the nose, made it bleed all over my lap. Why'd you do that? I asked him, but he didn't answer, just stood there laughing, so I laughed too a little, bleeding. It's crazy, but you couldn't ever stay mad at the kid. He was just one of those people, the kind you wanted to be forgiving all the time.

We used to walk to the bus stop together, only a block from our house, but Mom still made me promise to hold his hand the whole way there. Soccer was six and I was eight, and Mom didn't want him getting hit by a truck, or raped by a perv or something. Anyways, I hated holding his hand. It was always wet and sticky no matter what, like he'd just dipped it in a jar of honey. I'd ask him why his hands were so sticky, but he'd mostly just ignore me. Like he never talked much. He hummed though, songs from that Disney version of Peter Pan, the one where Peter's got a knife instead of a sword. That was Soccer's favorite movie. I remember one year he even dressed as Peter for Halloween, while I was Captain Hook. But Soccer kept stabbing all the neighborhood kids in the butt and balls with his cardboard dagger; they'd been saying we were poor, having homemade costumes and all. Mom made us go home early when Soccer refused to cut it out.

So we weren't millionaires, but it's not like we were a bunch of dirty hobos neither. I mean Dad had a decent enough job. He was in charge of the tools department at a store called Home Repair. He'd been there as long as I can remember, ever since I was born, working the same eight to five shift, five days a week, or sometimes six, wearing that same grey uniform, steel-toed boots, black socks and digital watch, and a name tag that said *Trig* because his boss thought his full name was too violent.

Mom on the other hand hadn't had a job in years. It's not because she was a lazy fat-ass or nothing, but because she's a religious idiot who doesn't believe in birth control. Like both my parents are only in their early thirties now, still young I guess, but they've already had five kids, six if you include Soccer, and I can pretty much guarantee more will be on the way eventually, after they get back together and all. But I was the first. Mom was seventeen when she had me, and had to quit high school, and her job at Little Caesars, but it didn't matter much back then because it was just the three of us—Mom, Dad, me—so we could afford it. But then Soccer was born a couple years later, and Quinlynn after that, and then the dumb twins, Minster and Hermia, and finally, Birdie, who's still just a baby because Mom only had her a couple years back, the same year Soccer disappeared. So Mom's been basically looking after babies half her life now, which is pretty crazy when you really stop and think about it, like a big responsibility for just one frizzy-haired lady, trying to make sure all us kids don't grow up to be assholes, teaching us about God and consequences, and about how to be good people, and everything else important in life.

Sometimes I'd see Soccer at recess at school. He'd usually be playing by himself, maybe throwing a tennis ball against the wall, whipping it hard like he was trying to put holes in the bricks. Or other times he'd be throwing other things, like sticks, small rocks, whatever he could find, dead birds and bigger rocks, until a teacher eventually came over and yelled at him to stop.

One day I saw Soccer standing near the swings on the playground, and this old lady teacher named Mrs. Flemberger was yelling at him in her annoying Newfie accent, and she was wagging her ugly finger in front of his face like he was a bad dog. I went over to see what was happening and Mrs. Flemberger told me Soccer had cut off a girl's ponytail with a pair of scissors and tossed it in a puddle. She showed me the ponytail lying there in the dirty water. It looked like a dead snake. Mrs. Flemberger had been in the middle of lecturing Soccer about the dangers of scissors, and how important a girl's hair is, and she was really letting him have it, probably trying to make him cry, but he didn't. The school did phone our parents though. He got in big trouble. Mom said he wasn't allowed to watch *Peter Pan* for an entire two months, and Dad took away the box of army men, and melted a ton of them on the grill even though like half of them were mine.

A couple years after that I was ten, in grade five, and got my first girlfriend, the beak-nosed Rachel Perkins. She ran cross-country, and also played on the girls' volleyball team. I went to see one of their games after school. This is before Rachel was my girlfriend. Her coach kept yelling at her because she was sliding on her kneepads every ten seconds. Keep on your feet! he was saying. I swear to God, Perkins! You'll be the death of me if you don't start keeping on your damn two bloody feet!

It was funny because Rachel Perkins basically started crying right there on the court. Her face scrunched all red and gross-looking, and she kept saying, I hate you all, I hate you. Everyone was laughing pretty hard, and my best friend Daniel even tried throwing the rest of his Ring Pop at her head, but missed.

One day I was sitting at my desk, when Rachel's cross-eyed friend Bethany Freeman approaches during indoor recess. She gives me a note that says *do you like rachel? yes or maybe (circle one)*. I looked over at Rachel, and she was pretending not to look back, chewing her lip to keep from smiling, but she was basically smiling, and all of a sudden her beak nose didn't seem so beaky. I circled *yes*.

We never kissed on the lips or held hands, but Rachel Perkins did hug me a couple times, and sometimes she'd even sit beside me on the bleachers near the softball diamond, lean her head on my shoulder and breathe slow, and my penis would tingle like crazy until she sat back up again.

She gave me three candy canes for Christmas that year, and a dreidel because she knew Dad's Jewish, and I drew her a picture of a skeleton riding a pig-faced dragon. She kissed my cheek and said, Merry Christmas and Happy Hanukkah, Carver, and my penis was spazzing out. I basically had to go home right after and rub myself against the corner of the mattress forever. Soccer kept asking what I was doing, but I just told him to shut his fat face and mind his business.

Soccer and Quinlynn got pretty close around that time. He was eight and she was six, so now it was his turn to be holding some little kid's hand on the way to the bus.

A lot of the time though, they'd be with Eddie too. He was an only child who lived in the house above our basement. He was eight like Soccer, this long-limbed ginger kid who kept a toy gun tucked inside the waist of his sweatpants. The attic room of his house had a balcony overlooking the backyard, so Soccer and Quinlynn used to go up there to drop parachute men off the ledge, while Eddie stood aiming his gun from the grass below.

Since Quinlynn was old enough to go to school now, I'd usually see her playing with Soccer at recess. They'd build snow forts in the winter, roll boulders until they had enough to surround themselves with. Nobody was allowed inside their forts except Eddie, but Soccer did tell me the password was Robin Hood Riding Through the Glen in case I ever decided I wanted to join.

One day at recess Soccer climbed on top one of the boulders, pulled his pants down and started pissing in the snow, trying to spell the word KOALA, which was Quinlynn's favorite animal, only he ran out of piss halfway through the L. Rachel Perkins told me about it. She said she saw it happen, and it was her first time seeing a penis other than her dog's, and she was asking a ton of questions about it, wanting to know if mine looked as weird as Soccer's.

The school called our house again. They told our parents about the piss, so Soccer got punished, no TV for a week, and Dad even broke the *Peter Pan* tape we had, pulling all the film out of its plastic shell, and crumpling it in his hands, and chucking the ball at Soccer. But Soccer didn't seem to mind. Like he hardly ever watched that stupid movie anymore.

I remember our family was struggling pretty badly around that time as well. Dad had to ask Uncle Tony and Aunt

Jane for money, which he hated having to do. Complained about it nonstop for months after. And I think he was suffering some kind of depression too, because if he wasn't complaining, he'd stop talking altogether, even to Mom, and paid less and less attention to the twins as well, who were two then, and basically his favorite kids out of all of us. He'd get home late from work, eat cold dinner, then leave again, not coming back until one or two in the morning. Soccer and me would wake to the sound of him coming in the door and kicking his boots onto the mat. Mom asking where he'd been, but he'd just grunt and go to bed.

Rachel Perkins broke up with me a few months after we started going out. She got her friend Bethany to give me a note that said *i don't want to be your girlfriend anymore. i like dylan mcguire instead.* The note pretty much meant the end of the world, so I ran to the creek behind the grocery store plaza, lay flat on my stomach and dipped my face in the stream, swallowing as much water as possible because I figured it was dirty, and would poison me, and I would die.

I didn't die though, just got really sick. It felt like sharp rocks scratching the insides of my belly, and also, I kept having diarrhea. Mom was at church with the twins, and Soccer and Quinlynn were playing with Eddie in the house above us, and Dad was watching *Who's the Boss?* on TV. I came out of the washroom and lay on the other couch across from him. Curled my legs against my body and lay on my side, holding my stomach. Dad didn't notice, so I started moaning.

What you moaning like that for?

My tummy hurts.

Tummy?

I drank dirty creek water.

Well why'd you do that for?

Rachel Perkins broke up with me.

Perkins?

My girlfriend.

Since when you got a girlfriend?

I don't anymore.

Course. Well quit whining, Carve. I'm trying to watch this stupid thing.

I was so angry, I ran outside and broke the mailbox beside the Hendersons' front door. Murray Henderson saw me do it through his window, so he came over afterwards and told Dad we had to pay for it. Dad dragged me into the furnace room after that. He whipped me with his belt about a million times, and I was crying, not so much because of the belt, but because Rachel Perkins didn't like me anymore, and also, my stomach was still hurting like hell.

Later I showed Soccer the lines on my ass and back, and he told me some of them were bleeding a little, and others looked like a tic-tac-toe game. He asked if Dad used the brown belt or the green one with the snaky designs, but I wasn't sure. Soon Quinlynn came in the room, dressed in her footed pajamas with the white horses galloping all over the sleeves. The three of us sat in a triangle on the floor and played Jenga for a while. It wasn't much fun though, because Soccer kept getting bored and knocking the blocks down on purpose.

Mom got pregnant again a couple years later, and had Birdie in the fall, right after the new school year began. Quinylnn and the twins were looking forward to having a new sister, but Soccer and me were fed up with babies by then.

We sat in the waiting room with Uncle Tony while Mom pushed Birdie out, and then Dad came and got us, and we all went inside to see the stupid baby, but it wasn't too exciting because she looked the exact same as Quinlynn and the twins had all looked, just this bald, clammy little thing with a bunch of yellow crud in her eyes.

Dad needed to start working six days a week after Birdie, longer hours each day. On Sundays off he'd go out for breakfast, either by himself, or sometimes take the twins, and then come home and nap for the afternoon. So we didn't see much of him during that time. But sometimes I'd go see him at work, because Daniel and me liked getting hotdogs from a cart outside Home Repair. The vendor was this blotchy old guy named Lou. He gave Daniel and me pop for twenty-five cents while everyone else had to pay fifty.

One time we were sitting on the curb in front of Lou's cart, and Dad came outside to help a customer load a gazebo onto the back of a truck. When he saw me sitting there, all the lines on his forehead turned in, his eyebrows pointed sharp at his long nose.

Carve, he said as he came over.

I'm eating a hotdog, I said.

Where'd you get the money? he said.

Daniel gets allowance, I said.

No skateboards, he said, because Daniel was sitting on one.

You want pop? I said.

Where's your brother?

At church with Mom and the kids.

Your mother's got her hands full, he said. You gotta quit coming here and start helping. Go be with Soccer, Carve. Scram.

Daniel and me said bye to Lou and then walked down the backstreets behind the store, the streets with all those houses that aren't semis or townhouses. There was a white car in front of one, and I didn't know much about cars then, but I knew it looked expensive, so I poured the rest of my pop all over the back windshield, then spit on the trunk.

Your dad's a jerk, said Daniel.

Yeah, I agreed. He's a stupid motherfucker.

There was a dance at my school later in the fall. I was in grade seven, so it was my first dance, and that's where I met my second girlfriend, Aja Mistry. She had black hair and brown skin and the tiniest hands you'd ever seen, fingers the size of worn-down pencils. She was in the grade above mine, thirteen years old, a teenager.

I'd been standing against the wall with Daniel when she walked up during that LL Cool J song about needing love, reached her hand out, and it looked so small and so harmless, I couldn't help but grab hold. She pulled me onto the basketball court, started wobbling with me, and I guess we were dancing. Our feet teeter-tottering real stupidly. My head was close to her shoulder. I wanted to bite it. I wanted to kiss her on the lips, and then bite her lips and shoulders. She smelled good, real clean, like maybe she'd showered recently.

Quinlynn started getting bullied that same season. I didn't see it, but Soccer told me kids had been giving her a hard time for wearing boy clothes to school, like hand-me-downs from Soccer and me, and also, a couple of those same little bastards had been making fun of the way her forehead looked. When Quinlynn was littler and got chickenpox, she dug nails under the pox to pick them off her skin, mostly her forehead, so now she's got all these little dots scarred above her eyebrows. Soccer told me this one kid, Joey Sission, kept calling her Crater Face. It got me so angry I could've exploded and died. I made a stupid mistake then, and told Soccer to fight Sission the next time he saw the kid being mean to our sister. Soccer grinded his fist against the palm of his hand, nodding like crazy.

Probably less than a week later Soccer got suspended for punching Sission in the face eight times, one hit for every syllable of Don't call my sister Crater Face, knocking two of Sission's adult teeth out. The school called our house for the hundredth time. Dad wrestled Soccer into the furnace room and whipped the piss and shit out of him, literally. Like they were in there for a good half hour, maybe more, and I could tell by the sound the belt made that Soccer's pants and underwear were pulled down.

When Mom realized the beating was going to last longer than usual, she decided to take Birdie and the twins to the park. All four of them were crying as they left, and Quinlynn was crying too, so I brought her outside and we walked around the semi to the back. It was windy, and the grass was covered in shriveled leaves. We sat down on a couple piles of bricks. They were back there because

Eddie's parents had started building a path from the back door to their vegetable garden. The bricks were pink like the lox at the bakery where Aunt Jane used to work, and not very comfortable to sit on.

Quinlynn stopped crying eventually, started licking the snot off her upper lip, and I thought about how she was too young to be feeling so sad. I told her she was pretty, and that the scars on her forehead were pretty too, because they made her different, and imperfections were the most perfect things about people sometimes. Then I farted so she'd laugh, but the fart came out silent.

The back door opened. Eddie came out. He'd shaved his head around that time, so the baldness mixed with his pastiness made him look sick and dying.

Does your dad know we can hear him through the vents? he asked us. My mum thinks it's real wrong, hitting kids the way your dad does.

Eddie was ten now, the same age as Soccer, but he still kept that toy gun tucked inside his pants. I told him to shoot me. He pulled the gun out, aimed and fired. I fell off the bricks and onto the leaves, all of them crunching under me, making my neck itch. Quinlynn told Eddie to shoot her too. Another loud snap. She dropped beside me, laughing so hard she snorted. Her forehead crinkled so you could hardly see the scars anymore.

I lay on my back and stared at the sky for a little while, but there was nothing much up there. I pressed on my elbows, angled myself so I could see the top of the house, the balcony on the fourth floor where Soccer and Quinlynn used to drop the parachute men from, and I thought about how Soccer's face had looked, eyes and mouth opened gigantic as he'd lean over the railing to watch them fall.

Dad shaved his beard for the first time since his final year of high school. Mom thought this meant he was having an affair. She accused him one night after a rare family dinner, right in front of Soccer and me as we cleared the table. Dad denied it, but Mom refused to believe him. Pretty soon she was yelling. But it was practically to herself because Dad wasn't saying much back at her. He just sat there at the table, staring at the dirty plates in front of him, the ones we still hadn't taken away. So Mom kept yelling, and eventually Dad picked up a fork and squeezed it. I got nervous he might try to stab her, because if he did, all the kids would see and they'd probably have nightmares forever.

Dad let go of the fork. He picked up a knife.

Mom was standing at the sink, and Quinlynn and the twins were in the TV area, and Soccer and me were next to the fridge, and I could tell Soccer was trying not to laugh. Mom demanded to know where Dad went at night and on Sunday mornings, and when he didn't answer, she stomped over to the plate cupboard and opened the door just so she could slam it back shut. Dad continued to sit there and not say anything, just stared at the knife in his hand. I walked over to Quinlynn and told her to take the twins to the bedroom. Soccer poured himself a glass of grape juice. Mom started talking about how she knew her body wasn't the same after having so many kids, but that it wasn't her fault, it was God's way, and Dad kept sitting there, shaking his head, but barely, and at one point he whispered, I'm tired. He got up and put his boots on and left without saying goodbye or telling anyone where he was going, like always. He didn't slam the door.

Mom told Soccer and me to go get Quinlynn and the twins, and then all of us gathered in Mom's bedroom in the cramped space between the bed and Birdie's crib. She made us close our eyes and pray, and thank God for food and shelter, and for each other. By then I was already old enough to know most of what Mom believed in was crazy bullshit, so I wasn't thinking much about God while we were in there. I was mostly thinking about running away from home, maybe with Soccer, or Aja, wondering what size and color Aja's nipples were.

After awhile the twins got restless, so Mom brought them to bed, and then returned and made Soccer, Quinlynn and me perform trust exercises with each other. She had us stand and take turns falling backwards into each other's arms. Eventually it was my turn to fall into Quinlynn's arms, but I didn't want to because I was too heavy for her. But Mom told me to fall because we needed to learn to fall into one another, whatever the hell that meant. So I told her she was acting like a retarded lunatic, and left the room to go watch *Doogie Howser M.D.* I could hear Mom crying, so I turned the volume all the way up and it was practically blasting, and then Quinlynn and Soccer came to join me. We were going to make popcorn but the popcorn maker was broken, so we watched TV without popcorn, until Dad came back, and told us to hurry the hell to bed, and we did.

That was the last time we were together as a family, because a couple days later was the last time any of us saw Soccer. It was a Friday evening, close to the end of

November, but the weather wasn't too bad yet. No snow or rain, not even wind, and I remember because we'd all worn sweaters to school that day and left our jackets at home.

Dad was out that evening, and Mom was in her bedroom with the twins and Birdie and the door was closed. I'd invited Aja to come over, so the two of us were in the TV area, seated so close we were touching hips. She wore a knitted sweater with a big blue A on it, and her lips were red and smelled like red candy.

There was a knock at the door, Eddie checking to see if Soccer and Quinlynn wanted to go play in the backyard. So the three of them went back there and it was just Aja and me, the two of us alone on the couch. I think the Hulk Hogan/Undertaker rerun was on, but neither of us was paying much attention to it. She looked at me, and her mouth made the whitest smile I'd ever seen, teeth shining the same as bright colors at a glow-in-the-dark mini putt. She asked if I'd ever done anything sexual, and I nodded, even though the closest I'd ever come to sex was when Rachel Perkins kissed me on the cheek.

Aja said she'd sucked on Bret Bastian's penis at a party the previous summer, but it was only for a few seconds and no semen got in her mouth. I already knew about it because everyone knew about it, and I told her I didn't care. After that she started rubbing my crotch, like moving her palm against the outside of my pants along the zipper. It hurt at first, but then the pain started to feel good, and I was smiling because I was so happy, and she got pissed and told me to take things more seriously.

Later I waited with her on the front steps in front of the house above us. It'd gotten colder out, and the moon was full and bright white, like a big spotlight, shining big and bright on no one but us. Her dad pulled up in front of the walkway. I asked Aja if she liked me a lot, or only a little, and she told me that some guys are babes, while others are just cute, and while I'm only one of the cute ones right now, not to worry too much, because one day I might be a babe. Then she skipped down the walkway and got in the car, which was jet black and didn't have any back doors. I waited on the steps, hoping she'd look out her window and smile and wave, but she only looked.

I went around the house to see what the kids were up to. It was dark back there, only a single bulb above the door that led into Eddie's kitchen. A body lay in the glow of the light, with arms and legs sprawled on the grass, all of them not moving in a very scary way. I ran to the body to see who it was, but the body didn't have a proper face because the face was broken and bloody and one part caved in.

There was a brick beside the body, dark brown smeared across a corner of it. I threw up. I also pissed myself like a pansy. The piss ran down my legs, it felt warm and cold at once. There was a toy gun tucked inside the body's sweatpants.

I ran inside Eddie's house, his parents were in the living room, Evening, Carver, his mom called to me.

I sprinted up the first flight of stairs, down the hall and up a second flight. I kept burping because my body wanted to puke more, but there was nothing left to come out. I ran into the attic room, out the door and onto the balcony. Quinlynn was bunched in a corner, her arms wrapped around her legs, her body ball-shaped and shaking non-stop.

Where is he? I asked, but she didn't say anything, just sat there squeezing herself. I looked over the railing and saw Eddie's faceless face looking back and I burped again.

Is Eddie hurt? she said, still not looking. She had her eyes pressed against her knees.

Where's Soccer? I said. Where'd he go?

He threw the brick not thinking it'd hit him but it hit him, she said.

Go home, Quinlynn. Go out the front.

I ran. Stairs. More stairs. Eddie's hurt in the backyard, I yelled as I ran past the living room and back out the sliding glass door and past the body and over to the shed.

Zach Wagman from next door told me later that Eddie's mom Sylvia completely lost her shit when she saw it, started cursing God and Jesus, while kneeled beside Eddie, touching his face like she was trying to put it back together with her hands.

My board was useless because one of the axles had busted, so I had to run. I ran in the direction of the main street where everything was, the buses and cars, because I thought that's where Soccer might be, trying to get away from what he'd done.

I passed the elementary school. There was a man sitting in the dark on one of the benches out front, and the man was Dad. He wore his jean jacket, one hand tucked inside a pocket, the other holding a cigarette. I stopped running. He stopped smoking. We looked at each other for a moment, and in that moment hatred poured into my body like lava, and I burned, and I swear to God I could've gone over there and killed him. He stood, started walking towards me, but I remembered I'd pissed myself and didn't want him to smell it. So I ran again, down the street, the main street, the backstreets, everywhere. I searched forever, but never found him.

Eddie's funeral happened a week later. Mom thought the body might scare the kids, so she waited with them in the hall while Dad and me lined up with everyone else. It felt like all the other people there were staring at us, burning holes in our bodies with blame and bullshit thoughts about Soccer. When it was our turn to look at Eddie, Dad put his hand on my shoulder and the two of us stood there like father and son.

They'd fixed Eddie's face, but not entirely, because it looked like a face, but the face wasn't Eddie's. It was more powdery, and hard-looking, like if a brick got dropped on it now, it'd be the brick that broke.

Eddie's dad Harry stood beside the casket with his hands folded in front of him, chin tucked to his chest. Dad walked over and put his hand on Harry's arm. So I stood in front of the casket alone for a minute. Stared at Eddie's lanky body and weird face. The bridge of his nose was too thin, his bottom lip too big. The skin on his face like the surface of the white rocks in the garden at school. He'd lost a lot of freckles too. And there was no toy gun poking out the front of his goddamn stupid sweatpants, just a nice tucked in shirt I'd never seen him wear when he was living.

They started putting pictures of Soccer on light poles around town, and in the windows of pizza shops, grocery stores, the bakery, other places. A picture of him was even shown on the news, and Mom got interviewed, and everyone at school was talking about it.

One day Rachel Perkins came up to me during middle recess. She was wearing pink earmuffs and a pink jacket and pink boots, and her cheeks and nose were pink too because of the cold. I'm sorry about your brother, she said, but, well, like, did he really murder Eddie Price? I didn't answer. She asked if I wanted some nibs because she had an entire pack of them, and I took one, but then whipped it in the snow, gave Rachel Perkins the middle finger and ran. I ran inside the school, into the boy's washroom, kicked open a stall. I unzipped my pants and pissed all over the toilet seat and floor, and even on the roll of toilet paper. Then I took out my pocketknife and carved *fuck u* in jumbo letters on the wall.

A month after Soccer disappeared there was a Christmas party at a kid named Allen Stager's house, in his unfinished basement, with its hard floors and walls that weren't there. I only got invited because Aja was invited. There were bowls of Cheetos and cans of orange pop, and everyone's mouths were orange too. Eventually we played spin the bottle, and Allen's bottle pointed to Aja, who was wearing a white dress with red polka dots, and they kissed with their tongues, eyes wide open so they were staring at each other from only an inch away. I picked up the bottle and tried smashing it against the ground, but it didn't break because it was plastic. Allen Stager still got pretty pissed though, asking me, What's the deal, Carver?

Everyone was staring at me the same way people did at Eddie's funeral. I started walking backwards, towards the door that led upstairs. I called them all a bunch of stupid asshole white crackers, only it didn't make sense because I'm white, and also, Jason Tam and Charlotte Lorvell were both there, and Jason is Asian and Charlotte is half-Asian, and also-also, Aja was there too, and she's brown.

I didn't bother calling Dad for a ride home, not that he would've come. I walked down the main street. The sidewalks were covered in slush. The heels of my shoes were broken, so the weight and wetness got inside them, soaking my socks, making everything squish.

There was a picture of Soccer taped to one of the bus stops. It was torn, the paper soaked through from snow, ink-smudged, Soccer's face a blur.

His name was still readable though, but not Beally, our last name, the letters blended.

So according to the poster he was Soccer. One word, and nothing more.

Yesterday I turned fourteen. Mom bought me a cake with caramel syrup and cookie crumbs sprinkled all over. The twins wanted to blow the candles out, so I let them. Grandma asked what they wished for, and they looked at each other, and Hermia said cancer medicine for Phoebe, her doll, while Minster just sat there staring quietly at the smoke.

Dad said he'd probably call, but by eleven he still hadn't, and I was getting tired, lying there in bed with the phone on the pillow beside my head, fighting sleep, and losing.

We don't really talk much about Soccer anymore, but every now and then I'll be with Quinlynn, either playing a board game, or maybe watching her draw a picture of him, and she'll ask if I think he's dead, or been raped and tortured by crazy people like Paul Bernardo on the TV. I normally shrug because I honestly don't know the answers to those questions, and Quinlynn shrugs too, even though I haven't asked her anything. Then she'll ask if I think Soccer's gone to hell, assuming he's dead, since he killed Eddie and all, and it was on purpose, debatably, but I don't know how to answer that question neither because I'm not sure I believe in hell.

Quinlynn's ten now, the same age Soccer was when he disappeared. The twins are six, and Birdie's two. We all live with Grandma Currie in Aurora, a suburb south of Port Woodlot. Mom serves at the chicken wing place on Wellington, and Grandma takes care of Birdie in the day, and sometimes Dad will pick us up on weekends, and I'm almost as tall as he is now. Also, I've been lifting weights at my new high school.

It's stupid, but last night I was thinking about the future, about being an old man, like seventy-five, hunched and wrinkled. My parents will be dead by then of course, and my siblings will either be dead too, or old like me. I imagine myself walking down the street. I don't know where I'm going, but all of a sudden I run into Soccer. Only Soccer isn't old like the rest of us. He's still ten, with curly hair and chubby cheeks and fists for hands. He tells me he's been in Neverland this entire time living with Peter Pan. He tells me I can come back with him, fly to Neverland and be young forever. But it's too late. I'm already old. So he turns to leave, but before he does I tell him some things. I tell him he's my little brother and I love him and I miss him. I miss you, Soccer. And maybe he tells me he loves me too, and that I was a good big brother, and he forgives me for not watching him more closely that night the brick fell on Eddie. He tells me I was only a kid, and that we were all only kids.

I moved my hand, checked to see if the phone was still there. The finger holes felt cold as I turned the dial in the dark, once, twice, a third time, and stopped, hung up, pushed the phone off my bed and onto the carpet. I fell asleep to the sound of the dial tone.

2

He used to sit at the corner booth in the smoking section. Every Sunday morning, rain or blizzard or shine, he'd show. Sat there with a cigarette on his lips, reading the paper. Drank his coffee black. Sometimes he'd order toast, jam, maybe eggs and sausage, but mostly just coffee. I'd pour him up to eight cups during the time he was there. Never thanked me once, neither. Just sat there, giving a smile that wasn't much a smile, then turned back to his paper. He tipped lousy, too.

The other ladies thought he was handsome. Angry-looking, but handsome. That's how Patti put it. She'd serve him sometimes when the place got crazy and I couldn't make it back to his table every two seconds. He doesn't got a ring, she said. You ever notice, Connie? Angry-Handsome's got no ring.

He looked around my age, thirty or so, but his eyes appeared older. Tired the same way my daddy's were. Bloodshot, and glassy, surrounded by browned, puffy skin. He was constantly rubbing them. I wanted to tell him to stop, that maybe he'd shed a few years if he'd only quit touching them. But it wasn't my place saying such things. I mostly kept quiet. Ma was always telling me to keep quiet, and mind my business. If only you'd mind your business, Ma'd say, maybe you'd quit getting in so much trouble. Ma hated trouble. It's the reason she kept threatening to kick me out come winter, saying a lady my age oughta learn to behave and exist on her own.

He'd been coming to the diner about six months when one Sunday he seemingly failed to show. So I ended up seating others at the corner booth, a couple of seniors with hair coming out their ears. You see the hairs on the old timers' ears? I asked Patti.

Hairs? she said. She was hardly listening. She was calculating something on a receipt, and then she was asking, Did you see your man?

What?

Your man. Angry-Handsome. Did you see him?

Wish you wouldn't call him that, I said. *My man,* I mean.

She pointed across the diner, at the corner opposite his usual spot. He was seated in the non-smoking section now, across from a couple little kids, a boy and a girl. I asked Patti what the deal was, but she didn't know. Old Marge's table, she said. She rolled the receipt pointy like a spliff and tucked it in her breast pocket.

I found Old Marge in the kitchen. She was leaned against the sandwich counter, picking dead skin off the palm of her hand. Marge, I said. My voice sounded a lot louder than usual. It rebounded off the stainless steel. Can I ask you something?

Ngh, she said.

What's the deal with the man at the corner booth? I said. The one seated with the cuties.

What about him?

What's the deal?

Deal with what?

Him, I said.

Ngh. What are you asking?

I'm. Asking. Who. The. Kids. Are. Marge.

Old Marge flicked a skin the size of a Frosted Flake, saying, How's should I know? His kids, I'm assuming?

They say anything?

To me?

Sure.

Ngh. No. I don't know, Connie.

Old Marge had a plate of eggs and sausage on one arm, and a serving of pancakes in each flaky hand. I followed behind with a bottle of ketchup.

He looked different. Better than usual. His dark hair slicked shiny to his scalp, wetted with good-smelling mousse. Oh hi, I said, pretending I didn't know he'd be there. Old Marge gave me a look. I put the ketchup on the table, and tried best to swallow whatever nervousness I felt deep down to my belly. He nodded, but wasn't looking. He looked at the kids. Four or five-ish, both with big eyes and dark, mushroom-shaped hair. Old Marge told him to holler if he needed anything. After that she left, and I was left standing there, watching the man cut the kids' pancakes in small, jagged pieces. Connie, I told him. I tapped my nametag with my thumb, giving the thumbs up, acting real corny. He looked at me, my chest, my nametag. Squinted as if it were all a bright light. Trigger, he said. I leaned closer. My hips pressed the edge of the table. Excuse me? I said.

Trigger, he said. My name.

It is not, I said.

Kay, he said.

Trigger breathed like it was a hard thing to do. Sounded the same as air leaking out a can of pop. He'd trimmed his beard, but it still grew high on his face, certain strands sprouted out his cheekbones. His hair was cocoa-colored, mostly, with random patches of red and yellow. His nails were long and filthy.

He'd finished cutting the pancakes. He poured syrup on a side plate, slid it between the kids.

So, I said, I guess it's safe to assume your daddy liked guns?

He held a hand over his coffee, blocked the steam. Dipped his middle finger in the black burning liquid. Didn't wince. He was telling the kids to eat their strawberries and bananas, not just the pancakes. The little boy dipped his own fingers in a glass of chocolate milk, and the little girl giggled. Trigger told me about his daddy's guns. They were kept in a room, he said, on stands. Pa built the stands from poplar. Gun stands.

It was the most he'd ever said to me. I could feel my face flush at the sound of his voice. My daddy named me after a folk singer, I told him. Connie Converse. You ever heard of her? She went missing back in the mid-seventies, and still is, missing, I guess. No one's seen her since.

Trigger remained focused on the kids, watching them soak pancake pieces, fruit, their forks, and tiny bits of napkin on the syrupy plate. He had four fingers in his coffee now. Steam escaped past the sides of his hand. Where's she? he asked.

Connie Converse?

Where's she missing?

It was a strange thing to say, at least how he said it. *Where's she missing?* I told him I wasn't sure. Just missing, somewhere. He nodded. Seemed satisfied enough, or didn't care. Thanks, he said, pointing at the ketchup. Coffee dripped off his trigger-finger. He picked up his mug and took a gulp without sipping first.

The next week they were back, Trigger and the kids, so I asked Old Marge if we could trade sections. She said no at first. Hated my section, the smoke. But I told her I'd cover her tables if she wanted extra bathroom breaks, so she agreed.

I prepped in the kitchen, checking my makeup on the microwave door. That's when Patti came in strutting all young and curly blond. Caught me powdering my nose, and pushing my bra way up. Cackled the way she does and said, Looking good, Connie!

Whatever.

You doing that for him?

Who's *him*?

Don't pretend you haven't noticed Angry-Handsome's looking extra handsome today.

His name's Trigger, okay? Trigger.

Trigger? Is not.

Yup.

Well, Trigger's looking awfully handsome, she said.

As if that means something, I said.

Trigger was wearing red plaid tucked in black jeans. Work boots. His hair and beard the same as the week before, slicked, shiny. I approached his booth with sweaty hands and feet. Trigger! I said. He looked at me, up and down, but not in a good way. More like he was measuring some sorta threat. I smiled extra wide to show I wasn't one.

What can I get you to drink?

Coffee and orange juice, he said, and two chocolate milks.

I want orange juice, said the little girl.

Trigger looked at the boy. You want juice, too?

The boy sat there.

Coffee, two orange juices, one chocolate milk, said Trigger.

Back in the kitchen I found Patti leaned over the chopping board, her butt stuck out, perfectly bulbous under that hiked yellow skirt. She ate coleslaw from a bouillon cup. Soooooo? she said, half-turned to me, licking spicy mayo off her glittery lips. What'd you say, Connie?

Nothing, I said. Took his drink order's all.

She turned fully then, sat herself up on the counter. Those legs. That hair. That face, so pretty, tawny, except around the eyes. She stirred coleslaw with a delicate wrist wrapped in slap bracelets and said, I can totally tell he's a widow, you know.

My face got hot and itchy. How can you tell that?

It's the way he carries himself. His manner.

Where you suppose the kids came from?

The wife, obviously. The dead wife.

No. I mean where were the kids before? Like before he started bringing them here?

Patti shrugged. Maybe the mom died recently, she said.

I pulled Trigger's coffee off the burner. Maybe so.

After eating, he went outside to smoke. Left the kids in the booth, but stood on the other side of the window watching them. I refilled his coffee and he nodded behind the glass. I asked the kids what their names were. The little girl pointed at herself and said, Hermia Beally, and then pointed at her brother and said, Monster. The little boy stared at the soggy pancake pieces on the syrup plate, not saying much, just like his daddy. Hermia said, We're twins, but Monster's older.

Where's your mommy? I asked.

With Baby Birdie.

Birdie? That your pet?

Nuh. She's my new sister.

He just had a baby? I said to myself.

Nuh, said Hermia. *She* had a baby. Mum did, and, taking care of Birdie's hard work, and uh, Dad needs it outta his hair!

Trigger watched. He blew smoke on the glass.

Monster licked syrup off a butter knife. I told him to quit it. Hermia said she was finally an older sister. Monster and Quinlynn and Soccer and Carver's all older, she explained, but Birdie's younger. I told Monster to quit licking the knife a second time, that he'd cut himself. Then I asked Hermia who Quinlynn, Soccer, and Carver were. Trigger tossed his cigarette and turned towards the entrance. Monster grazed the knife against his palm. They're uh, my other brothers and sister, said Hermia.

How old's your daddy? I asked.

Two-nine, that's almost thirty, she said.

Monster held the knife up. Not sharp, he said.

I brought Trigger the bill. Then asked Patti to cover my tables, and tell Barry I'd fallen ill. Migraine, nausea, cramps, the runs, didn't matter. I put on my windbreaker and waited a minute, two minutes, heard the bell chime above the door. I watched them through the front window. Trigger buckling the kids in booster seats. I collected four quarters off their table, ran out and hopped inside my car. I could see Old Marge in the front window. She was refilling a napkin dispenser and shaking her head. Her lips were moving, but there was no one there.

I caught up to them at the lights. He turned, so did I, and we fell into the flow of traffic. I kept checking my mirrors, eyes, nose and mouth. We headed south. Ten minutes. Trigger turned right on a cul-de-sac, drove, and then slowed down. He stopped in front of a house, blocking its driveway. I drove past. Pulled over in front of another house three homes ahead. Looked in my mirror, at him, me. My face was flushed cause I'd quit breathing. His car moved forward. His windshield grew giant in the rearview. It got so close his bumper gave mine a peck.

He kept the motor running, got out of the car, lit a cigarette and smoked as he approached. Tapped two knuckles on my window. I rolled it down. He stood straight up, so I had to lean in order to see his face.

What's happening here? he said.

Trigger, I said.

Why you following me?

I'm not.

Why you following me? He bent down on the window ledge, breathing smoke in my face. Why you following me? What is this?

I couldn't say. Kept trying to, but there was nothing. Pockets of air in my mouth. I considered telling him about Connie Converse, how she went missing on purpose. It didn't matter where she was cause that's where she wanted to be.

What is this? he said again. I'll call the cops.

Nothing, I said. Connie Converse is—nothing. I'm going home is all I'm doing.

Where you live?

None of your business.

You quit tailing me, he said, crazy cunt.

He flicked his cigarette across my lap. It landed on the seat next to me, burning black on the beige fabric. I picked it up, dropped the cigarette in the cup holder and rolled my window shut. His car backed onto the driveway behind it, and then turned left, and took off in the other direction. Augh, I said. The sound of a yell, but a whole lot quieter. Then I took off my windbreaker, bunched it, pressed my face against it and screamed.

Both of them were glued to the tube when I came in. Ma seated in the bowl chair, a pomegranate on her crotch, while my daddy lay across the couch, shirtless, a pale, hairy hill of belly. They were watching Ray Combs pit blacks against whites on *Family Feud*. I stood behind the couch a couple minutes. Ma kept looking at me, and then back at the screen. Wasn't until commercial break anyone spoke. Thought you're supposed to be at the diner til three, Daddy said.

Don't feel so good, I said.

What's the matter?

Tummy. Head. Pretty much everything, I said.

Ma rubbed a pomegranate seed across the crack between her lips. Staring me down, not saying much. She ate the seed. Daddy tickled his belly, massaged around the button with stubby fingers and told me to feel better. I told him I was going to go lie down. Ma watched me walk down the hall. I could feel her eyes follow me up the stairs.

I opened my bedroom window. Stood there and smoked the remainder of Trigger's cigarette. Thought about how old he must've been when he started having all those kids. The trees outside made the sky look shattered. I shut the window, put the nub of the cigarette on my shelf with all the others, turned the clock radio on and lay in bed listening until I smelled dinner.

Ma made beans on buttered toast, sliced cheese and liver. She chewed with her mouth open. Black and grey hair matted on the sides of her long, mean face. Eyes narrowed. She stink-eyed me the whole time.

I forked my food, not eating much cause I was supposed to be sick. Or maybe I was sick, for real. Chewed each bite about a minute before swallowing. Daddy made small talk, brought up the chipmunk in our drainpipe, always with the chipmunk, wondering what sex it was, what it would do come winter. And Ma wondered the same thing about me. I asked what she meant. Don't play the fool, she said. You thought about it, yet? What'll you be doing come winter, Connie?

Daddy nodded like the questions were aimed at him and the answer to all of them was *yes*. I asked to be excused. Ma said I needed to consider how soon winter was, and I did, considered it all night, while staring at shards of sky outside my window.

He quit coming to the diner. Angry-Handsome's a no-show, Patti said the first week, and the second, and then the third. But eventually she quit saying it cause his absence had become such a normal thing.

I considered taking work off one Sunday, to drive around Port Woodlot and find wherever he'd settled. But I never did. Learned enough to know that kind of thing got ladies in trouble. So I never saw him again. Not for a couple months, at least. Not until I'm watching the news one evening with Ma and my daddy and this lady appears on the screen. Caption says her name's Sherri Beally, and she's crying. She's saying her little boy's gone missing. Says her little boy Soccer's been missing nine days. And then there's Trigger, standing beside her. He's staring at the ground. He's wearing a necktie, his face clean-shaven. I nearly fainted. He was looking more angry-handsome than ever.

I was in the kitchen the next morning with Old Marge. She stood picking skin off her hand with eyebrow tweezers. Ngh, she said. I watched her, noticed how old she looked, like Ma and my daddy, only Old Marge still worked.

Patti came in carrying a couple empty plates and told us it was snowing. Big, beautiful flakes, she said. Doesn't even look real!

I pulled a pot of coffee off the burner and we followed Patti to the dining area. There was the sun outside, bright as summer, with a blizzard falling in front of it. I held my hand over the pot. Patti hummed It's Beginning to Look a Lot Like Christmas, and so did Old Marge. I dipped my fingers in the coffee. Let go. The glass shattered. Burning liquid spattered across our feet and ankles. Patti and Old Marge hollered, while I sucked my fingers and tasted fire under the nails. And looked back at the snowfall. Something about the sparkling beauty of it made the burns feel a helluva lot worse.

3

This story is almost entirely about a girl I used to know. Then I didn't know her for a while, but now I do again. We reunited a couple months ago at a sex shop on Queen called the Condom Shack. It was mid-October, sunny and raining. I was sifting through a cardboard display of rubber fists near the entrance door when she approached, tapped my shoulder with the tip of a black fingernail. Johnny? she said, and her voice sounded the same as I remembered, young and full of gravel. Johnny Kines? Is that you?

I turned, saw myself in the reflection of her Ray-Ban Wayfarers. My face appeared happy to see her. Hermia Beally, I said. I'm only in here as a joke

Sure, she said. You look different.

I have a moustache, I said.

You look like you've seen things, she said. You look like you've seen a lot of bad things since the last time you saw me. Have you?

We had sex that evening around dinnertime. Six O'Clock Sex, she called it.

But I'm hungry, I lied.

We'll eat after, she said, so you have something to look forward to.

We were in her apartment in the living room with the thirty-nine inch television and glass coffee table and the framed picture of her parents as teenagers seated on the hood of a sea foam green K-car. She unbuckled her studded belt, let her black jeans drop around her white ankles. She didn't step out of them. The pants lay there like a cat curled on her feet. She wasn't wearing underwear. There was a tattoo of the word Tattoo on the front of her left thigh. I'll never get used to the way the labia looks when a woman is standing up.

I'm going to fuck your pussy good, I said.

I pulled down my pants and underwear and let them hug my ankles the same as her. Then I took off my shirt. I wish I'd taken my shirt off first in retrospect.

You have an okay body, she said. Better than I expected.

But you can see the veins on my chest, I said.

Blue's my favorite color, she said. And I like veins.

Take off your shirt, I said.

My back is whipped to shit, she said. Don't let it bother you.

She lay naked on her stomach on the loveseat. I knelt in front. Her face turned to me, half-sunk in the cushion. I scratched her, but my nails were cut short; they barely left a mark. I yanked the belt from the jeans around her ankles and started hitting her with the non-studded side. She kept saying, Harder, more force, and my penis remained soft and sick-feeling. She pressed her face deeper into the cushion. I stared at the soccer ball tattooed between her shoulders. I slapped her ass with the belt and it jiggled. New lines soon appeared on top of the ones already there. They were pink, purple, red, and then stayed red. She flipped onto her back and asked me to use the gadget we'd purchased at the sex shop on her. I had difficulty ripping it out of its package. She grew impatient, so kicked the jeans off her feet and then used her mouth on me until there was something to work with. The time blinked on the Blu-ray player. I lasted eight minutes.

Later she made breakfast for dinner—scrambled eggs, veggie bacon, hash browns, a small bowl of chopped fruit. I didn't eat anything except the fruit.

Sex ruin your appetite? she asked.

No, I said, I'm just afraid of dying.

She didn't react to this, only nodded, and squeezed more Tabasco on top of everything. We sat on the floor on opposite sides of the coffee table. She drank black tea out of a plain white mug, pink lips whistling steam off the surface. I watched her catch the liquid on the back of her tongue so it wouldn't stain her teeth.

Do you work? she asked.

I write articles for a fake news website, I said. They're meant to be satirical. I poke fun at people, and politics. Murders. Natural disasters, and tragedies in general. They want me to focus more on Canada, or specifically, Toronto. Our daily hits have quadrupled since all of this Rob Ford stuff started happening. Have you been following it? There are some very funny videos of him on YouTube. Would you like to watch some?

Do you have a girlfriend? she asked next.

No, I said, shaking my head.

She stabbed a piece of egg and bacon and potato and kiwi, had them packed on her fork. This was a one-time thing, she said, pointing at herself, then me, herself, me.

I nodded with too much enthusiasm.

She took a bite.

Do you remember when we used to play House? I asked.

She didn't respond because there was too much food in her mouth.

I don't make much money writing for that website, I admitted. Only some. But it's fun. I mean I really enjoy doing it, I just need to work other odd jobs on the side to keep afloat if you know what I mean. Like money's tight right now if you know what I mean.

She swallowed and said she did.

My mother normally calls on Sundays and so the following Sunday I mentioned I'd run into Hermia Beally.

Hermia Beally, said my mother, again and again. Hermia Beally. Hermia Beally. Hermia Beally. Then she remembered. Oh, Hermia Beally!

Hermia Beally, I said.

How is she? my mother said. Does she still smile with all of her teeth?

I told my mother that Hermia Beally did in fact still smile with all of her teeth, only those teeth were bigger now, and whiter, and they left pussy-shaped bite marks on my neck and thighs, but I didn't mention that last part. I did mention however that Hermia Beally lived by herself in a one-bedroom close to Toronto City Hall, a twenty-minute walk from Ryerson University where she was attending grad school and employed as a teaching assistant for a class called Introduction to Women's Studies. I told my mother Hermia Beally had dyed her hair black, and that it was cut medium-length and dropped to the fifth knob of her spine, and that she had a perfect little nose, and bronze eyes, and was five-foot four, the height of my heartbeat, but I did not mention the lashes on her back, or that having rough sex with her made the room smell so spicy it made my eyes prickle. My mother wondered what Hermia Beally's mother Sherri was up to, and I told her Mrs. Beally still lived on Spruce Street in Aurora and was working at the Boston Pizza on Commerce Drive, and then my mother wondered what Hermia Beally's grandmother was up to, and I told her she'd died three years prior due to diabetes mellitus.

I stood on the balcony of my apartment observing myself in the sliding glass door. I had shaggy brown hair, a moustache, and what my doctor often referred to as an *alarmingly lean frame*. According to my last appointment, I was close to thirty pounds under the standard bodyweight for a man my age and height. I also had an anus comparable to that of an elderly person. This was due to *too intense wiping*.

My mother asked about my anus and women and my roommate, Billy. And she asked if I'd been eating three meals a day. I held the phone between my ear and shoulder even though both hands were free. Billy sat on the couch inside. He had a dill pickle wrapped in a slice of twelve grain bread, and there was a cigarette burning on the ashtray on the armrest. He wore boxers and a buttoned shirt.

I told my mother the website I worked for had recently offered me a raise, which was a lie. I also told her I loved her. That much was true. She blew kisses into the phone that sounded like gunfire, and so did I, before finally reentering the apartment to tell Billy to take his smoke outside.

Hermia Beally had moved into her grandmother's house on Spruce Street in the spring of nineteen ninety-four when we were almost six. She arrived with her mother and four siblings—two sisters, two brothers. She'd also had a third brother at one point, but I'd been told he disappeared.

Disappeared? I said.

Like magic, she said. But Quinlynn keeps saying he's gonna come back.

It's true I knew Hermia Beally was pretty, even back then. I could feel her prettiness everywhere, in my head and chest, and groin, and would sometimes have to lie flat on the beanbag chair and press my bottom half into it for minutes at a time. I also knew she was different, dangerous. Standing beside her was like stepping on an insect, like I was doing something somewhat wrong, and kept having to turn, check over my shoulders to make sure no grown-ups were watching.

I lived four houses down from her. She'd invite me over on weekends to play House—Hermia Beally as the mother, and me, either the dog or father. And our daughter, a Cabbage Patch doll named Phoebe who had long yellow locks, fingerless hands, peachy cheeks, and slanted eyes that made it look like she had Down syndrome.

Phoebe's got *special needs*, said Hermia Beally. We should call her Special Pheebs!

We loved Special Pheebs, but sometimes grew tired of having to tend to her special needs, so it was decided she should be dead for the day. Hermia Beally had me dig a hole in the yard, gather dirt, grass, and clay under my claws, as she bowed her head to speak a few words, before tenderly tossing Special Pheebs in the ground. Cancer was normally the cause of death. We both knew it was bad because Mrs. Clark across the street had died from it, and also my great aunt Nancy had lost one of her boobs.

Special Pheebs's got heart cancer, Hermia Beally would decide, and want us to cry, only neither of us knew how to cry on command, so she'd bring out the adult shampoo from the upstairs washroom and have us rub it in our eyes until everything blurred and tears started falling out of them. It's cancering her special, special, special heart!

A lot of the time when we played, Hermia Beally would get me to taste her scabs as well. They'd normally be on her knees, elbows, but this one time she fell off Minster's handlebars and scraped her face, the chin. Soon a scab formed, and it was burgundy with a soft yellow border. She got me to lick it and tell her what it tasted like because her own tongue couldn't reach that far. I told her it tasted like the swings at the park, the scratchy brown parts on the chains.

Sometimes Hermia Beally hurt herself on purpose. She'd run and slide like a baseball player, grazing herself against the pavement. She enjoyed licking the wounds when they were still fresh, sucking the blood out, and even got me to suck on one once, but I didn't like doing it because there was gravel stuck to the middle.

Point is though, we used to play House, and be married, and mourn our dead daughter, and eat scabs together, and it was all a lot of fun, but then something happened, and it was something I still don't quite get, but it was enough to change everything.

It happened close to the end of that summer. Hermia Beally wore a turquoise T-shirt with a cartoon mouse figure skating on it, and the shirt said *If FIGURE SKATING was easy, it would be called HOCKEY*. Her hair was brown back then, and in two lopsided pigtails. We sat on the wooden frame surrounding the sandbox in her backyard, Special Pheebs buried between us, her cabbage head poking out of the sand. I was a dog that day, not the husband or father.

Here, boy, said Hermia Beally, patting her thighs.

Woof, I said.

I crawled across the sandbox and stopped in front of her with my tongue hanging out. She pointed at the scabs on her knees and said, Lick, boy. Dinner. So I was licking her knees. They were like sandpaper. My tongue stung. Hermia Beally placed two bloody-knuckled hands on my head and started running her fingers through my hair.

I angled my eyes toward the window above the back deck where Mrs. Beally sometimes stood watching. She wasn't there. Only the reflection of a cloudless blue sky on the glass.

I folded my hands behind Hermia Beally's knees, continued licking, started sucking the scabs. Hermia Beally started crying, but she wasn't moving. She wasn't trying to get away, so I kept going. She told me she didn't want to play anymore. You gotta go home please Johnny, she said, sobbing now, her teardrops dropping on top of my head. It was making me feel confused. I bit, twice, and pulled away from her legs. The scabs were gone and there was red running down her shins and I was chewing her scabs like bacon bits. I scooped sand in my hands and rubbed it in my face, in my mouth, and tried swallowing it, but the sand stuck to the back of my tongue.

I'm sorry, I choked.

Soon there was the sound of the screen door banging open, and Mrs. Beally, sprinting down the steps of the back deck, yelling, No! No more you little fiend! No more pain for my family!

Twenty years later—nine days after we had Six O'Clock Sex in her apartment—I asked about it. Do you remember when I ate your scabs in the backyard?

Yep, she said.

But do you actually remember? I said. Like do you remember with your memory, or just think you do because you're always hearing people talk about it?

Who the hell would talk about it? she said.

Everyone, I said, but that was a lie. No one even knew it had ever happened.

We sat in a Starbucks on St. Clair. It was the last day of October. There was a pumpkin on the counter next to the cash register, and fake spider webs were strung across the ceiling. Several baristas were dressed as slutty monsters.

We were seated at a table next to the front window. There was a dog outside. It was small and white and tied to a bike rack.

Dog, said Hermia Beally.

I nodded. Dog.

Hermia Beally wore her hair straight down. It was parted in the middle. She looked like a flower child, but without a flower. Her voice was husky, but soft, still feminine. She drank peppermint tea. She held her cup on her lap between sips.

Tell me about something, she said.

I told Hermia Beally about the time in college I was hazed by a group of guys who made me stick a bottle inside of myself.

She tore open a packet of sugar and poured its contents onto the table. She blew it at me. The sugar made a galaxy on my pants.

I don't like that, she said. Tell me something less depressing.

I told her about my roommate Billy, who I'd met at college, though he was not one of the kind gentlemen who'd made me bottle-fuck myself. I told her Billy worked at a place called The Stone Floor, which was a thirty-plus dance club on Bloor that attracted mostly middle-aged singles desperate to not die alone and looking to bust a move in the course of finding their one true later-in-life love, fingers crossed.

He's in charge of the coat check, I said.

I could tell Hermia Beally was interested in the club because her back straightened and eyeballs perked at its mention. Specifically for old people? she said. She lifted her tea to the table.

Thirty and up, I said, yeah.

We should go, she said.

They check IDs, I told her. We're four years too young.

Hermia Beally smiled toothily and said, Yep. We go tonight.

She took a long sip of tea. I stared at the nicotine patch on her neck, then the shape of her hands, the chains tattooed around each finger. She wore an Operation Ivy T-shirt under a tight leather jacket, black short-shorts, red stockings, and a pair of ratty, custard-colored sneakers.

She kept kicking me with them. I think she thought I was a table leg.

A man moved toward the other side of the window. He started tapping on it. Hermia Beally looked first, I followed her eyes. The man wore a plain blue sweater, grey work pants, boots, and a frayed Blue Jays cap that barely stayed put on his brown mop of hair. He chewed gum, or his tongue. He smiled so wide it pulled his eyes shut.

This is uncomfortable, I said.

Yep, she nodded.

He keeps looking at us, I said.

Because we're looking at him, she said, only she was no longer looking at him. She looked at me. I looked back at her, those unimpeachable eyes, the only part of her face that hadn't changed since childhood.

Should we give him money? I asked.

Food, she said.

I walked to the front counter and pointed at a couple slices of banana bread on display. I ordered a Venti Americano as well. When I looked back at the table, Hermia Beally had her hand pressed against the glass, like she was starring in some film about a chimp in a testing facility, and the man was the chimp, only he didn't touch her back. He just stood there, still smiling. I exited the Starbucks and approached vigilantly. He stank so badly of booze, I could almost taste the burn of alcohol in my own throat.

Happy Halloween, I said, and handed him the coffee and bag of banana bread.

Okay, he said. God bless.

I watched him walk off. He poured the coffee in a storm drain and tossed the bag of bread at a passing cab.

I turned back to the window to touch Hermia Beally's hand, but she'd pulled away.

I went back inside the shop. Hermia Beally was pouring more packets of sugar on the table. I blew it at her this time. I told her I'd go to the dance club.

Billy can get us in, I said.

She brushed the sugar off her T-shirt and into the cup between her knees. There are so many people, she said.

I wasn't sure if she was referring to the customers in Starbucks or the amount of people in the world in general, but I think she meant the world because there weren't many people in Starbucks that day.

So many people, I agreed.

There was a lineup of about twenty-five over-thirties outside The Stone Floor. Hermia Beally stood beside the line. She wore black pants and her leather jacket, hair greasy, spilling out the edges of a knitted toque with a fuzzy ball on top. Red lipstick. She smelled like pot and rain. She didn't hug or kiss me when I arrived.

Johnny, she said.

Hermia Beally, I said.

They look pathetic, she said, tilting her toque at the middle-agers.

Your hat doesn't match the rest of your outfit, I said.

Please kill me before I get that old, she said.

Can I strangle you? I said.

No, she said. Just kidding. I'm actually looking forward to it. Being old. Kids, grandkids, laugh lines, death, bullshit, bullshit, blah-blah-blah. She forced a laugh.

We used to be kids, I told her, which was a pointless thing to say. Then I said, We still are, actually. We are kids.

We fucked, she said. Kids don't fuck.

Kids make love, I said.

That's a creepy thing to say, she said.

I don't know what I'm saying, I said.

It was a chilly night. The sky drizzled. Wet leaves stuck to the ground, soaked in the gutter. I touched Hermia Beally's hip. She let me keep my hand there until it got too cold and I had to place it back under my armpit. We waited several minutes for Billy to come out. He ruffled my hair when he did, smoked a cigarette and poked fun at the way my moustache curled over my upper lip when wet. Then shook Hermia Beally's hand. Kissed between each knuckle.

The childhood friend I presume, he said.

Guess so, she said.

Billy led us inside, past the big-breasted door lady and a couple of thick-necked bouncers with forehead veins and tribal tattoos on their arms. He pointed at the bar, to a tall, dark man in a dark dress shirt with the top three buttons undone. That's the boss, said Billy, quietly adding, A real cock-nostril that guy is.

The dance floor was located in a different room. Much dimmer than the bar area, with flickering Christmas lights strung along the corners of the ceiling. Women drank margaritas, wore piquant perfumes, feathered scarves, fake eyelashes. There was more than one man sporting a mullet plus handlebar moustache combination. The DJ spun Kesha. One woman screamed, Kesha's my bitch! while another responded, Nuh-uh, she's *my* bitch, bitch! as a disco ball spun bleakly over all the fun being had.

Billy wore a tight white V-neck meant to accentuate his pecs and the broadness of his slender shoulders. He pointed at a woman in a grey dress, her hair dyed black, teeth dyed white. Fucked that broad, he said, and then pointed at another, this one with a bad perm, tube top, and sparkly hooker boots, and said, Her too. I butt-fucked that one up the ass.

Hermia Beally and I slid inside of a semi-circular booth close to the coat check. We sat facing each other. She put her sneakers on mine under the table. A waitress with wide hips and a snaggletooth took our order—vodka water for her, a beer for me. We drank, and observed. Most of the people seemed to be having a good enough time, this throng of soft, sweaty bodies bouncing on the dance floor. But a few didn't dance at all. They lurked. Creeping in the shadows along the perimeter of the room, maybe waiting, desperately, praying to be approached.

These people are god-awful, said Hermia Beally. Only she didn't say it. She wrote it on a napkin with an eyeliner pencil.

I took the pencil and added, *We'll be one of them in four years.*

She drew a picture of a hanged man.

Billy's having an affair, I wrote beneath the gallows.

With an old woman? wrote Hermia Beally.

She's forty, I said.

Hermia Beally drew a picture of a vagina on the napkin with bats flying out of it.

Forty's not that old, I said. We're almost forty.

Hermia Beally placed a finger in her vodka water and started twirling it, spilled liquid over the rim in an attempt to form a whirlpool.

Billy's bringing them back to your place? she asked.

What? I said.

His affairs, she said.

I folded the napkin and slipped it inside my pocket.

He fucks them in cars, I said.

By end of my ninth beer I feel falling and Hermia Beally's eyes is dumb and dopey but she's stunning man stunning with pieces of lights running past her and I tell her I've got three ribbed condoms in my wallet. There's a man standing at a tall circle table on the other side the coat check who's short stout like a little teapot that's got stains on his pits and hair that's thinning with round balds of crown then sadness everywhere like weighing him down everywhere so he's stood slumped with eyes slumped droopy. He's been there all night waiting and hoping for one these wench whores'll approach. Him holding that same bottle that's been empty so taking sips of nothing all night man these invisible sips of beer that's not there cause he's too cheap to go buy another so stands not dancing not bobbing not smiling not once all night standing sipping nothing and wanting love that's not ever gonna come.

Billy leans over the coat check counter with his slutty man cleavage slutting up the joint and flirting with these two old hags that got bleached hairs with leather skins in their forties probably and bodies pudged ways you know they've each shot a couple bratty shits out their vag. One them stumbles behind the counter to fall in Billy's arms trying to kiss him and his neck as the friend's laughing like it's so so sooo funny to take pictures of it on her iPhone the both them shitfaced and stupid and the lonely man's watching with pathetic lonely droopy drooping eyes as he tilts his bottle back to drink nothing for the bajillionth time tonight.

Hermia Beally stands then saying C'mon John! and she never calls me John but calls me John and it's weird. I follow cause I'm think we're leaving but not cause we're standing in front the lonely guy now man and Hermia Beally's on her knees in front him going I wanna suck your dick daddy whip it out let me suck it please! Up close his face's a bulldog's face with foldings and wrinkles and brown bags under each his beady eyes he's looking at me with and not her so I'm looking him back while Hermia Beally's on the ground sucking a gap of air between his bulge and her lips going Daddy daddy daddy you taste like sweet fucking candy!

Soon a bouncer's that's got biceps the size my head's pulling Hermia Beally by her arm practically dragging and it looks like we're getting booted so I try shouting bye to Billy but he's too blind to see by the couple skanks so not noticing what's going on like he's got no shit clue what's happened man not even.

What's happened's we're in back a cab on way to Hermia Beally's and she's sobbing makeup down down her face as the driver's keeping turning saying she better not barf man she better not mess his floor. The city's dazzling in darkness that many lights of buildings and ambulances to sirens and music to drunkards drowned in bagged bottles of pills and booze and men women kids yelling loud into the night at a sky and stars and moon clipped like a toenail.

Back at her place we're naked not fucking but holding and rolling sloppy on the small rug in front the television. She's on top me with stomach and chest pressed to my stomach chest and the warmth of our skins breathing and she's still crying but's got her face contorted over mine so I catch tears like acid raining on my tongue as the ceiling spins spinning round and around behind her and I nearly choke on my own blown chunks.

My mother called the following afternoon. She asked if I'd been eating well. I lied, told her yes, for breakfast I'd had three eggs, toast, cereal, a pear, bacon, oatmeal, and asparagus. The asparagus didn't make sense, but I wanted to cover all food groups and couldn't remember if vegetables were considered something separate from fruit. She asked why my voice sounded so strange. It was because I was hungover, still quarter-drunk, but I didn't tell her that. I told her I sounded strange because I was nervous about an important piece I'd been assigned to write for the website I worked for, a critical review of the Rob Ford crack video, complete with star rating, as if it were a legitimate film, containing plot, character, some form of artistic merit. She asked to hear more. I told her the website was paying me double what I normally made, which was a lie. I told her I was quote-unquote: climbing the ladder. My mother told me to climb, climb, climb my heart away, until I reached the stars, and I said, Will do.

I walked out to the balcony of my apartment. I wore a T-shirt, pajama pants and bare feet. My teeth chattered. My mother asked what that strange sound was and I said,

My teeth chattering. I spat over the railing, watched it fall to the frosty grass below. I spat again. Please stop doing that, said my mother.

The front door to the apartment opened and Billy came in. I watched him through my reflection. He wore the same clothes from the night before. Leapt over the back of the couch in our living room, lay on his side and lit a cigarette. I tapped the glass. He waved.

I told my mother I had to go, and she told me to make sure I kept eating properly, and then we blew kisses at each other until eventually one of us hung up. I stood on the balcony a minute longer, watching Billy. He was seated upright on the couch now, examining his wrists, which appeared to have bruises all around them.

I opened the door and walked inside.

Jeez. Weren't you freezing? he said.

I was talking to my mother, I said.

It's supposed to snow tonight, he said. Eight to ten inches, like my cock.

What happened? I said, pointing at his wrists.

You see the one wearing the blue dress? he said. She sorta looked like Dorothy from Oz, only older, and sluttier. Know who I'm talking about?

Did you see what happened last night? I said.

With your friend? he said. Yeah, I saw. Pretty funny.

He slid his hand down the front of his pants. I don't know what he was doing—scratching his balls, tucking his dick, playing with himself—but he was doing it.

What happened, I asked again, to your wrists?

Told you, he said. It was the Dorothy-chick. Tied me to her steering wheel.

I still had the phone in my hand, so I went back outside and dialed Hermia Beally's number. I wanted to explain to her that memorable and matchless things happened whenever I was with her. That it had always been that way, and I was so happy to have her back in my life. But she didn't answer.

This is Hermia. Leave a message after the—

A few hours later there was a knock at the front door.

Knock.

Knock. Knock.

-

KNOCK.

I opened the door and there was a man standing there. He was tall enough to meet my eyes. He shoved my chest and I stumbled backwards into the apartment. He stepped inside, gently shut the door behind him. He was old, like fifty. He had a gut, wide nose, dimpled chin, a crew cut. His cheeks were pallid and pockmarked. His fist was hairy, meaty, with fingers pressed into his palm.

Wait, I said.

He punched me in the face. My nose broke out of place. There was blood on the floor. It dripped into a spiral on the hardwood. I think I was on my hands and knees and he punched the back of my head and my face met the spiral. He tugged the back of my hair, pulling my head up, his fingers intertwined in the tangles of my shag, and forced my face against the floor, one, two, five times. I could feel my features engorge. Everything smelled thick and smoky. It was difficult to inhale, almost impossible to breathe.

I was standing. The man must've stood me up. He was holding me, guiding me towards the television cabinet, dropping me to my knees in front.

Please, I tried saying.

He forced my face forward so my mouth met the corner of the cabinet. It dug into the edges of my lips. I tried to speak, but there were no words, just blood and pieces of teeth. I lay on the floor in the fetal position, wondering what time Billy might return, hoping he'd remember toilet paper. The man pressed something cold against the back of my head. It made a clicking sound. He wanted me to think it was a gun. I wasn't afraid. I knew I wasn't going to die because there was nothing flashing before me.

He spoke.

You so much as look at my wife again, swear to Christ, coat check faggot, I'll come back here and kill you.

Then the front door opened and closed and he was gone. I lay on the floor for a little while longer, my face like a heartbeat. I fell asleep.

Later, Billy came home. He forgot the toilet paper.

I was in the bathroom. I was shaving my head and moustache. I didn't bother cleaning the cuts or icing any of the bruises. Strands of hair stuck to the blood on my face. I let the rest fall and gather in the sink, and clog the drain.

I went out to the living room. Billy smoked a cigarette on the couch. The Billy Specialty in a popcorn bowl on his lap—scrambled eggs mixed with fries mixed with melted cheese mixed with leftover pre-cooked grocery store chicken. He ate with chopsticks.

Hi, I said.

He put his cigarette out on the food. Johnny, he said. What the fuck, Johnny.

Are you working this weekend? I asked.

Did you get mugged? he asked.

How much blood is too much blood to swallow? I asked.

You need to go to the hospital, he said.

I touched my face, its new feel, and form, and textures.

Are you working The Stone Floor this weekend? I asked him.

What? he said. You need someone to fix your nose, Johnny. It's crooked.

I sat beside him on the couch. He offered me a bite of melted cheese and chicken skin, cigarette ash as garnish. I shook my head. It hurt to shake my head. He stared at the top of my head, kept telling me how pale and ugly it looked. I breathed through my mouth. I could almost taste his meal on my tooth-torn tongue.

I chipped a few teeth, I said.

Your mouth looks like a broken window, he said.

I started thinking about the things that happened afterwards. Like how I wasn't allowed to go play anymore. No more sandboxes or Cabbage Patch funerals. No more games of House. The summer ended and the school year began and my family moved to London, Ontario, miles from Hermia Beally and whatever had compelled me to do what I did to her knees in the backyard that one day. And I mostly forgot.

But halfway through the new school year, a girl in my class named Stephanie Groh approached the chalkboard for her turn at show-and-tell, and she said, I fell at tennis lessons and got this. She held up her arm so the underside showed. Between her elbow and wrist there was an egg-shaped scab. It looked oily. I like it, she said. I like how it tastes. It tastes good.

Our teacher stood up from behind her desk. Not a good idea, dear, she said. But it was too late. Stephanie Groh was licking the scab. A lot of my classmates were grossed out, but not me. It was the first time I'd been reminded of Hermia Beally in months. I raised my hand and asked if I could lick Stephanie Groh's scab as well, but my teacher said there were bacteria on the tongue that could make Stephanie Groh very sick. I asked if she thought Hermia Beally was *very sick*.

My teacher looked at the class, and me. Who's Hermia Beally, dear?

I never went to the hospital. Instead I took a cab to her apartment building and waited on the bench outside. I'm not sure how long I sat there for because I wasn't wearing a watch and I'd forgotten my cell at home. I'd forgotten my jacket as well, and it was snowing—the tree branches and telephone wires catching the snowfall. Everything looked beautiful, like it belonged on a postcard.

Next thing, I was seated in her apartment, on the loveseat we'd made love on two weeks prior. I was naked. A quilt had been placed over my shoulders, a different dinosaur stitched in each square. I wiped my nose on what she said was an elaphrosaurus. My freezing wet clothes hung on doorknobs, my socks folded over the back of a rocking chair. I looked around the room. Saw it like it was my first time seeing—the monochrome walls, cacti on the windowsill, framed photographs, one of her siblings, another of her late Uncle Tony, a bookcase with two shelves devoted entirely to texts about depression and other mental illnesses, Minster's composite novel, paintings of deformed babies and giant eyeballs, scenic landscapes, a house.

I sat in her bathtub. She assured me the water was lukewarm, but it burned like a thousand knives cutting into me. My penis looked small and ugly, nestled there between my thighs.

She didn't ask how it happened, just sat on the toilet lid next to the tub with one leg kicked over the other, foot fidgety. She was looking down at me, and I was looking up at her, and she was wearing a Daniel Johnston shirt under a black blazer, black skirt, black stockings, and a pair of fluffy mauve slippers.

You look like you've been kissing a sledgehammer, she said.

I laughed without smiling. I didn't want the cuts on my lips to stretch wider.

Should we pour tomato soup in the water? I asked.

That's to get rid of skunk smell, she said. It doesn't heal wounds.

Oh, I said.

And it's tomato *juice*, she said.

I slid so my entire body was submerged. The ceiling rippled and a crimson cloud formed before my eyes. I sat back up and wondered why there wasn't any hair stuck to my face. Then remembered I'd shaved. I licked my upper lip to see if the moustache was gone too, make sure I hadn't just dreamed getting rid of it.

I'm hairless, I said.

You look younger, she said.

Do I look like a baby? I said.

You look like a monster, she said. A baby monster.

The water had turned a misty red. You could hardly see my penis anymore. I slid back under and started touching the wounds on my face, picking at them until they bled more. When I sat up again she was gone, and the red in the water was no longer misty. It looked like tomato soup.

Bring spoons, I yelled.

The moon? she called back to me.

Dishes clattered in the kitchen down the hall.

Woof woof woof, I started barking.

She returned with a mug of tea in one hand, a plateful of buttered toast in the other. Two slices of bread were cut into four triangles.

I can't, I told her. Literally, I can't. It hurts.

She set the mug on the backend of the toilet, leaned forward and lifted a piece of toast from the plate to my lips. I nibbled the crust. She fed it to me like I was a child. It hurt to swallow, but I still did. I swallowed the food. She told me I wasn't going to die, and I believed her. She held the plate under my chin so no crumbs dropped into the water. She fed me a second piece of toast, and I swallowed, and I was still alive. She tipped the tea inside me. It burned, but everything burned. Burned until nothing hurt anymore.

I should probably go to the hospital, I admitted.

I already texted my cousin Kirby, she said. He works at the Rogers Center but can bail in ten. He's got a car. So you won't have to take transit or waste money on a cab.

Is it still snowing? I asked.

Yep, she said. Tis.

I fell underwater a third and final time, blinded by red, swallowing it. The taste was cold compared to the tea. She was still there when I resurfaced. But there was water in my eyes, so she appeared hazy at first.

I want memories, I told her. I want more memories with you in them.

She smiled, but it wasn't genuine. Her mouth moved, while the rest of her face remained wooden. She looked at the bruises instead of my eyes.

Johnny, she said, and her voice sounded clearer, so much younger than ever before.

Hermia, I said. Beally.

She touched the side of my face and dabbed the tears with her thumb. I handed her the bottle of shampoo from the side of the tub. She shook her head at me.

You don't have any hair, she said.

4

Every night, top of the fifth, we'd change and head to the Left Field Gate. The nine of us in Home Hardware hats and jerseys, and Nike running shoes, and Sandy with his EpiPen bracelet, and Adnan with a stick 'n' poked jay on his tricep cause he was the only one who cared outside the gig. Two Conversion guys pulled the gate open. We'd shuffle back, then sprint. Victor leading the pack cause he'd competed in the four-hundred meter dash in college and still had it in him. The rest of us laggards in comparison.

You could see two-thirds of the CN Tower from the turf. Lit light azure cause the run was eight forty-five-ish, on the brink of black sky. The moon and the stars and the Tower and me with a looper in hand like a war scythe. I ran past Third. Thought about Grandpa Dustin dipping pretzels in mustard in the stands, Mom at home chanting Go Kirby, Uncle Trig at a tavern on Dundas, the game on a TV mounted close to the ceiling, but him facing the bar, blinking impassively. The nine of us broke into groups of three. Me, Victor, George, on First. Sweeping dirt, replacing the base. Victor said, You tired, Kirbs? and I wiped my eyebrows with my forearm and spit.

Dad got tickets off a scalper once during the Joe Carter years. Uncle Trig was there too. I have five cousins but Trig only brought the twins. They sat either side of me and warned when the wave was coming, and when it did I stood A-shaped, and Dad laughed. Later Minster peed in the washroom telling me he'd hit Hermia with one of Trig's belts. He said, My dad never strapped us how he did Carver and them, so she wanted to feel what it's like. Then Minster gulped. Then splashed water on his face, gasping while fat-bellied men with foam fingers pretended not to hear. In the lot, Hermia showed us her nicked skin. We were behind the K-car as our dads drank beer and smoked cigarettes on the hood. That was two years after the Jays won their second Series.

Back in the Crew Room we'd eat Doritos and lounge on threadbare couches. Victor did heel drops. I'd brush the Turface off my knees. Soon the innings dwindled and the stadium emptied and we'd go back out and water the bases and throw a tarp on top. There'd be trash every-where, but the Tower kept pointed towards the sky.

5

So what I'm doing's I'm shopping by touching things. Look: me touching this and that and that and this going (la-la-la-de-da!) look at me I'm shopping! Normal. Normal-shmormal. I'm touching a bottle of grape seed oil. A zucchini. A container of pre-made bean curd rolls. Whatever. Point is it's normal. Point is I'm normal, touching this that this and occasionally putting this that this in my cart, lining up at the cash register, doing things perfectly good and perfectly perfectly normal.

But then: Poof!

Suddenly I'm being chest-pushed by this broad-chested fella calling me Old Perv. Y'Old Perverted Perv, he goes. Socking me hard in the ribs. And then I'm in cuffs!

See: after my Audrey died I got lonely. Real lonely. I'd be pacing. I'd be clipping my toenails again and again even when I got no more nails to clip. Picture this: me clip clip clipping away! I've got bloodstains on the toe-ends of my socks. I'm washing my hands a lot too. Hot hot water. Doing things that aren't the most healthy. I'm counting leaves on a tree, counting down days to the Y2K. I'm lamenting. Talking to bugs I think might be her. I see a mosquito on dog shit and I go, Audrey? I see maggots on a gutted raccoon and what I says is, I love you and I miss you and it hurts so so much so please please please come home my Little Matzo Ball.

Then I'm at the store one day and see her. Meaning: she looks just like her. And not mosquito/maggot her, but human her. Only a much younger version human her. This girl, the cashier at register six, she goes, I can help whoever's next. And I was in line at five and next and was holding a can of mung beans and a jar of broccoli baby food. This girl, this angel, she had the same dimples as my Audrey. The same smiley eyes as my Audrey. Crinkled her nose squirrel-like how my Audrey used to crinkle her nose squirrel-like, then Achoo! So I says, Little Matzo Ball? and she goes, Kosher stuff's in aisle sixteen, and I says, My hands (showing her how raw my hands had got), and she goes, That'll be six seventy-three if you're not grabbing matzo balls, dude.

See: after my Audrey died I was real lonely like I said so what I did's I got a rat. A gal rat. Called her John Wayne. A strong name for a rat. And I got John Wayne a big big cage like a dog cage then wrapped additional chicken wire around the bars then constructed her her own Ratty Mansion! Built a number of climbing mechanisms inside for her to climb. Hung a battery handheld fan from the ceiling. Put in a porcelain water dish, then an equally porcelain food dish. And more! Empty Girl Guide cookie box, toilet paper rolls, newspapers and strips of old undershirt, a dishrag hammock, a rope perch, a homemade wading pool. Picture it: John Wayne scurrying this way that way every which way going, Neat neat neat neat neat neat neat neat!

Going, Thank you Dustin!

And I says to her, I says, I'm gonna take good care of you forever.

That was two years back. Now she's dying same way my Audrey did. Got herself the shaky-shakies, poor thing. Has stopped eating her spinach, strawberries, yada yada, will not touch her biscuits. Her teeth and claws have elongated. Her fur's grown sparse and dull. I love her even though she's a rat and not something important like a human or brisket. Sometimes I'll hold her, feel those splayed footsies in my palm. I'll angle my own outwards out out until it hurts too much to twist my legs any farther.

I call Trigsly who hangs up.

I call Tony Baloney who doesn't. I says to him what's happening. He goes, I'll Google it. I says to him, Google-shmoogle! and he goes, Google-shmoogle? and I says, Yes yes Google-shmoogle, and he goes, Well, Google shmoogle's got some suggestions on how you can help her. So you want to know? You want to know how you can help the rat or not? and I nod, and he goes, We're talking on the phone, Pa. Remember, I can't see it if you're nodding right now.

Ah, Tony Baloney: a good boy with a sensitive heart and highly impressive Google-shmoogle capabilities! I see him at the funeral. He goes, I'm so sorry Pa, and I says to him, I says, Sorry-shmorry you are! She was your mother, Baloney. I'm the one who's sorry. And then he looks at me with eyes that were hers, my Audrey's eyes, putting a hand on the side of my neck, with thumb rested in front of my ear, and I just about break. Or do break. The only time I ever breaked! Breaking into Baloney's shoulder as

Kirby and Kelsey put hands on my hips as if to say, There there, Grandpa. There there.

I kissed the soil they buried my Audrey under. Then Purelled my lips!

Trigsly was a no-show. Not to that, or the house afterwards. It was just me, Baloney and his family, Trigsly's ex, plus some of their kids, all us in the kitchen or front room eating baby beef sandwiches and saying things such as Remember the time (. . .) or There was no better gal! or Wish Trigsly/Dad/Uncle Trigger could've made it.

One point Trigsly's youngest comes at me going, Hi I'm Birdie. Her hand out. And I shake it. And I says to her, I'm Dustin. I'm your Grandpa.

She cocks her head sideways, seeing me angled.

And I says to her, How old are you?

Seven, she goes.

And I says, Pick a hand, any hand! with two fists out. She chooses left. I uncurl my fingers to unveil a dollar coin. The truth: there was a dollar in my other hand too! She slides the coin in her sock cause she's got on a dress that doesn't got pockets.

Thank you thank you thank you! she goes.

And I pat the bow on her head saying, Think I'm gonna get myself a pet now that my Audrey's kicked the bucket. So maybe you can come back and see it sometime, no? Maybe you, your brothers and sisters, maybe even your daddy, you can all come back and see the new pet someday soon. How's that sound, Birdie?

Birdie said it sounded Super! while Trigsly's ex Sherri scowled eating potato salad next to the curio cabinet. I haven't seen either of them since.

But back to lately: Baloney told me the Google-shmoogle suggested feeding John Wayne baby food. High calorie, easy on the gob. So I was going to the store more and more and buying jars by the armful! Sometimes I'd say something to the cashier (Hello or Don't need bag, thanks or Not for baby; I got a sick rat), while other times I'd only look. She'd look at me look and not look happy I was looking. But I'd still look. Look at the face that was my Audrey's face fifty-some years ago and the cashier goes, I know I know. Something about matzo balls, right?

And I'd be speechless. Such disdain. It was uncanny!

I'd get home, and open the cage. John Wayne only ate it off my fingers. No spoon! she'd go. Spoon-shpoon! she'd go. Place your hand beside the bowl of sterile potting compost, please. Thank you Dustin!

Before she got sick though I'd take her out, put her on a pillowcase on my thighs. She'd eat escarole leaves as I told her things I'd never said before: Holocaust things, or when I fought in Israel type things. Things still very much in me. And I'd pace. And clip my toenails and burn my hands with John Wayne on my shoulder going Shhhh. She'd go, Shhhh Shhhh, mimicking my Audrey cause that's what she did. Gently, always a gentle Shhhh. Laid on her back with my head on her tummy so I could hear the rumble rumble. It made me feel better. Much calmer, made things more clear. My Audrey running fingers through my hair going, Shhhh. I'm here Dustin. I'm right here.

Months before she bit dust I found a lined paper folded under the photo book in our room. She'd written *On the Implausibility of My Making it to Heaven* at the top. And I'll admit: I had to look the word Implausibility up! I'm no Einstein! So I see what it means, then see what she's written below: *1. Made Don't pinch my darn cheeks! face whenever Mother pinched my cheeks, 2. Fed the Hyrtzacs' kittens antifreeze, 3. Time in grade school when long-haired lisping boy Christian Daluca got picked on for having long hair and lisp did not defend said long hair and lisp, 4. Swiped tobacco from Father's Do Not Touch! box then chewed tobacco then swallowed then upchucked tobacco onto Mother's daisies blaming it on the Gratons' dog who I later killed with antifreeze* (and yada yada). Then, skipping to the bottom, I see it. Most recent jotted reason: *63. Let Dustin be rough with the boys.*

I tried erasing it with spittle on my thumb but she'd written in pen!

Thought about it lots after she died, while at the store, touching those foods and reading those labels, shopping, being normal-shmormal, how I'd sometimes be rough with them. Sometimes. And I'd look at that cashier. Remembering my Audrey that way. With skin like that. A neck like that. Back when we were young and my temper got lost and she'd go, You gotta take it easier on them, Dustin. They're just boys.

On the day I'm about to buy a container of pumpkin and flax seed flat bread she sees me in line. Finishes serving the lady already paying. Then puts Register Unavailable sign up. Then speed-walks to customer service where she goes, Baby food guy's back again! even though I don't got baby food that day. Then rushes through Employees Only door as customer service lady lifts phone. Next thing: I'm being chest-pushed by this broad-chested fella calling me Old Perv. Y'Old Perverted Perv, he goes. Socking me hard in the ribs. Also asking lots of questions he's got no business knowing answers to. So I says to him, I says, The nerve! and what he does is he unfastens a taser from his belt!

I wanna tell him, I'm in pain! Don't you see my pain?

But instead I throw punches. He dekes them. Pushes me gut-first against the conveyor belt. Now I'm being cuffed with things that aren't cuffs. Correction: they're FlexiCuffs! And all I wanted was to see her. All I want in this world's to see her and the boys one last time, all together, so I can say I'm sorry. You all deserved so much better.

Hold still! the broad-chested fella bellows.

And I says to him, I'm an old man!

And he digs a fist at my spine. And I get banned from the store.

In the lot I thought: Good thing I've stocked up on John Wayne's food! Then thought about other good things too. Only the good things now, cause one more bad could've killed me right then and there, and I wasn't ready to be killed just yet. No no not yet! What I got's a rat to take care of!

So I walked to the bus stop thinking: Only the good only the good only only.

Thinking: Trigsly and Baloney ages nine and five, peeling bark off a bitternut hickory in the yard until they got themselves a couple gun-shaped pieces.

Smoke the Nazis! they go. Smoke 'em to ash and shit!

Meanwhile: me and my Audrey on the porch with my face on the side of her face. I says to her, Hmm. You a yummy little matzo ball? And she smiles. And I eat the dimples in her smile going, Num num num num num. And the boys see and go, Ew! but giggle while Ew!-ing,

then return to smoking Nazis to ash and shit as the sun
sets slowly on the fence in the yard.

6

The first thing I told her about was the swastika. Someone had spray painted it on the side of the synagogue in Hamilton where my parents live. I was driving to their place on Mother's Day weekend when I initially saw it facing the main road, this big black stain on the yellow stock bricks, pointed and precise as a throwing star. It bothered me, of course—in fact, it bothered me in a big, bad, burning way (!)—but I won't lie, the bother soon passed as my attention turned back to the point of my trip, which was my mother, taking her to Cora's and asking the server to serve us a side plate of banana slices because her doctor had recently revealed she'd been running dangerously low on vitamin B6. So I made sure Mom ate every last slice, and then hugged her goodbye, and headed back to Barrie, Timmies, my real life, assuming that was that.

I returned to Hamilton a couple months later, however—for Canada Day, as I try to visit my parents on every important holiday—and guess what I see? The gosh darn swastika (!). It's still there, still tagged on the side of the synagogue, only a little less bold now, faded like a tattoo that's maybe been exposed to too much sun. So I ask myself, Am I dreaming this? How's it possible for something so awful to exist for so long? I turned off the path to my parents and drove straight to the nearest Canadian Tire where I purchased two cans of spray paint, both of which were labeled Gloss Black, and then headed back to the synagogue, pulled to the side of the road, marched across the cut green grass and up to the building where I sprayed my buns off until the gosh darned thing had been covered entirely.

There was a black square on the synagogue now, drip lines hanging off the bottom like tassels. I looked around to see if anyone saw—keep in mind, it's four, maybe five in the evening, plenty of commuter cars and people passing by—but no one seemed to care, not a soul said anything to me. I'm just standing there under the hot sun with Gloss Black stippled up my arms and sweat in my eyes and I might as well be invisible.

That's how I ended the story, in present tense—*I might as well be invisible*—and she looked me square in the eyes and shook her head as if to say no, I wasn't.

Her name was Birdie Beally, supposedly, nineteen years young, with long brown hair and a face that got pretty so long as you were patient enough to learn to appreciate its particularities. She wore a black mesh hat, a black cardigan over a white tank top, and tight black jeans. Her sleeves were rolled to the elbows and her feet were bare, and perhaps her toes were a tad too long and a tad too curved for my liking, but hey (!), they were only toes.

Why'd you buy two cans? she asked.

I'm sorry?

Of paint. You needed two cans to cover the swastika?

Oh. No. There must've been a deal at the store, a two-for-one sale.

How much were they?

Uh, I don't know. I'm not sure, Birdie.

What'd you do with the other can?

What other can?

The one you didn't use.

Oh. Nothing. I don't know. Sorry. I can't quite remember.

She nodded, told me she understood, and so, naturally, I began to wonder what there was to understand. Perhaps I'd missed the point of my own story. It wasn't about a swastika or everyone's inability to see it at all; it was in fact about cans of spray paint (?).

Do you enjoy graffiti artwork? I asked.

She ignored my preposterous question by blowing a purple bubble between her lips. It smelled of grape candy, and I was instantaneously carried back to childhood, to that good ol sting of youth—the scraped knees, bruised elbows, getting Chinese sunburned in line at the drinking fountain. I rubbed my arm. Her bubble popped, but its scent lingered. She licked the splatter off her mouth and said, Lucy—that's what I'd told her my name was, earlier, while chatting online: Lucy Jones (Ha!)—Lucy, she goes, can I ask you a dumb question?

There is no such thing as a dumb question, I said.

I've never done something like this, she said.

It wasn't quite a question, but I still tried to answer the best I could. Told her yes, neither had I, that this was something new for everyone—by everyone, I meant *us*—but it was a good kind of new, an exciting kind of new even, and not the kind either of us should be at all worried about.

Don't worry, I said.

I'm not, she said. Just saying.

Our room was on the twenty-second floor. The curtains were drawn. We still hadn't turned on any lights. And so we sat there in the almost-dark watching the shadows shift shades on each other's faces—me seated on one bed, her on the other, a nightstand with a bible in the drawer between us. She kept her head straight, never turned profile. Online, she'd mentioned her *Jew nose*, oh how she hated it (!), the size and sharp bend, but, after several measured minutes of careful deliberation, I think I decided it was my favorite physical part of her.

You're pretty, I said. Just gorgeous, Birdie.

She sat with her hands flat on her upper thighs, shoulders hunched as if her head might soon retract between them. If she was what she said she was, then that meant I was close to two decades older (Yikes!). I looked at her hands. I looked at my own.

I told her to share with me.

Share what?

Anything. Whatever we haven't already tackled. I want to know everything, Birdie.

She straightened her hat, which hadn't been crooked.

A favorite childhood memory perhaps? Let's start there, shall we?

She looked at the television, and then the clock radio on the nightstand, and then the white crumbs of something surrounding the garbage bin beneath the desk, and then the desk, the paper bag I'd brought full of tallboys, bottles of wine, a ring box containing four ecstasy tablets, and she shrugged her shoulders with her hands still on her thighs and said, What?

Are you nervous? I asked.

No.

Are you disappointed?

With what?

Moi.

No. Why?

Maybe I'm older than you expected?

No. Not really. Thirty isn't old.

I'm thirty-seven, Birdie.

Yeah. Okay. Thirty-seven isn't too old. It's fine.

Fine?

I like the way you look.

But of course I inferred *I don't like the way you look* (!), and so my face immediately began to wash out at the thought of it—*the way I looked* (!!!)—my skin prickling, my lower back sweating through my grotesquely drab shirt. Oh how I hated what I had on (!)—that ol lavender sweater with the collared blouse attached underneath, and my ex-husband's lucky socks, and skinny jeans, for the first time ever, suffocating my cellulite, pinching my muffin top. Not to mention the oxblood nail polish and lipstick, the opaque eye shadow. My hair shoulder-length with straight-cut bangs and highlights. And black lace panties. Yes—Black. Lace. Panties (As if!).

Birdie? I said.

Sorry, she said. Sorry if I'm being quiet or something.

Don't be sorry, I said. All I want is to get to know you better. But if you feel uncomfortable, I understand. I understand if you want to leave. Please don't feel trapped.

She stood, peeled the comforter and sheet off the top corner of the bed and lay back down in it, covering herself, bunching her body beneath the blankets to pull off her pants (!), tossed them on the floor. She kept her hat on, however. It had MILL ST. BREWERY patched to the front. She turned on her side and lay facing me, head half-sunk. Her hat curved almost off her head. I remained seated on the other bed, but leaned in as close as I could, to catch her breath, that waxy smell of purple engendering so many tender recollections. My hands clamped firmly between my knees, I kept my eyes on hers, the left one—the only part of her face I could still see over the dip of the pillow.

Mom drove, she said. I don't know where we were coming from, but it was a residential area. I was only three or four. I remember though. It was late. The moon was orange. Mom kept telling me to look at it. She kept saying it looked like the sun. It did, too. I remember. Anyways, I was strapped in the back, diagonal her. She was driving and talking to me about stuff, and then she stops talking. She was looking out her window, so I looked too, and there was this woman running alongside our car. We were moving slowly because there were a lot of speed bumps on the road, and stop signs, but the woman still had to sprint to keep up. She was on the sidewalk. She was dressed in black. Or maybe her clothes just looked black because it was dark. I don't know. I remember she was ethnic though. Chinese, I think. I was little. It was a really long time ago, so I'm not positive, but I think she was Chinese.

She paused then to blow another bubble. I waited, wanting and-or dying to hear more, and embarrassingly so—so much so I was leaned so far forward my buns barely touched the bed anymore—I was practically squatting on air (!).

Mom stops at the next stop sign, she continued, tells me to make sure my door's locked even though she knows it is. Then waits for the woman to either run ahead or cross in front. But the woman doesn't do either. She just stands there on the corner in the cold—it's winter, by the way—taking these long-drawn, frigid breaths we see coming out of her mouth. Mom rolls down her window and asks the woman, Do you need help? But the woman doesn't say anything. Just stands there looking at us, breathing. So Mom presses the gas. The car starts moving, and that's when the woman moves too. She sprints in front of us. Sprints and leaps in front of our car. Mom hits the brake. The bumper knocks the woman's legs and she falls flat on the hood. Then looks up. She looks past Mom and at me. I'm like ninety-five percent sure she was Chinese. She runs around to my side of the car, to my door, and tries opening it. She's smacking the window yelling, I can help you find him, I can help you find him! I remember. Mom stomps the gas and we're off. She's driving fast, not slowing for any more speed bumps. I think we must've been coming from Aunt Charlotte's, Mom's sister. Probably. Her area had all these really wide speed bumps on the roads. So I guess that was it.

Another bubble, which popped much smaller, and quicker than the others.

What was *it*? I asked.

Huh?

You said, *I guess that was it.*

Yeah. That's what happened.

I don't understand, I said.

Neither did we, she said, and then, a second time, Neither did we—those three words repeated through a feigned half-yawn, their inflection insinuating a sense of ennui, although her eyes told of something different, much more electric, as if her vision had been newly recharged by the telling of her own story. I asked what made her share it, and she told me I did. It was her favorite childhood memory.

By then I was under the covers too, on my own bed, opposite hers, my pants and socks and shirt folded in a neat square at the end of it.

How come?

I don't know, she said. I just like it.

There has to be a reason, I said.

I think it was the last time I felt safe in danger, she said.

You weren't afraid that crazy woman might hurt you?

No. I don't think so. Maybe. But no. Mom was there.

I see, I said, then waited patiently for her to ask me something similar—*Tell me, Lucy, what's your favorite memory? Have you ever been put in a situation that had you feeling safe in danger?*—but no, all she did was lie there wordlessly with chestnut eyes dully concentrated on nothing, or the dark between our faces. Or, perhaps her attention was caught someplace else now, a spot of introspection, her mind redrawing it—illustrations of the woman, herself, and that thin pane of glass between them, smudged by perilous handprints, a *smack-smack-smacking* threat, but Birdie still feels safe, oh so protected. Her mommy's there. How nice.

She shut her eyes and said, Don't worry. I'm not tired yet.

It's okay if you are, I said.

Can you stop telling me everything's okay? she said.

Okay, I said.

Sorry, she said.

Kids called me Beaver Girl when I was younger, I said.

But I like your smile, she said.

What makes you think it was because of my smile? I said, smiling.

It's cute, she said.

It was about then I got out of bed wearing only my bra (!) and black lace panties (So bad!) and hurried to the washroom—a claustrophobia-inducing closet-like space with hexagonal tiles on the floor and a tumbleweed of pubic hair in the drain in the tub—where I parked my buns on the toilet, and felt my belly fold into three or four rolls that I squeezed and pinched until my entire tummy turned red. *Cute, cute, it's cute, my smile is cute.* I mouthed the words. The fan buzzed with dust balls obstructing its ventilation. I licked along the uneven outline of my teeth, breathed through my mouth, mouthing *cute, she thinks I'm cute* (!), more than just a teensy bit embarrassed my sensitive system had me having to be in there for so gosh darn dang it long (!).

By the time I'd returned, Birdie had switched beds, and there were more clothes on the carpet—her hat, bra, a pink pair of skid-marked panties (Awkward!).

But I don't want to touch yet, she warned.

That's fine, Birdie. That's just fine.

I sat at the foot of the bed next to where her feet made tiny teepees in the comforter. She asked me to lie down beside her. I said okay, but kept seated, my belly still reddened and layered like dough. My feet rested atop the luggage on the floor. I'd only brought one bag, my black adidas duffel with a string of anal beads and my work clothes inside. I was assistant manager at the Dunlop Street Timmies in Barrie five afternoons into evenings a week, the thankless three to eleven shift.

Wish I didn't have to work tomorrow, I complained.

She cracked her ankles under the comforter.

There are cockroaches in the Iced Cappuccino machine, I said.

Gross, she yawned.

A man yelled at me at work the other day because I put both of his donuts in the same bag, I said. Apparently one of the donuts was for a friend. So he says to me, Now I gotta touch my buddy's donut to get to mine! You should've seen his eyes, Birdie. He was actually angry about it, like really furious. I must've made a face too, because he goes, Don't make that face at me, bitch! Ha! I wonder what kind of face I was making. Wish I could've seen it.

Birdie buried her face under the covers.

Do you have a job? I asked.

Uh-huh—her response stifled through rose petal-patterned fabric—I told you online. I work at Yogen Fruz.

I placed one hand on the comforter where her right ankle was. She uncovered herself quickly, turned to look at me, and appeared provoked, as if she'd just now discovered I was there and didn't like it. Puzzled, I apologized. She rested her head back down on the pillow and asked why. She was asking why I was sorry, but what I heard was *why are you here?* The question kept repeating in my head. Why am I even here?

To be touched, I whispered creepily.

What?

By you.

I was acting very creepy, a little horny. It was almost entirely dark in the room by that point. I kept blinking for no reason. The thermostat lit green.

Do you like your job? I asked.

What? No. It's boring and cold. I need it though. Tuition. Booze.

Do your parents help?

Mom gives me money for books and bus passes when she can.

Well that's good.

Yeah.

Well, you know the old saying: A job's a job ya dirty slob!

What?

Ha! Yes siree, Bob. I'd be lying if I didn't admit my job can be boring sometimes too.

She turned onto her back and looked at the ceiling and sighed and said, I saw an old neighbor of mine at Yogen Fruz the other week. Sylvia Price. She didn't buy anything. I hoped she would, but she didn't. She just used our washroom. Her hair was really messy and she wore sweatpants. She looked bad.

Did you speak to her?

No. She doesn't know me. I was a baby when my family lived under hers. I probably would've said something though, if she'd come to the counter. I would've told her I was someone who knew who she was. Or *knows* who she *is*. Or maybe I wouldn't have.

How'd you recognize her?

What?

If you were a baby.

I've seen her online. Mom showed me a website she's got. For grieving parents or something, like she helps people with dead kids. Sylvia's son died.

Oh, I said. I see. That's hard. That's really hard.

Yeah.

How'd he die?

Doesn't matter.

That's really hard, I said.

I guess.

They say that's the hardest. I wouldn't know because I don't have children, let alone dead ones, or, like, a child that's passed—sorry—but I can only imagine, like. It must be so incredibly difficult to go through, get through. So hard.

Birdie asked me to please stop repeating myself. I apologized, with one hand on each of her ankles, rubbing them softly, wishing I hadn't just kept repeating myself.

Does that feel good? I asked.

I'm starving, she said.

It was pitch dark in the room, so we turned on the television and several lamps. Birdie was vegan, or *a* vegan—I never know how to gosh darn say it (!)—so there were very few options for her to choose from on the menu. She chose salad. Me, the chicken Parmesan, scalloped potatoes, and garlic (!) snow peas. Room service arrived promptly. We sat at a circular table next to the window with a bottle of red wine uncorked between our plates. Ate slow and drank fast, my brain spinning—spun until my thoughts tangled, and made tongue-tied pre-sentences that got tethered behind my teeth. We hardly spoke. *Two and a Half Men* was on television and it was unbearable. She played footsy with the stubble on my shins—unbearably unbearable (!). I took another swig of wine. I wore a bathrobe, and so did she, and neither of us had anything on underneath, and another swig, and I asked if she'd ever been in love.

She said she had, once before—a girl named Tess, who Birdie described as *the total worst*, with orange hair and a nose ring and a tattoo of a bell jar on her ankle and oh gosh was I jealous (!). She said it was an on-again off-again thing that went on and off again and again until eventually it turned off without end.

What happened?

Her feet slid away from mine, left cold bites from her toes on my ankles. She broke her salad down with the side of her fork, chopping lettuce leaves into tiny seed-sized portions, and eating them, one at a time to make the meal last forever. And forever stretched longer by the tale she told, about Tess—I think her last name was Gartner, Gardener, something *Gar?*—how they'd started seeing each other in secret their first year of high school, and then second year, and third, which is when Tess cheated on her with a boy—Phil or Bill or Will or something that makes me *ill* (Ha!).

Birdie didn't forgive Tess. Then Birdie forgave Tess. On and off and ongoing.

It was one of those, she said.

Been there, done that, I said, laughing a little, a little too loud and unaccountably.

Grade ten and eleven and twelve, she said, and we were together and not together the whole time. And I loved her. Like a lot. I was miserable.

Then winter. Graduating year. During a period they aren't dating *like technically*, Birdie receives a phone call around three in the morning. It's Tess. Tess asks Birdie what she's doing, and Birdie says nothing, and Birdie asks Tess what she's doing, and Tess screams, Don't pretend you don't already know!

Click—followed by a slithering sound of dead air.

Tess is still stuck in a mental facility, one Birdie described as similar to those I'd seen in cinema, with white padded walls, and cameras recording Tess's every move from the top corner of every room. She is strapped to a bed because she poses a risk to her own well-being. Believes aliens abducted her the night before she called Birdie, and operated on her face (!), or more specifically, her eyes (!!). She believes the aliens surgically removed her eyeballs and placed tiny cameras inside the sockets, then put the eyeballs back in place (!!!). Now everyone in the world has access to a secret channel on his or her television that allows them to see whatever Tess is seeing at any given time (!!!!), which, nowadays, must include a whole lot of padded walls (Ha!).

She can't be left alone, said Birdie, or else she'll try to cut them out.

The cameras?

Yeah. Her eyes. She has green eyes.

I swallowed a forkful of scalloped potatoes and said, Tragic. A tragedy is what that is.

It just happens like that, she said, and snapped her fingers. It happens overnight sometimes. Your brain fucks you over. It's totally terrifying.

I shook my head, agreeing. Her salad looked like crushed glass on the plate. She poked at it with her fork, packing shards tight along the tines. I fell to my knees in front of her, parted that uninvitingly off-white bathrobe she wore to reveal her legs, and kissed her shins, which she despised—not so much the kiss, necessarily, but shins, a close second behind *Jew nose* for the feature she hated most about herself. They were a tad dry and very slightly bruised and I very very slightly may have given one a little suckle (!). My eyes, throat, heart, stomach, lady parts (!) all tightened, but in a good way, and it was then I knew this encounter was different, unique compared to all of the others I had had on other nights in other hotel rooms. I suckled her shin again, relished its flavor—shin to ankle to foot to those awfully long and curved toes, my suckles not quite so very very slight anymore (!). I worked my way back up to her scrawny thighs.

She swept her thumb across my hairline, and pressed my forehead, before tracing down the bridge of my nose to my nose—Honk, she said—then touched my lips, my smile, ran her thumbprint over my teeth.

Beaver Girl, she said.

Don't make fun, I said.

Our eyes lethargic from too much wine, we ogled each other, dopily.

You drunk? she said.

Nope, I said.

You happy? she said.

Very much so, I said.

Are you happy in general? Are you generally happy?

Yes, Birdie. I'm so very generally happy.

She covered her legs back up. You know that lady I saw? My old neighbor Sylvia? I could tell how unhappy she is. I could tell she's done. Just done. You know? Existing. Using the washroom in places like Yogen Fruz and waiting to die. I could see it. You ever want to die?

The tightening in my body tightened tighter, tightened too gosh darn tightly (!), and I had to stand, shake the tightness out of me. I was perspiring buckets. My bathrobe stuck to the back of my thighs. I rushed to drop the temperature on the thermostat, as Birdie slid a beer across the table, and said to sit back down. She snapped the tab of her own can then, allowed the head to froth through the wide mouth and onto the carpet, landing foamy white, and dissipating into a stain that stayed there. She chugged.

I'm so happy, I said. I'm so happy to be alive right now.

Back under the covers on the same bed with our lips almost touching, breathing the food and alcohol, and other things, on the other's breath, like remnants of purple gum, her eyes gazing so deeply into mine those unbounded black pupils could've swallowed me whole. She reached a hand around to feel the top of my crack (!). We pressed chests. She told me to turn off the lamp on the nightstand. Her eyes twinkled in the dark.

I haven't seen Tess in two years, she said. After she lost her mind, her parents wouldn't let me talk to her. They say she was never gay. Her love for me wasn't real, they say, just an illusion, same as the aliens. All part of her mental illness. Two years. I don't even know if she's still got eyes in her fucking head.

Birdie nuzzled my breasts and let it out. I stroked her hair and said, It's okay it's alright it's okay, until perhaps she believed me, and began to quiet, pressing herself up so we were side by side again, face to face. I didn't kiss her. Just looked, my sight having adjusted enough to the night, to see each other, as the two of us drifted in and out of sleep, and dreams, seeing and not seeing, until the morning.

She parted the curtains a couple of feet, the sky a pearly plum hue. The rising sun still hadn't risen over all the tall buildings, but squeezed between them. The CN Tower on the skyline seemed to be directing the light where to go.

She hopped back in bed, our legs wrapping over and around each other's, and asked if I was too tired to do something, which I was, groggy with bad breath and only half aware, but I shook my head nonetheless and asked, What *something?*

Something.

Yes. What, Birdie?

Uh, she said. I don't know.

But she did, because immediately after saying she didn't she said, Watch porn?

Really?

Yeah. If you want.

Okay. Okay, sure. Okay. Yeah, I said.

I tried sitting up, searched disquietly for the television remote, but Birdie suggested we watch it from her laptop instead. So I waited in bed as she darted to her luggage, which was on the floor next to the footstool. She bent in the nude (!), flat-chested, hairy between the legs, with ribs like stiffened knuckles, and two jutted hip bones, everything about her naked body just as defined as her face. She asked what I liked. I told her it didn't matter, so long as there were no men involved, and she typed *gaping ass interracial lesbian yoga* into the search engine.

We cuddled for the next twenty minutes or so, cracking jokes about how phony it was, those oddly-shaped breasts and duck lips, the heavy breathing, kissing, cunnilingus, screaming, rubbing and tugging. Moist, meticulously groomed lady parts, scissoring. Birdie commented more than once on their skin, the lack of sweat, how each woman's face appeared *dry as a powdered sponge*, and even built up the audacity to ask at one point if I sweated during sex (!), if, to use her words exactly, my *tits got all slick and shiny when boning* (!!!), cackling as she said it.

But eventually the situation stopped being funny, and we watched the pornography in silence, counting freckles, pimples, moles, herpes sores (Oh god!) on the performers' bodies, keeping track of the bogus orgasms and the amount of times each girl glanced dead eyed at the camera. Several instances I felt the need to look away, and so looked at Birdie, seated beside me, so close I'd begun to notice new things—her earlobes, for one, how tiny they were, attached to the sides of her head and pulled firmly with hardly any flap. A middle-aged black woman squirted between a teenager's clavicles, and Birdie snickered, as I decided right then and there that those earlobes were my least favorite physical thing about her.

Nevertheless, I wrapped my lips over that sliver of skin, and held there, earlobe in my mouth, breathing through my nostrils and into her ear canal, and savoring it, her, yet another young girl, who tasted of virtually nothing.

By the time the pearly plum sky had brightened and become an even pearlier shade of watermelon, she'd placed her laptop on the nightstand and begun touching herself under the covers. I tried demanding her to stop, but she wouldn't, kept at it, that utter lack-of-earlobe glistening with dribble and leftover lipstick smears. I turned to the table where our half-eaten meals remained, malodorous. She climaxed, and leaned over to tweak my chin with wet fingers. Kissed my shoulder.

Hey! I said. Don't do that.

Why?

No kissing. We're not kissing.

You kissed my ear.

It wasn't a kiss.

You put your mouth on it. That's a kiss.

No. I didn't kiss. There was no kissing sound. There's a difference.

She tossed the covers off her legs and got out of bed, stood beside her bag beside the footstool, kicked the bag open but didn't start packing. She looked at it, and me.

What? I said.

Why'd you talk about the swastika?

I'm sorry?

Why'd you tell me there was a swastika on the synagogue?

What? I don't know. I was just telling a story.

Is it because my dad's a Jew?

No. What? I didn't know that.

Yeah you did. I told you that. Is that why you told me?

Please, Birdie.

Is it because my dad's a Jew?

I don't know what you're getting at, but you're upsetting me.

Was it supposed to impress me? Because it did.

I don't know what you're trying to do, Birdie.

She started clapping.

Stop it, Birdie.

Bravo, she said. Seriously. You're my hero. You painted over a swastika. Thank you so much. Can we fuck now? Tell me we can. Please, Lucy Jones. It's already tomorrow,

Lucy Jones, and we haven't even fucked yet. I'm totally legal and horny for you.

I curled into an S under the covers, started pinching and scratching the fat on my belly until the pain grew to be so gosh darn gargantuan I forgot who the heck I was (!).

When I reemerged I remembered—I am me. The curtains were all the way open and the television was turned on and there was a breaking news bulletin about Osama Bin Laden having just been found (!). Birdie was brushing her teeth in the washroom. She stepped out once she heard me unzip my duffel, and stood there on the carpet, still naked, scraping the brush against her tongue and watching me stumble into my tacky Timmies uniform, those slacks, that hairnet, frantically collecting whatever else was there, and leaving. And that's how I left—frantic, and in a rush—her words on a fiery loop inside my head, but only the ones with serrated edges— kissed, swastika, bravo, fuck.

I slapped my steering wheel with an open hand. The horn beeped, and others beeped back at me—one portly gentleman even went as far as to flash me his fat pickle-finger (Gag!). I said I was sorry, but not to him, not to the drivers around me, but to myself, perhaps, to my own eyes, oh so desperate in the rearview as I sped down Highway 400. I'm sorry, I said. And I kept imagining her back there—not at the hotel, but in the back seat of my car—three years old and unafraid, and seated beside the two cans of spray paint, rolling side to side on every turn.

7

My Eddie lay flat with his ear to the floor vent.

Mr. Beally's at it again, he said.

I was preparing egg and cheese sandwiches at the stove, and curly fries, celery sticks, cucumber slices, even a sugar-free strawberry milkshake, because it was the last day of summer and I wanted my Eddie to enjoy something special before his lunches turned back to cold cuts and boxed milk. But, as it so often did in our household, said specialness lost color in a jiff, and became depleted posthaste.

Floor's filthy, I told him.

He squeezed his eyes shut and gritted his teeth, as if doing so might make his hearing grow. I can't tell who's getting it, he said. I think it sounds like one of the girls this time.

I turned off the stove. It was oddly instinctual, how I had the knob back to zero before he had even completed the sentence—*I think it sounds like one of the girls* [click] *this time*. It should not have made a difference, but it did, having it be a girl, this time. The floor's filthy, I repeated, only louder, and much more meanly. It got him to his feet, which were big and pigeon-toed. He remained gawking fixedly at the dusty brown vent.

I apologized for having yelled.

He brushed the crumbs off his shirt and asked if lunch was almost ready.

Soon, I said. Five minutes. You go wash up, and don't touch the pans. They're hot. You go wash your hands and the food will be ready in five minutes tops. Okie dokie pokie? Go on. Five minutes. Don't touch the pans.

He looked at me like there had been a *blip* in my brain and I had malfunctioned. The same expression he gave his grandma who could not remember she was his grandma anymore. Don't shoot me that stare! I said, flouncing over to him, in a fraught effort to simulate everything-is-okayness by making believe things were not. You've got artwork on your face, I said in mock-anger, licking my thumb, attempting to wipe Crayola scratches from his freckled chin. But of course he was not having any of it. Mum! Mum! He squirmed, reiterating the word: Mum! Mum! Mum! Mum! as if my name were a repellent.

I told him to go wash up, to not touch the pans. Five minutes, I said.

He scuffed socked feet across the linoleum in cross-country fashion. My poor precious Eddie, cursed with his mother's clunky stride, dumpy bottom, ragweed allergies, and a spastic colon. He had recently turned ten. A Leo, as if that meant anything to anyone other than my sister, who taught classes on how to weave a dream catcher, and believed in genies. Eddie wore his blue sweatpants that day, with the monochromatic Tasmanian Devil spinning a twister on the left thigh, his beloved cap gun poked out at the hip. I had to sit down. I waited until he had left before I did, and then did it, butt on heels on floor with chin on knees, trying to breathe, just breathe, Sylvia, breathe. Focus on other, more pleasant, less nerve-racking things.

Pink posies. Haagen-Dazs. Kevin Costner. Scrapbooking. My Eddie's hair.

His hair.

The same red mine was before middle age turned everything dark.

Harry in the upstairs bathroom, still in his Starry Night pajama bottoms, and shirtless, a frenetic jolt to his eyes as he mulled over the sink. I stood behind him. It was the smell of mildew and unventilated morning. Black sandy water filled to the brim.

Drain's clogged again, he muttered, not turning. Eyes fastened to the shingle in the water. And my eyes on him. The M-curve of his hairline reflected in the oval mirror above the sink, and then his wide, fleshy, pimpled back, and plump neck, gradually melding into it.

Would you like to do something today? I asked.

Like what?

Anything. To celebrate the end of summer with Eddie.

Sure. That sounds good. Will you let me finish here first?

Of course. How long will you be?

Not sure.

Can you give me an estimate?

Sylvia. I'll be done when I'm done.

My head was pounding. I massaged my temples counterclockwise and thought about daffodils, saltwater taffy, my Eddie's red hair, youth. Sweet, edible youth.

Harry saw me in the mirror, finally. He sat me down on the toilet lid. I love you, he said. I love you. It's not our business what goes on down there. I love you. His wet hands on my collarbone. He kissed my mouth, my nose. He kissed each lens of my glasses. He brought my fingers away from my temples.

Take an aspirin, he said.

The veins on his forehead like cracks in an egg.

I'd like to celebrate the end of summer, I said again, always again with him, that is what it took, with certain men, again, again. Please, Harry?

When I'm done, he said, and following a *beat* of silence, or not quite silence, but a *beat* filled by the bark of the Millikens' collie in the street, Harry added, It'll pass.

My Eddie asked to eat in front of the television, which normally I would not allow, but, to recap, it was the end of summer, and I was feeling extra generous. So I set a tray for him. Folded a paper towel over his collar, kissed his sweaty hair, and said, Enjoy. I sat on the other side of the couch with my feet curled under me. He ate the cucumbers first. He ate the fries. My brain, minced. I watched him watch *Leave It to Beaver*. He smiled buck-toothed whenever Eddie Haskell said something snarky.

I used to watch this show when I was your age, I said.

You've only told me that a googolplex times, he said, chomping celery.

A googolplex?

Yes.

A whole, entire googolplex? You sure?

Yesssssss, Mum. Crunching his food. Yes!

Well, I'm sorry then.

I stayed put until the first commercials came on. An ad for Burger King. Wish I was eating a whopper instead, he said. My vision undulated as I bent my neck this way and that, but no direction could help ease whatever it was I was feeling.

You okay, Mum? Your head hurt again?

My Eddie's gun rested on the cushion between us. I picked it up as instinctively as I had turned off the stove, like I did not realize what I was doing until it was done. He said there were no caps left in the cylinder. I tried sticking the barrel in my pocket, but the pocket was too small, too tightly pressed to my thigh. So I unbuttoned my jeans and slid it down the front. The handle visible above the waist similar to how my Eddie always had it. Mum? he said. I stood straighter, and took off my glasses. It did not matter the world appeared muddled. I looked better. I would march back upstairs and try again, looking better. Much more confident this time. That is the key, Sylvia. Confidence!

Uh. Can you move, Mum, please? I can't see the TV.

Neither could I. I put my glasses back on.

Harry shirtless and barefoot on the bathroom floor. His cheeks mottled from stress. His nostrils flared. Fat ankles and foot fungus, and more hair on his gut than head, and that voice, the routed syllables, Why is this so hard?

I stood outside the door because the bathroom floor had become one pungent puddle. He sat soaking in it, leaned against the side of the tub, his face more sickly than mine, and with a whitewashed expression. A hammer on the floor beside him. And a drill. And a slinky, and a wooden spoon, and a shoelace, and a clothing hanger, all prepared to render something jerry-rigged.

I'll do it, he said.

Harry, come downstairs.

I love you, he said.

I had known him since we were kids. His father had been the same, a hard man, the kind who would rather perish than tolerate a tricky drain. Sometimes, steadily shifting to oftentimes, Harry reminded me of the old man. He would walk stiffly on purpose to widen his shoulders, drink scotch from the bottle, eat Pringles off the carpet, and avoid the primary problem by choosing to obsess over something else.

It's the pipes, he said. The insides of the pipes are peeling. They're disintegrating, I think, and the pieces are what's clogging the drain, I think.

You should call a plumber.

A waste.

But Harry.

Why pay a stranger when I can do it fine?

Please, Harry.

Quit bending your neck like that! he snapped. If your head hurts, hon, take a pill. Another aspirin. How many have you had? I'll be done in no time and then we can go have fun with the Edster. Okay? So go get rid of that headache. Lie down. I love you. You've got a gun in your pants, by the way. Heh. I love you.

Be the better dad, I said.

What? he said. Am I not? He stood, hammer in hand, water trickling off the face and claw. Tell me, Sylvia. Tell me. Am I not? He turned to the sink. I chose not to stick around for the racket. Downstairs I found Eddie slurping melted cheese grease off his plate. I asked if he would like to join me on a walk to the convenience store. How's that sound? You can choose a candy for school tomorrow! He strapped on his rollerblades, Ren & Stimpy-stickered helmet, elbow and kneepads, and skated in front the whole way there. A good number of the sidewalk squares were broken, but my Eddie skated speedily, around the cracks, or bunny hopping over them, and never stumbled, not once.

At the store, he could not decide between a Kit Kat, Twix, or Jawbreaker, so I said I would buy him all three if he made a funny face, and another funny face, and another funny face, and honest to God, my Eddie made three of the funniest faces I had ever seen. On our way home, he glided on one foot, both arms outstretched at impeccable right angles. He skated with his eyes shut. Skated backwards. That clunky stride of his employed a newfound elegance when wheels were attached to his feet. Maybe he would grow to be a famous figure skater, like Elvis Stojko, humble, handsome, curly-haired, Canadian. But would the other boys make fun? Ridicule those gaudy hand-stitched costumes he would have to wear, equipped with sequins, and giant dragonfly wings? Kids could be so cruel. *So what* if my Eddie had wings?

I drew the cap gun from the front of my jeans and loaded it with caps I had bought at the store. Handed it to Eddie once we were on the driveway, handle-out, as if passing a pair of scissors, and told him to shoot.

He aimed at the high window, where the noise was coming from. Harry swinging his hammer and making everything so much worse. Eddie fired in retaliation.

Not ten minutes later I found Harry in the kitchen boiling a pot of water. He stood next to the stove with a saltshaker in hand.

Cooking noodles? I asked.

No, he said. Burning water's supposed to unclog the drain.

He had put on a shirt. It was a brown button-up with the breast pocket half-torn, flap dangling loosely by a couple threads. He also wore shorts. His knees showed, cracked and grey. I squeezed my fingers so forcefully my nails punched holes in my palms. I showed him the indents, and tried to express with my eyes that something bad, no, downright dreadful, was building, a dire edifice inside me, brick by culpable brick.

Why are you looking at me like that?

It hurts. My headache keeps getting worse.

Did you take one aspirin or two?

Enough with the fucking aspirin! I wanted to scream. [bubbling]

Harry asked if I was okay.

No. I felt bombarded. By him. By the thought of aspirin. By the too many tawdry details of our kitchen. It was hog-printed wallpapered walls, and checkered countertops, and all that dust and grime, and stains from spills, that garroted me. It was capers on the floor, or stuck to my feet. It was the sound that emanated from the vent. Breathe, Sylvia. Think pink posies. Haagen-Dazs. My Eddie's hair. Youth. My own hair. Red. The red my hair used to be. Kevin Costner. It was the sound of those children, trapped under us, and me, my own pitiable, enabling performance. Breathe.

The kitchen curtains looked like an enormous orange bat roosted on top of the pane.

Please, I begged.

Harry sprinkled salt in the water.

What are you doing?

It'll help it boil better, he said.

I moved to the door that led to the backyard. The sky was bright blue, almost white, and there was an airplane creeping across the clouds like a fly on a sheet of glass.

The water will scald whatever's blocking the drain, he said.

The airplane was not a plane at all, but a fly on the screen glass door.

Scald it to nothing, he said.

I slid the door open and the fly took off, and when I slid the door shut I was on the other side. And the calm was remarkable. A Sunday quiet. But the yard was the same as the kitchen in the sense it demonstrated some hodgepodge of unprepossessing detail. And so I took a moment, to think, to picture . . . flagstones. They would lead toward a vegetable garden on the other side of the enclosure. The path delimited by blanket flowers, perennial sage. At the end, big bright beautiful tomatoes. I breathed.

The desiccated lawn pricked my feet, but I still ventured barefoot, circled around the side of the house to the front and stopped at the steps that led up to my front door, while looking down the steps leading to theirs. I counted eight in total. I stood on their welcome mat. We had lived above the Beallys' basement apartment for six years and I had never once knocked. My hand pressed flat against the door and held there. The wood was cold, coarse as oil paint dried on canvas.

I sat on the cement steps outside my front door. Was not exactly sure what I was waiting for until he had returned, car pulled to the curb with Shiny Happy People coming out the windows. He turned off the ignition. Stepped out. He walked around the front, ran his fingers across the hood, his steel-toed boots and work pants caked in broken dirt.

Mum!

My Eddie's muffled voice. I turned to see him standing at the window. He must have heard Trigger's car pull up, the screech of tires, the R.E.M. in the tape deck. He waved, and I waved back, and the sunlight reflected off the glass and into my glasses, and I was blinded, momentarily, while sightlessly musing over the excitement I once felt seeing my own mom or dad on the opposite side of a window.

Trigger treaded dirt off his boots down the paved walkway. He was pushing thirty, close to a decade younger than me, but his face was in rough shape. A couple of bags under each eye, and a sun-burnt nose, and his hair peppered with dead skin, his beard bristly as the grass in the yard. I could feel the beat of my heart in my chest and the beat of my brain in my skull as Trigger tried to smile. He held a cigarette between two fingernails tainted black underneath. Sucked in. Afternoon, he exhaled.

Hello, I said.

Garden looks good.

I purchased most of my tools from your store, I said.

Not my store, he mumbled. Just work there.

I turned to the window, but Eddie was gone. Handprints on the glass, and a curtain the color of unbleached silk, and that was all. Sweat tickled my eyebrows.

You mind? he asked.

My eyes watered as I looked up at his face. I told him I did not mind, though I was not quite sure what he had been referring to. He tossed his cigarette in my garden.

The door screeched open at the bottom of the stairs. One of his children stepped out, the youngest boy, Minster. He carried a Tupperware container of Cheerios. Trigger's face softened at the sight of him. Little Minster, he said. Minster nodded in accord, that was in fact his name, and Trigger said, You eating a feast, buddy? Another nod. Minster shoveling cereal in his mouth. Little Minster, Trigger crooned, eating a delicious and nutritious feast. Look at him go, folks. It's Little Minster!

Minster tilted the container toward his mouth. Most of the Cheerios fell past his cheeks and onto the ground.

Trigger looked back at me. I'm gonna go inside, he said.

Alright, I said. Be good.

What?

Minster on his hands and knees, picking Cheerios off the welcome mat and eating them. I could only imagine how filthy that mat was. Minster's drool, Trigger's cruddy boots, the plantar wart on my left heel. I wanted so badly to tell him to stop, to stand him up and take him and the others home with me.

How's your boy? Trigger asked.

Pardon? Oh, he's good. He's been well, thank you.

I can hear him shooting his gun sometimes.

Oh. It's just a toy.

I know it's a toy.

Oh. Sorry. Of course.

Yeah. Well, I'm gonna go inside. How's Harry?

He's fine. He's fixing the sink in our bathroom.

What's wrong with it?

It's clogged.

Tell him to flush the pipes with hot water. If that don't work, use Drano.

Yeah, I think that's what he's doing. That's what he's planning to do.

Kay. I'm gonna go inside.

He walked down the steps to Minster and lifted the boy by the back of his shirt. Little Minster, he said, eating food off the floor like a doggy. It's Little Minster, folks!

Arf-arf-arf-arf-arf.

Their door opened and then slammed shut.

8

She used to cut herself. Sometimes with razorblades, other times with safety pins, or scissors, or X-Acto knives. One time she even stabbed herself with a metal fork. She was washing the dishes, and after cleaning this one particularly filthy fork, she just started doing it; she started jabbing herself with the fork, over and over, directly in the pit of her left elbow. Red polka dots appeared on her arm like little bleeding freckles, and they started leaking every-where, staining the oaken tiles on the kitchen floor. Blood got on the fork as well. She had to wash it again.

It may seem weird, but sometimes I felt like I under-stood why she did those kinds of things. When I was younger, like nine or ten, my mom used to make me read the bible for a half an hour every night before I went to sleep. And there was this reading lamp beside my bed, and sometimes I used to sit there and press different parts of my body against it, the burning bulb. Like one time I touched it with my ear, and then another time I rubbed my thighs against it. It always hurt a lot. Then another time, I cupped my entire hand around it, grabbed the bulb like it was a stress ball, and squeezed. I pulled away as soon as the pain got unbearable, which was pretty quick, but then I just did it again. I kept burning my hand and my fingers, over and over, like I couldn't stop doing it. Is that weird? I used to think it was pretty weird, but then I just assumed that's what everyone does when they're forced to sit beside a lamp. I don't know though. I haven't done it in a while, but I did it when I was young. And I guess that's why I feel like I understand the whole cutting thing in a way, because maybe the light bulb was the same sort of thing as the cutting. Was it? I don't know. A bit maybe, but probably not.

The first time I met her she was wearing socks on her arms. They must've been soccer socks or hockey socks or some sort of sports socks, because they were really long and bulky, pretty much covering her entire arms, stretching from her wrists to her armpits. She cut off the foot part of the socks so her little hands could pop out the ends, and it looked funny, but I didn't care much. I mean I guess I thought it was weird she wore socks on her arms, but not entirely. It was probably her own unique style or whatever, so who was I to judge?

What are you reading? I asked her, even though I could see she was reading a book called *Tales of Mystery & Imagination* by Edgar Allan Poe, and it was a really thick book, maroon cover, vintage, leather bound.

A book, she replied.

A book? I said. What kind of book?

The kind you read, she said.

I don't like reading, I said.

She didn't say anything.

Oh, I said.

It was lunch period, grade ten, and it was the beginning of fall. There was a breeze, but it wasn't too cold yet. I guess it was jeans-and-sweater kind of weather. She only wore a T-shirt, but she was probably kept warm by those socks on her arms. She sat beneath a tree in a field behind Williams High, cross-legged, with her back against the stump. All of the leaves on the tree were red and yellow and orange, and it looked like the tree was on fire and pieces of fire were falling all around her.

Is it for school or for pleasure? I asked.

What? She already seemed annoyed I was talking to her.

Are you reading that book because you have to read it for school, or is it for pleasure?

For pleasure, she said, but I don't seem to be getting much pleasure out of it now that you're standing here bothering me. No offense.

She was a bitch. It made me like her even more. I don't know why. I decided to leave her alone though. I turned to leave, but then she asked, What the hell's your name, again?

I turned back around, probably smiling like a dumbass because she wanted to know my name. Minster Beally, I told her.

Murder? she said.

Minster, I said. I know it's kind of a weird name. My sister calls me Monster.

Murder? she said again, only this time she was laughing a little. Your name's actually Murder? I've never met a kid named Murder before. Are your parents fucking demented or something? She was really laughing hard now, like calling me Murder was the most hilarious thing to ever happen. I think she was making fun of me but I'm not sure, and honestly, I didn't care if she was, because she was smiling, and she had a really nice smile. Well, Murder, she said, I'm Eloise.

I think we're in the same science class, I told her. Mr. Webb's science class.

No, really? she said. I've been in the same class as a kid named Murder and didn't realize? Guess I'm finally fucking losing it, huh?

No, I said, sort of nervously. I just really liked her by that point. I don't know why. She was just so weird, and bitchy, yet lovely. I don't know. Maybe it didn't make sense I liked her so much, but I did. I even tried saying it.

I like, uh.

She kept looking down at her book, but I don't think she was reading. I think she was smiling again, because her lips moved a little. It was pretty difficult to see her face.

Uh what? she said.

Eloise wasn't beautiful the way the models on *America's Next Top Model* are beautiful, but she was pretty in a normal person kind of way. She had dark brown hair. It was cut short, like halfway down her neck. It was really straight, and always hanging in front of her eyes. She'd blow it away, and it'd fall back down again, and she'd say something like, Fuck off, hair. Her eyes were medium grey, sort of like an elephant's skin, or the sky before it rains. They were really nice looking. Her body was a bit small though. She was short, and her arms and legs were kind of short too. She usually wore boys' clothes and never any makeup, and I guess from a distance she looked like a boy, but up close, her eyes were big and her eyelashes were long and there were faint freckles on her cheeks and nose. And her teeth, even though they were a bit square, were snow white and perfectly straight. I don't know why, but I just thought she was really pretty sometimes. A lot of the time, even. You just had to notice it.

I didn't even realize there were cuts on her arms until wintertime. Her skin got pale and the scars turned dark purple because of the cold. She didn't wear socks on her arms anymore, so I saw the cuts one weekend when we were hanging out in her basement.

What are those lines from? I asked her. For some reason I didn't want to use a word like cuts or scars or anything like that to describe them.

Nothing, she said. Just stupidity, I guess.

Did you do that to yourself?

Cut myself?

Yeah.

Yeah, I did.

How come?

Don't know. Don't worry about it though. It's no big deal.

But why? I said. Why would you do that to yourself?

Murder. Seriously. Stop asking me why I did it. She stared at the floor, probably at one of the stains on the carpet. Maybe I don't know why. Maybe I just felt like it, and that's all, and there's no other reason. Why does there always have to be a fucking reason for everything?

We were on the couch. It was covered with clear plastic, and there was dog hair stuck to the plastic, and it was starting to stick to my clothes as well. I sneezed, and then she laughed and told me my sneeze sounded like a queef, and then I laughed.

She got up and walked over to a huge wooden shelf on the other side of the room. It was packed full of her dad's records. Eloise pulled out an album by Bob Dylan called *The Times They Are A-Changin'*, and there was a black and white picture of Dylan on the cover looking pretty peeved. She slipped the record out of its case, put it on the player, turned it on. She kept the volume low, maybe because her parents were sleeping upstairs. She'd recently gotten into folk music. It was because the U.S. was talking about invading Iraq soon and Eloise was against it. She said what we needed was a good protest song to protest the idea, but all we had was slutty bullshit like Christina Aguilera, or insanely retarded bullshit like Eiffel 65, so the songs written forty years ago would have to do. Anyways, I liked the record. The music was soft and mellowy, sort of like the opposite of her. She started dancing, but not really. She snapped her fingers to the strum of the guitar, making her way back to the couch, walking with more grace than usual. Like there was more rhythm in her step, if that makes any sense.

I was trying my best not to sweat or be awkward. Eloise sat down beside me and leaned her head on my shoulder. Her face was near my armpit and I hoped I didn't smell bad because sometimes I'd smell bad out of nowhere. She held my left hand in both of hers. Her nails were colored green with permanent marker. There was a drawing of two stick figures having ass sex on the back of her right wrist. She spoke quietly, maybe whispering. Some boys like girls with scars, she said.

How come?

Because boys like to think they protect girls, she told me, and when a boy sees a girl with cuts, he thinks that means she's fucked up and damaged, or needs to be saved in some way. It's lame as hell, but boys go crazy for girls like that, ones they think are sad or lost or troubled, whatever. They always want to feel like they're protecting us, you know? Even though there's mostly nothing to protect us from.

I thought I understood what she was saying, but not entirely. Funny thing is though, after seeing all those scars on her arms, I sort of did feel like I wanted to save her, protect her, do all the things she was just talking about. And I wanted to kiss her as well, like kiss the scars, and then maybe after I kissed them they would disappear.

Don't worry, I said. I wouldn't ever try to save you.

I think she smiled. I didn't see the smile, but I felt it. Her cheek moved against my shoulder. I can swim, she said, so if you see me drowning, it's because I want to be drowning. Sometimes people need to chill the fuck out and let other people drown.

Yeah, I said, nodding as if it all made perfect sense. Then we just sat there for a while, not really talking much, just listening to the music, and listening to each other breathe, and the sound of the furnace, and other things. Occasionally I'd kiss the top of her head, maybe every ten minutes or so. I wanted to be doing it every second, but I didn't want her to think I was super needy or anything like that.

So that was around the time I decided to start hurting myself too. Eloise did it, and it's not like I was a follower or anything, but I guess I sort of followed in a way. I didn't cut myself like she did, but I beat myself up a bit. I only did it when I was feeling extra sad about something, or if I hated myself that week. Like the week I couldn't stop washing my legs. I kept feeling like my legs were so dirty, like I could see bacteria on the skin and in the hairs. I punched myself in the face a lot that week.

Then there was the week I got scared my penis might cut open if it touched anything. I was even concerned about it rubbing inside my boxers. So I started wrapping masking tape around it every morning, to protect it I guess, and peeling the tape off in the shower every night. It's kind of funny to think about now, but not at the time, like when it was actually happening it got me feeling pretty upset. I mean I knew how crazy it was, wrapping tape around my penis and all, and yet, I still had to do it. Or felt like I had to. And the routine of standing there in the shower each night, taking the tape off wet so it wouldn't hurt as much, well, I gave myself two black eyes that week. I even called Kids Help Phone, for help. The woman who answered sounded angry after I'd told her what was wrong. She said, Listen carefully, sir. Kids Help Phone is not a joke. Then hung up on me. I thought it was funny she'd called me *sir*. I told Eloise about it, the call and the masking tape. Is your dick taped now? she asked. I told her it was. Her ears wiggled when she smiled. You're more fucked than I thought, she said, like a less cool Sid Vicious or something.

It wasn't until a little before spring that we started getting really intimate. Truth is, I tried putting off sexual things as much as possible. I was fifteen, and pretty inexperienced, and there were rumors Eloise had been with a few boys before me, and they were older, and she'd done things with their penises, and I wasn't sure how I felt about letting her do things with mine, never mind the fact I was a recovering penis-taper.

Her parents went away for a few nights, so she invited me to sleep over. I told my mom I was going to stay at Carver's new place, and then walked to Eloise's house because it was only a few blocks away. She hugged me when I got there, and gave me a hickey. Then we made dinner together—macaroni and two root beer floats. She wore a plaid dress shirt and jean shorts and mismatched socks, one black, the other rainbow. Her hair was longer around that time, and sort of resembled a mullet. She wore red mascara and it made it look like her eyes were bleeding.

After dinner we watched her favorite movie *The Princess Bride*, only we didn't really watch it. She talked mostly and I just listened. Sometimes she talked about normal things like music, or her part-time job at Country Style, or exams coming up, but then other times she talked about other kinds of things. She told me that sometimes her body felt real fragile. She asked if I'd ever hurt my funny bone, and I told her I had, and she told me to imagine my entire body feeling that way. A quivering pain, she called it, but the pain isn't just in your elbow. It's everywhere, and sometimes the twinge grows to be so bad you can't move. You just lie there in bed and wait it out and wonder if what you're feeling is real or just in your head. You know what I mean, Murder? What I'm trying to say is I think I understand you.

Eloise led me to her bedroom. It was my first time being up there because we were normally only allowed in the basement or main floor. There were posters on the walls. Most of them were of stuff like world maps, or diagrams of human bodies. There was also one of Viggo Morten-whatever from *Lord of the Rings*. Eloise sometimes told me she wished I was more rugged like him.

Do you want me to strip? she asked.

I nodded.

Her bedroom was full of candles. None were lit, but the room still smelled like burning cinnamon. She was naked. She skidded over to the closet and opened it, looked at herself in a mirror attached inside one of the doors. She played with her boobs a bit, telling me not to look. Then turned to me, blushing. Just wanted to make sure they're nice and perky for you, she said.

I pretended to be cool and started undressing.

She walked over to me. I noticed there were cuts on her stomach, each about an inch long, streaked below her bellybutton. They looked new, only beginning to scab. I told her I used to burn myself with light bulbs. Eloise kissed my mouth. I was naked. She stuck her tongue in my mouth and moved it around, rubbing it against my tongue, and our tongues tasted sweet and sour. She pulled me towards her. She reached for the light on the night-stand and switched it off. She lay beneath me. I started kissing her. I kissed her mouth, her neck, her breasts, her stomach. She moaned approvingly, and I sort of had a boner. It was fun. She grabbed one of my hands and placed it on top of one of her boobs. I kept kissing her stomach with the one arm stretched over my head, playing with her nipple, pinching it sort of. It was more rubbery than I'd imagined it would be. I liked it. Blood rushed to my face, and I felt hot, and I sweated. She thrust her hips. The cuts on her belly tasted more sour than her tongue.

I was kissing my way back up. Suddenly everything felt different. Stomach, breasts. They were wet. I kissed her neck and it was wet as well, and I could feel the wetness on my face, and in my mouth. It was like she'd smeared herself in grease or something. Still, I didn't stop. I kissed her lips, but they were wet also, and the wetness was getting in both our mouths now, so I said, Wait. Wait. What's going on?

Eloise reached for the nightstand. Turned on the light. My eyes adjusted and I could see she was covered in blood. Completely covered in it, like maybe she'd slit her wrists and just started lathering herself in it.

You're covered in blood, I said, a bit traumatized.

You too, she said.

It was all over the bed too, on the pillows and the sheets. The room looked like a scene from one of those French horror movies. What's happening? I said.

She squinted at me for a second, and then started laughing.

What? I said, about ready to cry.

Dude, she said, your nose is bleeding.

It was. It was bleeding all over the place, all over her bed and her body and her pretty little face. And all I could think about was SARS. Everyone was making such a big deal about SARS around that time. Quinlynn's friend's boyfriend's grandma even died from it I think. And I think a bloody nose was one of the symptoms. Was it?

Oh shit, I said. I am so, so, so sorry. Oh my god, I'm sorry.

Eloise kept laughing. Why the hell's your fucking nose bleeding?

I don't know. Oh my god. I think I have SARS.

Maybe you're nervous, she said. I hear people get bloody noses when they're nervous about something. And the air's pretty dry in here.

Maybe, I said. I don't know. Ugh. Oh god. I'm trying not to faint.

She hopped off the bed. I considered killing myself right then and there. I pretty much ruined her sheets. She wasn't mad though. She actually made me feel a lot better. She just kept saying, Don't worry about it. It's actually kind of funny when you think about it.

I was about to put my clothes back on, but she told me not to. She grabbed an old style camera off her desk, and asked if we could take some pictures.

For what? I asked.

I don't know. This just seems like the type of thing we should capture.

The photo session lasted about an hour. By the end of it the blood had dried, and we took turns scratching flakes off each other's shoulders. I sat down on the side of the bed, pulled my boxers up, feeling a bit weird about the whole thing. Eloise walked over to me, put her hands on my cheeks the way my dad used to, and kissed me on the forehead, real gentle and cute-like.

You're funny, she said.

I never really spoke to her again after that. Not sure why. It was just one of those things that ended. Occasionally I'd maybe pass her in the halls at school, or I'd see her reading under some tree during lunch period, but that wasn't too often. Truth is, I mostly forgot about her.

One day nearing the end of that school year though, I opened my locker and there was a yellow envelope on the top shelf, and it said *MURDER* across the front. I opened it and there was a photograph inside. A black and white photograph of the two of us, and we were naked, and there was blood all over our faces and bodies. You could tell I was the one who took the photo because my arm was stretched out of frame, holding the camera. Then I had my other arm around her waist. I was leaning downward, and she was on her tippy toes and looking upward, and in the photo we were kissing. I don't know much about photography, but it was actually a really nice looking photograph. Our bodies were pressed against each other and they just sort of fit nicely together, like our bodies were meant to be together. I think that's why she wanted me to see it. So I could see it for myself, the curves of our bodies connecting like that. The photo turned us into something important, I think, like something you could hold, not just another fleeting thing.

I ripped the photograph though. I couldn't risk bringing it home because if my mom saw, she would know I'd been naked with a girl. So I tossed the pieces in the garbage, on top of some applesauce. That way I knew no one would try to pick it out and see.

Eventually I told my Uncle Tony about me punching myself. He promised not to tell anyone, then phoned the school. So I had to go to these group meetings the last couple weeks of the semester, and sit in a circle with a bunch of other kids who hurt themselves too. Most were girls who cut, like Eloise. They wore bracelets and fancy sweatbands to cover the cuts. When it was my turn to talk, I said sometimes my hands felt dirty no matter what, even right after I washed them, so I'd get stressed about it, the dirtiness, and start punching myself in the face, or hitting myself in the face with a mini-stick. They made me start seeing a counselor one on one after that. Her name was Barb-something. She looked like a Hispanic Monica Lewinsky. She made me talk about a lot of difficult things, like Soccer, or my dad. She also asked a ton of questions about Eloise, as if Eloise was one of the reasons I hurt myself, but she wasn't. Eloise was actually what made me want to be normal. Like I'd think about her, and girls in general, how pretty they all were with their ears and smells and the way they cared about their hair and stuff, and it made me want to be as normal as possible.

Sometimes Uncle Tony called to ask how I was doing. I'd tell him I was good, that I wasn't mad at him for calling the school, like I knew he was just trying to be a good uncle and all, so it was fine. He'd ask if I'd spoken to my dad recently, and I'd tell him no. It's not because he doesn't love you, he'd say, and I'd tell him I know. Love's a hard thing, he'd say, and I'd tell him I know that too. And I'd always feel a bit better and a bit stronger after talking to Uncle Tony because he had the same voice as my dad, telling me I was a good kid, that I'd be okay in the end.

I'd hang up the phone, go find my mom. One time she was loading the dishwasher. I wrapped my arms around her. She dropped the spatula she was holding and started crying right then and there. I don't know what I'd been expecting, but not that. I held her for a while. When I let go, she made me tomato sauce and melted cheese on Triscuit crackers.

Exam day was the last time I saw Eloise. She was seated on the bleachers beside the football field. I was standing in the Williams High parking lot with Hermie and her boyfriend Ollie. Eloise was far away, but I knew it was her. She was wearing a baggy sweater and some high cut, polyester shorts. I think she was smoking a cigar, but I'm not positive. I could see smoke around her face though. She was sitting by herself, smoking the maybe-cigar, occasionally tilting her head back to look at the sky, probably to see what the clouds looked like.

I love her.

Hermie and Ollie weren't even listening. One of them said, What?

I love her, I said. I really love her so much. I love Eloise.

I kept saying it, like ten times in a row. I probably sounded like a mental patient, but I still kept saying it. I honestly believed I truly did love her in that moment, but the funny thing is, I didn't even know what love was last year. Like, I didn't really understand what the word meant. I still don't, actually. But I know I loved her. And it wasn't in some lame, sappy, corny, stupid, romantic way either. It's not like I wanted to marry her or anything. I didn't even want to be boyfriend-girlfriend with her anymore. I just loved her, I really did, and that's all there was to it, and after that there was nothing else.

So I was watching her from the parking lot. Like I said, it was from a distance, but it looked like she was rolling up her shorts a bit. Then it looked like she was pressing the burning end of the cigar into her thigh. Like she was putting out the cigar by pushing it into her skin. I can't be sure, but that's what it looked like.

Hermie and Ollie got in the car. I got in too, and Ollie drove us out of the parking lot. We had to pass the football field once we were on Dunning Avenue. She was still sitting there on the bleachers, all by herself, arms crossed, just staring down at her thighs. I don't know why, but it bothered me she was sitting there alone. Not a lot though. I mean, if she was sitting there by herself, then it was because she wanted to be sitting there by herself. Still, a part of me wanted to go over and say hi, and hug her, maybe even kiss the burns on her thighs. But I didn't go over there, of course. We just drove past. Eloise disappeared behind the plazas in the back windshield of the car. Then I faced forward, and opened my window, and let the sun touch my face like a billion burning light bulbs. But the heat came from so far away. I mean I could hardly even feel it.

9

Next night I'm Tony the Worm Picker. Flashlight strapped to my forehead. Empty coffee cans duct taped to my ankles. A Vietnamese man with a grey goatee and scraped knuckles filling the left can with so much sawdust I can hardly lift my foot. He keeps the right one empty, says it's for storing worms. I think about the worms, their weight and texture, the taste of them. It's past ten o'clock. I still haven't eaten breakfast, lunch or dinner. My stomach rolls like thunder. The sawdust looks like Parmesan cheese.

Finally the truck stops and the back doors pull open. The road outside is rutted mud. I go first and others follow. All of them wear ponchos, none of them speaks English. The rain falls and clatters and sounds like spilt bullets, popcorn popping. I watch the other worm pickers start to disperse. Their yellow ponchos like flames burning out in the dark. I rub my eyes with cold, clammy hands, and stay standing next to the five-ton truck. My body swabbed in tail light, head bowed at the steel toes of my boots. They're sunk in the stink of saturated manure. I should've worn rain boots, but don't own any. I ask the Vietnamese man what the sawdust is for.

Worms, he says. They slip, he says. Sawdust better grip, he says.

Ah, I say.

Yah, he says.

Hah, I say.

He doesn't say anything after that. Just sits inside the truck on an upside down bucket of grip primer. He looks at the rain, the dark, me. Sips coffee from a stainless steel thermos and holds a cigarette between his thumb and pinky. I breathe his smoke, the manure, the worms and coffee. It all plays tricks on my appetite, tugging it back and forth. I ask to bum a cigarette. The Vietnamese man taps his wrist and tells me, Time-a-tickin. I bend down, pull a worm from the earth and hold it up to him. The worm curls like the feeling I've got in my gut. I pinch it end to end and start stretching the poor thing until there's blood. The Vietnamese man asks what I'm doing. I tell him not to worry, I'll stanch the blood. I tell him I'm making money.

I walk with the weight of my boots sticking heavy to the soil. Dip my fingers in sawdust and pluck worms like unwanted hairs. My back already burning. The fire spreads and catches inside my ribs and calves and eyes, eyes to the ground. Bunches of worms like moldered brains. There are hundreds, thousands, hundreds of thousands of them. Within minutes I could feed the ocean.

My brother once told me an anecdote about the ocean. This is when I was eleven and he was fifteen and his story was about something he saw floating on the water. It was suspended far off, a speck on the horizon. But my brother knew the speck was a girl. He didn't know how he knew, but did. A certainty had taken root in him. He kicked off his boots, dove in, swam out to her. She was floating at a distance too far to swim, but he swam it. Made it there in under an hour, aches cutting every inch of him. Said he found her laid across a wooden raft. She was naked, body buried under a thousand deep cuts. He told me she was dead, but her eyes were open. She was looking at him. Her lips were moving and she was saying things. That's what my brother told me to picture—a dead girl speaking to him on a raft in the middle of the ocean.

And what she's saying's important, he said.

He didn't describe the girl in detail, other than the cuts. But I imagined her with blond hair and eyes. Eyes so blond they were almost white. Pupils dilating on only white. Blue, broken lips. It was an image that bothered me worse than closet monsters or the cobwebs on the ceiling ever did. Kept me up more nights than Pa's holocaust tales. Crept like a shadow on the wall of an empty room.

Rain snaps against the plastic hood of my poncho. I've got Trigger on the brain now. That's my brother. Trigger. Pa's idea. He wanted to call me Bullet, to go with it, but Ma wouldn't let him. She said it was her turn to name a kid, and called me Tony after a mutt she owned when she was little. Tony Baloney, Pa used to say.

Tony Baloney, I say.

Brown puddles collect and spill over wet folds of dirt, stretching far across shadowy farmland. I follow their paths. I feel forever away. Turn back around and see the truck, but barely. It's a speck the size of a raft that's not a raft, but a speck. Fuck. I'm tired and starving and my mind's crashing harder than the rain. I sit on the muddy cushion of the soybean field and feel everything move faster than it should. Tony Baloney, I say. Baloney, I say. Baloney.

Trigger and I were kids in Toronto in the early seventies. A neighborhood people called Bush Flats. It was the antithesis of Forest Hill, where the wealthy Jews lived. Bush Flats was tarnished land. Made up of dirt and broken glass.

Our bungalow was in essence a brick box. It had a corrugated roof and front steps that weren't there. The door stood more than a meter off the ground. Pa had to leave a stepladder outside, but people kept stealing it. He assumed it was teenagers at first, but once caught a grown man trying to take it. So Pa didn't have to feel too guilty about beating the hell out of him. Punched the guy in the face until both his eyebrows split open.

Pa replaced the stolen stepladders with ones he bought at yard sales. There was always a sale happening on Haldoupis Lane, even during winter. People propping their shed doors open and calling others to come peruse their junk. Most of it was worthless—rusted chains, gun powder, padlocks missing keys, paper bags of twigs and dead shrubbery—but every now and then you'd find a gem. Like one time Trigger got a goalie mask, and another, Ma brought home a dozen aluminum glass bottom beer steins.

Then Pa found the boxing gloves. A couple old ratty pairs. Faded red, strings missing, camel padding bled out small tears. In our house there were two rules: One) never question Pa's behavior, and Two) always punch a kid who says something anti-Jew. Pa was teaching us how to properly follow both. A few times a week, he'd call Trigger and me to the damp cold of the basement, boxing gloves on our hands, nothing on his, and have us take turns punching him.

Trigger was ten. I was six. Pa wrapped electrical tape around our wrists to prevent the gloves from slipping. Then he'd count down in Hebrew—gimel, bet, alef.

Hit me, he'd say. C'mon, Baloney.

Sir, I'd beg.

Look at me, Baloney. You look at me.

I looked at his slippers.

You look at me, Tony Baloney. Let me catch your eyes. I ain't the sun.

He was shirtless, breasts and belly under dust bunnies of brown hair. I'd aim for his nipples. They were too wide and too red, made me feel angry. Pa took each punch like it tickled. He chortled. He hit us back. Hit our faces. He didn't hit mine hard, but it didn't have to be. Tapped me with two fingers across the cheek, flicked my ear with a fingernail. I was always in tears by the end, running up to my room, punching the pillow until all the feathers gathered in clumps on either side of the case.

I wake. A cluster of worms beside my face. Worms the color of sunburns. Wiggling spaghetti messes drawing into the ground at the flick of a finger. You need to get a good grip or they'll slip. You need to hold on.

Are you okay?

A woman's voice. I rub the water from my eyes and off my eyelashes and lean to look. She's standing at my feet, toeing the soles of my boots. Flashlight crooked on her forehead. She's Asian, like the rest. Boots are black rubber and up to her knees. She wears a poncho on top of a jacket, a garbage bag on top of the poncho.

You need help? she asks.

No, I say. I don't think so.

I sit up. And stand. Feel the blood rush to my head and fall back down. On my knees barfing, the taste of acidified rain, fists fingering soil.

I'll go get help, she says. But doesn't. She stands there, scoping the ground for worms.

I'm okay, I tell her. It's gone now. The sick feeling's gone.

She bends over, picking worms and asking if I'm sure. I tell her I am. The buckets on her ankles are near full. She doesn't bother with sawdust. Wears a can of worms on each ankle. Gathers eight worms at a time between the knuckles of each finger on each hand and drops them inside the cans without looking.

Perfect night, she says. Cold and wet, she says. Just perfect.

I stand back up. See the isolated light of the truck we rode in on. I think about the bench seats inside it, the windows cut in the cargo hold. Think about the coffee, the cigarette, a view of the fields from the truck's dry, heated interior. I think about the Vietnamese man, how he's got it made.

Excuse me? says the woman.

I don't answer. I'm staring down at the dozen or so worms inside my can. Try lifting my ankle to see them better, closer. I'm hopping on one boot.

Excuse me? she says again.

I look up.

May I ask how old you are?

Twenty-one.

A baby, she says. What are you doing here?

Her voice barely audible under the hard rain and thunder. She's stopped picking worms. Standing straight in front of me with her face ashen in the glow off my forehead. Appears older than I'd originally thought. Mid to late forties, maybe. Short in stature. She's got small hands, but rough, like a working man's. I tell her I'm here for my brother, my sister-in-law, and their three kids, soon to be five. I'm here for my nieces and nephews, I say. And then picture what happens next. The woman cutting the cans off her ankles and handing them to me, telling me she wants to help, telling me to be safe, to stay true. Piano music plays as she says, Good luck, and strides off into the stormy night.

I watch her go. She waddles over the mud, plump under all those layers. Her body bent, picking worms like a pro. I look back at the lonely dozen on my ankle. The others must've escaped when I was asleep. Only the still remain. Bits of dirt sticking to their bodies like chocolate crumble and I think they're probably dead.

When Trigger found out he was going to be a dad, I was the first person he told. This is close to ten years ago, when he was seventeen and I was thirteen and we were sharing a cigarette on the smoking patch in Bush Flats. The smoking patch was a square plot of withered land close to the Laundromat. Teenagers used to go there to smoke cigarettes and pot, light garbage on fire.

It was a hot day. The kind of heat you feel in your eyes. I kept rubbing them. Trigger told me to quit it. Quit touching your eyes, he said. Your hands got dirt, he said.

Sherri's pregnant, he said. He slipped it in there like it was anything else. She won't get the thing abortioned cause she thinks it's a sin.

He kicked his boot to the dirt and made a dust cloud between our knees. I could feel it in my eyes worse than the heat. Started crying. Lifted my shirt over my face to hide. Spoke against the cotton. I asked Trigger if he was going to teach his kid how to fight.

Don't know, he said. Maybe. If it's a boy, maybe. Quit crying, Tony.

We stayed on the smoking patch longer than usual, watching the sun drop. Trigger had a box of matches. He burned them one by one, holding each until the flame grew too close to his fingers and he had to let go. Blew on his fingers and lit the next. But eventually he stopped dropping them, the flames. Let the fire stretch on the matchstick until he was practically pinching it. Then he'd blow it out, make a fist, squeeze his burnt fingers to palm and let out an exasperated breath. I watched and wondered what kind of dad he'd be.

Trigger was wearing blue jeans and a white T-shirt with Pa's blood on it. His hair was big and curly and there was the start of a moustache under his nose. I remember hoping I might grow to look like him. Prayed to God in my head I would. Prayed I'd end up looking like Trigger, and that my name had been Bullet instead of Tony.

I asked Trigger what he was going to name the kid.

Carver, he said, without having to think. If it's a boy, Carver. Remember Pa carving the gun stands? Or that fish?

He cut the worm, too, I said. Chopped it like Ma did carrots for soup.

Chopper, he said. Chopper or Carver?

Carver, I said.

Right, he said. Carver, he said.

We left the smoking patch at dusk, but our footprints remained. Stamps of no-name boots and sneakers beside three Hebrew letters Trigger had carved in the dirt with his comb. They were the numbers Pa used to count down before we fought him. All that, and black matches everywhere.

Occasionally Janey will propose the idea of us having kids of our own. Not soon, but one day, she says. Then adds, I want to have a boy and a girl. Not soon, but one day. One day when we're older, Tony, like thirty or something. After we've achieved other dreams.

I live in my parents' basement at the house on Haldoupis. It's finished now, with carpets and ceilings and even a toilet. No rent. Not yet. Not until I finish school and get a job. But yesterday I told Ma I needed cash quick. And Ma mentioned worm picking. Think it was supposed to be a joke because she was laughing, but Janey wasn't. She leaned against the sink with her arms folded giving me that *don't you dare even think about it* look. Already thinks I do too much for Trigger and the kids, but I don't believe in *too much* when the too much is for family.

Your father used to pick worms before we had you boys, Ma said.

He like it?

Who could like it? she said. No he didn't like it. But it was good, fast money. That he liked. That was something we could all get used to.

Janey turned the tap water on and started scrubbing dishes even though no one had asked her to. She made a lot of noise and even broke a plate.

The black sky brightens. Scratches of lightning. I cut the cans off my ankles. Press them in the dirt to make little latrines. Worms emerge around the rims of the cans and slop inside them. But I walk away. I leave the worms behind. Turn off the battery-charged light on my head and walk without sight. My hands in front of me, catching raindrops, feeling them slip through my fingers to gather into puddles.

A year before Trigger became a dad, we were seated on the curb outside Coen Convenience, eating Popsicles, when we saw Pa's car enter the lot. He parked far, but we knew it was him. The brown Austin Allegro with a diamond-shaped dent in the driver's side door. The black exhaust.

Trigger was sixteen. He'd later refer to this day as the one that came sixteen years too late. The day he dropped his Popsicle in the gutter between our shoes, stood with his shoulders back and his chest pressed out, and charged.

Trigger with his arm drawn in, Trigger with his arm swung forward. Pa's nose breaking.

I was halfway between them and the curb. A car honked at me. Trigger's Popsicle in my hand, speckled with ants and tiny stones. I tossed it at the car and sprinted in the direction of my family. Pa grabbing Trigger by the ears and headbutting him in the face. Real fights aren't like the ones in movies. Real fights don't last long. Trigger fell. His face turned black in an instant. Cheeks swelled with so much blood it looked like his skin might pop. He lay on the ground, both eyes webbed with broken vessels. His right arm reached for the seagulls overhead.

I still held my Popsicle. It was banana-flavored. I'd sucked it sharp by then. Pressed the cold sharpness to Trigger's face. He flinched, then relaxed. He relaxed to the sound of Pa's car pulling away, and so did I, relaxed, and took a better look at Trigger's inflated face, and broken fingers, and flecks of Pa's blood stained in a sneer on his shirt.

There's a home video of Trigger playing with his first born, Carver. The two of them in the backyard at Sherri's mother's in Aurora. Sherri's the one behind the camera. My boys, she keeps saying. Here they are. My two boys.

Trigger sits on the grass while baby Carver crawls around him. He stares at Carver like the kid's some gimp dog he doesn't know what to do with. The camera zooms in on Trigger's face. One boy, says Sherri. Then she turns the camera to Carver. And the other boy, she adds. Zooms out. That's them. My two beautiful boys.

Eventually Carver tears the head off a dandelion. He's about to eat it.

Stop him, Sherri says.

And Trigger leans towards Carver and tells him, No sweetie, we don't eat that.

No sweetie, we don't eat that.

No sweetie, we don't eat that.

No sweetie, we don't eat that.

I had to rewind the tape several times. Listen to the sound of Trigger's voice, convince myself it was true. He takes the dandelion out of Carver's fist. Carver doesn't cry. He laughs a goofy baby laugh, and Trigger smiles, so stiffly and discomfited it looks like it might be his face's first stab at it.

Two years later Trigger and Sherri had another kid. Then two years after that they had another. The home videos changed. Trigger no longer appeared in them, for one. Only kids. Clips of kids sitting. Carver on a bed, Soccer at the kitchen table, Quinlynn on the steps in front of their basement apartment, and Sherri's shaky voice behind the camera telling them to be cute, be cute, be extra cute for Grandma Beally!

And then the videos stopped coming altogether. No more tapes in the mail. Just a short letter informing Ma Trigger had hocked their camera for thirty-five dollars and a couple of steel sais.

My eyes open. The sun is white with pink sky surrounding it and there's an old man standing over my body. He wears overalls and a Christmas sweater, green trucker's cap and muttonchops. He carries a pitchfork.

Shit, he says. I nearly shat myself thinkin you were dead.

Who are you? I whisper.

This is my property, he whispers back. You were worm-pickin on my field last night, you and all those Chinese folk. They must've abandoned you. All of em packed in that truck and left more than a couple hours ago.

I look at the holes in my socks. Big toes poking through. I need to cut my nails. I don't know where my boots are. I ask the old man if I can borrow his phone.

He leads me across his land. Walks about ten feet ahead, humming a tune I don't recognize. Notes bend like they're coming out of an accordion that's been pierced through. I hum along, but not really. My socks are drenched. Water squelches under and around my feet. The pink sky burns red apart from that white hole at its center. Reminds me of the girl's eyes. Blond hair and blond eyes and blue lips.

She was dead, Trigger had said. But she talked to me.

He was serious. Dropped his cigarette on the ground to show how serious he was. So serious there could be no distractions, no more blowing smoke. He told me the basis of what the girl had shared. Told me she told him what happens after we go. She was dead, he said, so she knew. She could see it. Death. She could see what happens cause she was there. But alive too, he said. She was talking on that raft, he said. It's the truth. She was telling me what she saw in the afterlife.

What did she see? I asked him.

He didn't answer. Shook his head and lit another cigarette and looked deflated, like I'd really let him down. He told me that wasn't the point of the story.

The farmer turns, walking backwards. How come you don't got worms? he asks, pointing at the tape torn at my ankles. I tell him I don't know. Maybe they got sucked inside that hole in the sky, I reply to be cryptic, or uncooperative, or I don't know what.

The farmer looks at the sky. That's the sun, he says.

The sun, I say.

The early mornin sun, he says.

He's right. It's early, it's morning. The sun so soft you can stare right at it.

Yesterday I drove two and a half hours to Port Woodlot to hear the news in person. Trigger telling me Sherri's pregnant, for the fourth time. She's gonna be having another baby, or babies, he said. She's having twins.

Five kids, I said.

Five little bastard fucking shits, he said.

We were standing outside Home Repair. At twenty-five, he's their youngest manager, tools department. Says his boss has been promising a raise for close to a year now. Says he needs it. He's been waiting. That's life, he told me, little bastard fucking shits and a whole lotta waiting.

We walked around the side of the store to the back. There was a storage shed built next to a dumpster with a couple plastic chairs inside. I sat across from him. He lit a cigarette with a match from a motel matchbook. It was cold out. Wind kept finding its way inside the shed. Trigger held his jacket shut instead of zipping.

I'm in trouble, he said.

I told him not to worry.

He stood and turned to one of the walls of the shed and started punching. The sound clanging. Cigarette still in his mouth. The dent getting bigger until Trigger's hand was too sore to keep going. He sat back down on the plastic chair, bending his fingers in and out. I saw his forearms were speckled with tiny pink pricks. He sat inspecting them. Brushed his thumb against their pattern like it might rub off.

What is it? I asked. A rash?

No, he said. I was loading a truck full of blue spruces. Pine needles kept poking me, so now I'm itchy as fucking fuck.

I'm going to help you, I said.

He squeezed his arm. Put strain on the dots like blood might seep and release some tension. But the pine needles hadn't punctured the skin, only irritated it. He looked at me with genuine disappointment. Started slapping his arm until the entire thing turned pink and you couldn't see the pine needle pricks anymore.

Kay, he said, how? How you gonna help?

I found Pa on the wooden rocking chair in the living room. His nose was crooked, a grey goose egg on his head. Still wearing the same T-shirt. It was tight turquoise and bloodstained. He asked where my brother was.

Gone, I said.

There was blood on his lips, chin and neck. His hands were wet. He asked if I was okay. I told him I was fine, that I wasn't the one he'd hit. He told me to follow him. We walked past the master bedroom where Ma was seated on the end of their bed, shaking her head at the wall. We walked downstairs. Pa's breathing squeaked like the rats in Bush Flats, the ones always putting holes in things.

He yanked the string. The light bulb swayed. Pa took his shirt off. Told me to do the same. I took stance, twelve and half-naked with fists in front of my face.

Why'd he do that? he asked.

Who?

Him. Your brother. Trigsly. Why'd he do *this*? Pa pointed at his nose.

I don't know, I said. But I think I did. I think I knew. I think it was the shock of seeing Pa unexpectedly, as someone who existed outside our home. Trigger saw Pa posing as just another person in a parking lot and didn't know what to make of it.

I'm not the enemy, Baloney.

I know, sir.

The light bulb had stopped moving. Our shadows at rest on the wall. Pa placed one hand firmly on the back of his head, the other on his nose. Shut his eyes. The squeaking stopped. He'd stopped breathing. He was holding his breath. I counted down from three in my head because I knew that's what he was doing. Gimel, bet, alef, and Pa tried to snap everything back to place.

10

It didn't feel like we were breaking any laws cause we weren't planning on stealing anything. We just wanted to look around, see what she had in there. Open a few dressers and drawers and then be done with it. Simple. We didn't even bother being sneaky about the whole thing. We did it in the daytime. Sat there on the curb across the street from her house and waited til she came out. When she did, she was wearing a nightdress, cords, rain boots, and orange earmuffs, the kind you wear when you're learning to shoot a gun.

Good Ol Crazy-Ass, said Carver.

We watched her shuffle down the walkway, the driveway, and then the sidewalk, hunchbacked, and with these awful limp wrists that made it look like she had no bones inside her hands. On her way to the corner store on Burke to buy bread, milk, and ham like always. And like always, we watched her go, and grow small in the distance til she was finally out of sight. But that day we didn't just sit there after she left. We got up, crossed the street, and went straight for her door. The number on her house said 16 in gold metal, same as our age. Carver pulled the spare key from out the drainpipe. It was attached to a keychain the shape of two cherries. He tossed it to me. I unlocked the door like it was my own and we went inside.

The air in there was rancid. Sewage, spoiled food. Carver covered his nose with his shirt collar and said, Mother-fuck. It stinks.

The front hall was difficult to see. The light sockets were empty and the windows were covered with detached cabinet doors and pieces of bristol board. Carver pulled his pocketknife out his pants and stabbed one of the boards, ripping a piece and letting sunlight drop inside the house triangularly, pointed down the hall. We walked farther. Floorboards whined under our shoes like old cats.

Carver, I said.

What?

Imagine she dies, I said. Imagine being the next person who lives here after she dies.

What about it?

She'll haunt it, I said. Imagine how creepy it would be living here with her ghost.

I don't believe in ghosts, he said, his voice cartoony cause he was still plugging his nose. Then let go. His nostrils thinner. His hair like Eddie Vedder, and a peach-fuzzed face, and plaid shirt, and shredded jeans with holes between the knees and ankles. I looked him up and down. His nostrils stretched back to normal.

What you smiling at? I said.

You, he said.

I think it'd be scary, I said, living here after she dies.

Carver held the knife. It was small and the blade was dull grey. It's scarier now, he said, because that crazy bitch is still alive, she's just down the street. That's what's scary, Daniel. All these nut-fuck weirdos running loose in the world. Alive people are way worse than the dead ones, man.

We entered the kitchen. Black pots hung from the ceiling like bats. There was a clutter of dishes sticking out of orange bubbles in the sink. Chipped counters, broken elements on the stove, gashed tiles, nothing in the fridge but the smell of bad meat. Carver opened the oven door. More meat stink, plus cooking spray, vinegar and gas. There was a baby blanket folded in a rectangle between the racks. Carver pulled it out and unfolded it, stabbed it a couple times with his knife, and then stuffed it back in.

Why'd you do that for?

Bored, he said.

None of the rooms on the bottom floor had a door, but duvets were draped across the gaps. We yanked them down. The rooms were empty. We stepped inside and made loud sounds to hear the echo. Carver yelled his brother's name. He also called *Eddie*. He also called *Kurt Cobain*. We sang Rape Me in honor of him cause he'd died the year before. Our voices hit between hardwood and wall paneling, and landed in dust.

We went upstairs. The staircase creaked louder than the floors. Carver noticed a couple strands of hair coiled around the railing. Looks like the house is growing fur, he said. Ah shit, Daniel. I think it is. I think this place is coming alive.

The rooms upstairs were emptier than the emptiness on the bottom floor. The biggest bedroom had chunks of wall missing, and the toilet had been torn from the ceramic slabs and put inside the tub. The guest bedroom was the only place with anything inside. A cot, desk, cooler, a leopard-printed lounger. Carver walked to the desk. It was covered in pencil crayons and lots of loose papers. Looks like letters, he said. He lifted one off the pile. His eyes skimmed. All these letters are addressed to God, he said.

I crouched to see under the cot. There were about a dozen shoeboxes under there, all belonging to boys' shoes. I also saw a revolver.

Daniel, he said.

What? I said.

I think they're letters to God.

I lay flat on my stomach and crawled under the cot. There were bread crusts, cockroaches, grape stems, a whiff of more meat stink. I wondered about the boxes, but only had my eyes on one thing.

Carver was seated on the desk. The letters gathered in a stack on his lap as he flipped through. No lights, and boarded windows, so he had to peer at the words so hard his eyes looked furious. I watched him read a couple minutes. Then got fed up and told him to look, and he looked, and I was pointing the gun at him.

You scared? I said.

He asked if there were bullets in the gun. I wasn't sure how to check, so he told me, and I checked, and there were none. Carver brought his eyes back to the letters. I looked at the revolver. It was heavier than I'd expected. Wondered how people even shot the things straight without having their arms weighed down. I looked at Carver again, watched him read letters some more. He murmured lines. He was asking for forgiveness. I pressed the barrel of the gun under my chin to feel the coldness of it. Then considered crawling back under the cot to see if there were bullets in those boxes, but didn't feel like getting dirty again. I dropped the revolver and kicked it away from me.

Let's go, I said.

She's planning on bargaining with him, he said.

Who? What?

Carver held up one of the letters. Lines scribbled in pencil across the paper. God, he said. He let go of the page and it wafted to the floor. Then he got up and walked over to the lounger, lounged, and said he was gonna stay.

What for?

Her.

Old Crazy?

Yeah, he said.

Why?

Why what?

Why?

He didn't say anything else. Just sat there.

Whatever, I said. I turned to leave. I walked downstairs, out the front door and across the street to where we were before. I pulled out a cigarette. I lit it and smoked it. I pulled out a second and smoked that too. Smoked a third cigarette. I kept smoking til my head turned dizzy cause I was smoking so many so fast.

Half a fourth cigarette later she returned. I could see her coming from far away. Orange earmuffs and white hair and poor posture, shuffling. I looked back at the house. Really looked this time. The brown bricks and garage door, and garbage bags covering the tree branches, making noise in the wind. The grass on the lawn was long, knee-height. There were weeds and white dandelions. I stood and walked onto the street, finished my smoke. She was close. I could see the bread, milk, and ham in her bundle buggy. I watched her shuffle up the driveway. She shuffled up the walkway. She entered the house.

It couldn't have been more than twenty minutes before Carver came strolling out. He carried a glass of milk and had a cigarette between his lips. I handed him my Bic, and we started walking, already a block down the road by the time he told me she'd made him a sandwich.

Serious? I said.

A sandwich, he repeated. He took a sip of milk.

I noticed we were walking slower than usual, like we were barely moving. A couple kids passed on bikes, and a few cars drove by too, and birds flew overhead. It felt like the whole world was getting ahead of us in a lot of ways.

What'd she say? I asked him.

Jeffrey, he said. She thought I was someone named Jeffrey. Must've said it a hundred times, telling me how much she loved and missed me and she was crying pretty hard, making me a ham sandwich and calling me Jeffrey, Jeffrey.

We stood in front of a house with a garburator on the driveway. Carver kept looking at it. A stick of ash hanging off the end of his cigarette.

I think she wears those orange earmuffs to muffle the things people call her in town, I said. Did you know that?

Carver nodded at the garburator. He flicked his cigarette. Dead ash to the ground and he stomped on it. He said, I think we should cut her lawn.

Why?

Does your dad have a mower?

She say she'd pay us?

No. She didn't ask me to do it.

He was acting strange, not really looking me in the eyes. C'mon, I said. I started walking again, but Carver didn't follow. He remained in front of the house with the garburator on the driveway, staring at the ground like something real good was going on down there. I walked back to him. He poured the remainder of his milk on top of an anthill burgeoning from a crack in the sidewalk. We watched the ants panic under all that milky white. Then Carver tossed the empty glass onto the street. It burst on the pavement. I looked to see if people saw, but there was no one. Carver held the cigarette on his lips as he dug both hands in his pockets and pulled out a couple handfuls of crumpled twenty, fifty, and hundred dollar bills.

I took this from her, he said. They were in the boxes.

She know?

There's a whole lot more in there.

She know you took it?

She doesn't know shit, Daniel. She writes to God. She thinks I'm Jeffrey.

I stared at the money. I'd never seen so much.

You want to grab burgers? he asked.

Yeah, I said, and more cigarettes. And lotto tickets.

And ham, he said, for Good Ol Crazy-Ass. Bread and milk and ham.

11

We all used to cram into seats on the left side of the bus. Some kids who got on at later stops had to stand in the aisle and look over our heads and shoulders. The driver's name was Helga and she'd turn off Spruce and onto Catherine Avenue and ask if we were excited. Only the little kids answered. They'd yell yes or yah or yaw or yay in shrill voices while the older kids kept focused on the water-stained windows.

The Greys lived at the end of Catherine. Their house was third from Yonge. It was a medium-sized two-story with ecru-colored bricks narrowly sectioned by three A-framed rooftops, each of which had umber slates, bird nests on the chimney, and wind chimes fixed into the eaves, but we hadn't noticed any of that yet. All we ever saw were the three men out front. They weren't real. Mr. Grey had built them out of maple boards, wooden spools, and wire hangers he'd distorted to form ribcages. Their bodies draped in cast-off clothing, with nylon heads and hands stuffed with cotton. Their nylon skin was grey. That's why we called the family the Greys. We didn't know their real name.

Mr. Grey was a black man who wore a beaver felt hat so a lot of people thought he was crazy. He'd be up every Monday morning before the sun, out on his front lawn in the dark with his coffee and cigarette and gut bulging out of an open bathrobe as he strutted flatfooted across the grass to set the men in position. It was something different every week, a new stance to reflect the titles and lyrics of well-known songs. Like once Mr. Grey had the men assembled in a row in a claw tub on the grass. There was a sign set on a painting easel beside them that read *Splish, splash, I was takin' a bath* in black acrylic. Or another time, on the verge of a particularly heavy April shower, we witnessed the three men huddled under a spiraled umbrella, the sign sheltered under a pop-up canopy, the words on the sign warning *A Hard Rain's A-Gonna Fall* in purple pastel. Or another time, the three men had been decorated with angry melt-on eyebrows, flat bill hats and black hooded sweatshirts, big gold chains, and grills, and the sign spelled *AIN'T NUTHIN' BUT A G THANG* in glue and glitter.

Ain't nuthin but a G thang, said Quinlynn, as she tapped four fingers against her window and exhaled, drawing a G on the fog on the glass.

One occasion Mr. Grey even went as far as to include himself in the installation. He'd set the three men around a Styrofoam cake, festooned them with cone hats and a bouquet of helium balloons. Then Mr. Grey positioned himself apart from the three men, maybe four meters away, or five, six-ish. He wore a poncho with a kaleido-scopic design on the front, and lime-colored, lensless cat-eye glasses, and a cone hat like the others, only his was bent at the peak. He stood with his shoulders bobbing as he rubbed two fists over his eyeballs and pretended to sob.

The sign said *It's my party and I'll cry if I want to.*

We debated long and hard about it for many hours that day at school. All three recesses squandered by questions like: Does he stand out there all day? Is he still there now? Why didn't he set up one of the men to cry instead of himself? Won't his eyes get sore?

Sophie rolled her own eyes and *tsked* and said, God, Mr. Grey is so weird.

No, said Quinlynn, her voice fluttering because she was jumping rope. Mr. Grey's not weird one bit, Soph. He's an artist.

Quinlynn and Sophie were my two best friends when I was ten, which was two decades ago, but I still see them plain and clear—Quinlynn folding bologna and biting a hole in the middle, Sophie with oleander-shaped beads in her hair, Quinlynn tonguing the inside of her left cheek as she draws pictures of pine trees, rocket ships, her family, tombstones, Sophie eating garlic croutons out of a freezer bag, Quinlynn this, Sophie that, on and on as if they were still right there.

We first spoke on the bus, which drove past the Greys' one fall morning, the three men clad in fur coats and monster masks, carrying pumpkin-printed pillowcases beside a sign that said *I want candy.* Quinlynn read it out loud, as she always did, and I happened to be finger-scooping my way through a packet of Fun Dip at that moment, so I handed it to her, and Sophie saw and laughed, and then we all laughed, together, and started walking with our arms interlocked from then on. And doing other things too, almost everything. Swapping sandwich meats, trading barrettes. Arguing over who was going to marry Jonathan Brandis first. We'd even pee together, squatted in a triangle in the woods near Quinlynn's house, back to back to back with our pants tight around our ankle bracelets, giggling at the static sound of us spraying against the dried leaves.

Quinlynn said her father once beat her with a rolled-up towel.

Sophie said she masturbated.

I said I slept with the overhead light on.

We confessed these secrets under the slide at the Lester B. Pearson playground, seated on the mulch. Put our pinkies in to swear we'd never tell, and shook on it, hooked to one another. Then got up and played. It was the time of tag and grounders. Hide-the-name-of-the-boy-you-like-and-go-seek. Truth or Dare on occasion, four square on others. We even Stella Ella Ola'd like we were five. Prank-called mean girl Rosie Payne to call her a no-good chubby lesbian prostitute. Electronic Mall Madness at my house, Super Mario Brothers and Duck Hunt on Sophie's NES.

I admitted I cried at the town play production of *Rumpelstiltskin*.

Sophie said she stole fifteen dollars, three Werther's Originals, mascara, and skin cream off her grandmother's vanity.

Quinlynn said she used to live beside a little boy who died and she saw the dead body and ever since then the boy's bludgeoned body floated in her dreams.

We carved these secrets and others on the underside of the black walnut planks that formed the playground's bridge. Then crossed them out, and let the secrets live there under the scratches we cut with a pointed nail file attached to Sophie's keychain. She kept the file on her as commonly as we wore underwear, shaping her nails under the desk at school, or using it to scrape down a wart she had on her thumb. Or for scratching secrets into wood.

Guys. You guys. I'm gonna start smoking.

I remember when she told us. It was the most full-fledged secret yet. We were seated under the ash tree in the field next to the playground, Sophie presenting us with a quarter-full carton of cigarettes she'd stolen from her grandmother's James Dean cookie jar, planting one at the corner of her wily grin, then grinning wider.

My dad smokes, said Quinlynn. My Uncle Tony used to.

Sophie lit the cigarette with a barbeque lighter she had holstered in one of the belt loops of her flared jeans. Inhaled, and coughed twice, patted her belly as if her appetite had been satisfied. Inhaled again, coughed. What I love's the taste, she said.

I think Carver started smoking too, said Quinlynn. He's in high school this year and's been smelling lots more like Dad.

It's bad for you to smoke, I said to Sophie. Like, it's always bad, but especially like right now, cause we haven't gone through puberty yet. They say if you smoke before and when you're going through puberty, like, as you're growing boobs and getting bigger and all that, then your chance of getting cancer's like doubled. It gets, like tripled.

Sophie's eyes rolled from me to Quinlynn to the playground, where a group of teenagers in baggy pants and with metalhead mullets were applauding one of their own as he fingered the back of his tongue, gagged, and eventually barfed on top of the baby swing. They all cheered and fist-bumped one another. Most were smoking cigarettes.

Sophie said she only planned to smoke until she turned twenty-five. Because that's when I'm gonna have my first baby, she explained, and it's bad to smoke when you're pregs because the baby can come out sickish with crummy asthma lungs. I don't wanna hurt my baby. I want it to be strong and look like Jonathan Brandis. I don't want it to be ugly and retarded. And oh! Also, it's bad to say things are retarded, because if you do, your baby will come out retarded.

I don't ever, ever want a baby, I said. They come out the vagina. Your vagina. Whole baby bodies making your vagina the size of a baby.

Baby-sized vagina! Sophie laughed.

Baby, Quinlynn repeated, then started humming. They call me Baby Driver.

Call you what? I said.

They call me Baby Driver, she said again, or sang it; she was sort-of-singing, always finding a way to sing-steer the conversation back to what mattered to her most: Mr. Grey, the three men, the titles and lyrics of songs we'd stockpile in our heads until five p.m. when our parents returned from work and explained where the words came from.

They call me Baby Driver, I repeated to my father that night.

Simon and Garfunkel, he replied. Paul Simon and Art Garfunkel.

I told him the three men had been dressed in diapers that day. Hairless. Bright blue baby bibs. They were sucking soothers. Packed in one of those red Fisher Price cars with the yellow roof, a mass of plush limbs hanging out the front, sides, and back of it.

I see, said my father. But he didn't see. Swiveling his chair back to his Sudoku to examine the squares less quizzically than he did me. Tapping the puzzle with his pen ten times and biting the cap off the back and holding it in his mouth and breathing through the hole, forcing a soft, strained whistle. Give me a minute, Sarah. Just a few more minutes. You're cutting into yer Dad's me-time here.

Mr. Grey's an artist, I told him. I'd stolen the line from Quinlynn, but my father didn't know. He tapped his pen three more times, then drew a circle, gave the circle a smile and a pair of black shades, straight lines poking out all around it, encircling the circle. It was a sun with sunglasses on.

Me too, exclaimed my father. I'm an artist too.

He is! I yelled. Then I let him have his me-time so I could go have some of my own. I ran upstairs two steps at a time, to my bedroom, where I made my bed and then lay on the floor. And thought about how lucky we were to still be small enough to see how big those three men truly were. They were inimitable, high over everything. A snowflake that felt as though it was drifting only onto us.

It was a Monday in mid-May. The bus stopped in front of Quinlynn's house on Spruce. She boarded with the twins, and a couple other kids, and then took her usual spot next to Sophie on the seat behind mine. Helga drove past Mark Street and Maple and turned onto Catherine and asked if we were excited and the little kids said they were, like always, and the big kids just sat there silently, like always too.

Maybe it was the sun, how it settled too close to the horizon that morning, its light barren, blocked by trees and pressing lumps of shadow on everything, because I knew something was off, even before I saw what.

There was nothing on the Greys' lawn. No men, no painting easel. Only plotter paper curved around a garbage can at the roadside with red words scrawled across.

they were stolen!!

Quinlynn read it out loud. Then asked, What was? as if it wasn't clear.

We turned onto Yonge. Kids in the aisle returned to their seats on the right side of the bus. Some of the younger ones wept. Helga said, It's all good! Everything's all good-good-good!

Good. So we didn't discuss it. The day and week progressed as we jumped rope and drew hopscotch squares in silence. Pitched in quarters and nickels to buy wine gums in silence. Practiced triple jump, read to reading buddies, wrote on our arms and in our agendas, on Kristen Steep's leg cast, on the mirrors in the girls' washrooms with Sophie's grandmother's lipstick, without words. And then fell asleep at night to the crash of it, this dearth of conversation. Its volume mushroomed in the dark. Made our friendship feel contaminated. The men were gone. Sophie smoked cigarettes and no one cared.

The following Monday Helga asked again—Are you excited?—and the little kids answered as if the previous week hadn't happened. But when we looked out the window there were still no men, no sign. Only Mr. Grey in his thermal underwear and beaver felt hat. He stood buried to his thighs in a hole he'd dug with a trenching shovel, the muddy instrument held over his shoulder as he watched the bus pass.

Jesus, said Sophie. What the heck's he doing?

Yeah, what's he doing? I asked Quinlynn, because she was an artist too, but her attention kept her pressed to the window. It wasn't until we arrived at the bus loop in front of the school that she managed to turn her gape to us and say the first thing it felt like she'd said since the men had disappeared.

My mom thinks we should write a note to tell Mr. Grey we liked what he did.

What he did? I said.

To thank him for it, she said.

Blerg. Why even bother? said Sophie.

That weekend we convened at Quinlynn's, the three of us gathered on one side of the kitchen table, and attempted to write something grown-up and grateful, replete with meaning. Mrs. Beally served tuna fish on saltine crackers as we worked. A pitcher of cold water with a lemon grass teabag inside. Quinlynn inscribed *Dearest Mister Grey* as we ate and drank, and then crossed it out because we remembered that wasn't his real name. Dear . . . The crackers were stale but I was hungry. Quinlynn sighed and said, What should we say? By the time the pitcher was empty the paper was still mostly blank. Quinlynn let her face fall in the fold of her arms on the table, then hammered the letter with her fist. She'd written *To whom it may concern*, and underneath that, nothing.

God I'm buh-buh-bluh-blored, Sophie sighed.

I suggested Quinlynn draw a picture for Mr. Grey instead. She was talented, the only student Mrs. Croker regularly referred to as a peewee Francis Bacon.

How about you draw him a picture of the three men? I said. That way he'll, like, have something to look at whenever he gets sad they got taken.

She agreed it was a decent idea. Rushed out of the kitchen and returned shortly with art paper. Pressed her tongue against her cheek and drew a picture of her baby sister Birdie. She used a mechanical pencil. She cross-hatched instead of shaded. Added an explosion of circles surrounding Birdie's body that I think were supposed to be snowflakes. Then scribbled *Baby, it's cold outside* at the bottom of the page even though it was a spring that felt like summer. She flipped the drawing over so we could sign our names on the back in blue crayon.

Quinlynn, Sarah, SOPHIE xoxoxo

I didn't know how to draw the men because they always looked different, she said.

I think he'll like this better, I said.

The Greys lived three blocks down the road. We marched under the reverberated chug of electric mowers, that hot smell of clumps of cut grass. Our sandals clapping sidewalk. Sophie smoking a cigarette, Quinlynn cradling her art in a manila envelope, and me, imagining what Mr. Grey might do upon receiving it. Would he invite us inside his home? Would his wife bake us cookies? Maca-roons? A plate of snickerdoodles?

We arrived at the end of their driveway, which appeared pulverized. As if someone had taken a jackhammer to it. What the F? said Sophie. Has it always been like this?

It's so hot out, I replied. As if heat could cause such damage.

As if heat could be responsible for the other things as well. Like solidified bird droppings on the plumbing vent, or water damage and cat-scratched glass. That stench of something, coming from somewhere.

A honey locust grew on their lawn. Its wilted limbs sagged over the hole Mr. Grey had dug, a hundred skeletal branches curved like arthritic fingers, pointed everywhere, accusing everyone. I wondered how long these things had been there, the bird droppings and accusations. Were they new, or something we'd failed to notice until now.

I blamed it on the heat. I used my hand as a fan. We stepped over the fissures in the pavement. There was a dead squirrel close to the walkway. Most of its remains had been lacerated, but its head was still in one piece. We stood and stared at the squirrel, the pavement, our toes painted puke green. Sophie said she couldn't do it. I can't. I, just can't. She'd decided she didn't want to see Mr. Grey anymore, so she hurried back down to the sidewalk where she waited with her head hung, beaded blond tresses drooped in front of her face.

I looked at Quinlynn. Her hair was pulled back, a rare thing.

I keep thinking they'll be in there, she said.

Who will?

The men, she said.

I counted scars on her forehead. There were a lot. They were the same size as the snowflakes in her drawing. She looked at the squirrel. I counted six, seven scars. She said,

I keep thinking the men'll answer the door, you know? They'll tell us not to worry. *We were found,* they'll say. *We were found. Don't worry.* They'll be real, Sarah. I can see them real. They're moving and blinking and everything. They'll be talking to us, real and alive. Do you get it?

I didn't like being where I was all of a sudden. I decided once I reached fifteen scars I'd go join Sophie on the sidewalk. Create good distance between me and the house, that slaughtered squirrel, and any of the scary things Quinlynn was saying.

Twelve, thirteen, fourteen scars.

Are we even at the right stupid place? yelled Sophie.

Quinlynn rang the bell, which bonged. The door grated open. Mr. and Mrs. Grey side by side as if attached at the fleshy hip. They answered Yes? in unison, carrying the s too long, a whistle out the gaps each had in their teeth. They were older than I'd thought. From the bus Mr. Grey had appeared my father's age, but up close, he was elderly. Black skin cracked with a crisscross of deep-set wrinkles. I followed the lines on his face like they belonged to a maze I was trying to get out of.

Mrs. Grey hunched with her hands in the pouch of her apron. She was round, borderline circular. She licked the white whiskers over her upper lip with an equally whitened tongue. What'cha got there? she asked Quinlynn, who shuffled one step back, clutching the envelope tighter to her T-shirt. Mr. Grey then lifted his hat. He held it upside down in front of his belly and asked Quinlynn to drop the envelope inside. She shook her head as he nodded his. A glob of something meaty in his hair. It slopped down his face and got caught in his caterpillar eyebrows, stained the front of his I HEART NIAGARA FALLS sleeveless sweater.

Oh John, sang Mrs. Grey as she delightedly clawed the shepherd's pie from her husband's curls. Some of it dropping, plopping. A splatter of mashed potato on the straw doormat. The sound of Mrs. Grey sucking food off her fingers. And then that whimsical song of wind chimes as Quinlynn turned, and started running, almost stepping on the squirrel but managing to leap over it, a soft whimper through the air until she landed and stood bent and breathing next to Sophie on the sidewalk. I looked back at the Greys. There was a sliver of space between them. A view inside their squalid home. The front hall strewn with body parts—arms, legs, decapitated cotton-stuffed heads, in tatters, tears in the grey nylon, torn. More failed attempts at people.

Sarah! Sarah, let's go!

Mrs. Grey rested a hand on my shoulder and asked if I was okay. I told myself I was. Tilted my eyes to see her husband from the ground up. Those bare feet and piss-stained long johns, his love for Niagara Falls, that shamballa cross necklace, scarred philtrum, and eyes, sunken and yellowed, and then the shepherd's pie.

We-really-really-liked-the-things-you-used-to-do, I almost finished saying. But my body had turned before the sentence was through, and I was making my escape too, across the grass and past the hole in the lawn, which was deeper now, six feet underground with a heap of body parts inside. Some were kid-sized, our size.

We ran side by side by side down Catherine but kept having to stop because of Sophie's sandals slipping off. She yelled Whoore! each time. That's how her father pronounced whore. Stupid whoore bitch-ass sandals! she'd say.

Back on Spruce we stood in a small triangle to catch our breath. Quinlynn whipped the envelope against the ground. It smacked flat. She picked it up and wiped the grit off with her arm. Ripped the seal, pulled out the drawing—her little sister Birdie caught in a snowstorm as the sun burned carroty orange above us. I hate it so much, she said. A car was coming so we moved to the sidewalk. There was a ghost carved on one of the sidewalk squares. It was a cartoon ghost, the bed sheet kind, not the scary human kind. I wondered if it was someone's secret. We looked at the ghost like we did the squirrel. Eventually Sophie suggested we go light Quinlynn's drawing on fire. It was stupid but it was something.

She pulled a catalytic lighter from her pocket. She lit a cigarette and smoked as we walked, while describing a book her father had recently read her about King Arthur. She said King Arthur had been laid to rest on a funeral pyre. There was a picture in the book of a wooden structure floating on water, and another of it after being set ablaze by a flaming arrow. She suggested we make our own pyre out of grass and twigs and other things.

We travelled by foot then bus to Salamander Pond where the water was mucky brown inside a boundary of mud and reed grass. There were dragonflies, larvae. We wandered the damp shore, covered half the pond's perimeter before Sophie yelled, Faaaack! No more walking. I'm gonna die. My ankles are killing.

We stood in a triangle; there was no other shape. Quinlynn held the picture in her fingers and shook. I moved closer. Our triangle angled more acutely. I began braiding her hair. Sophie used her nail file to cut the grass. She piled strands in intersecting sets. Also included a quarter-cigarette, three Double Bubble wrappers, and her change purse, which was dollar store-bought, stitched out of tacky multihued lining fabric, and coinless. The finished pyre was the size of a cereal box.

It looks real, I said as if I knew.

It is, Sophie replied.

This is pointless, said Quinlynn. She put the picture on the pyre.

Sophie tried setting fire to the grass first but the strands wouldn't catch. She tried setting fire to the purse. There was an overcooked smell of fabric, a smooth skid of inky smoke. But nothing lit. It was all burn, no fire. Quinlynn kicked the pyre, the picture. She played soccer with the drawing until the corner patted the water, signature-side up.

Stop it, I yelled. Then, to quote Helga, It's all good. Good-good-good.

The water pulled the paper off the shore, so there it floated, a couple meters out, and ugly, real ugly, saturated with singed edges. Quinlynn stomped the change purse. Her drawing sank. The braid in her hair untwisted. She punched at nothing, or the tips of the reed grass. Sophie rolled her eyes, but there were tears in them. I tried to spot baby Birdie in the snow but the water was too murky. Soon the whole thing had sunk. Quinlynn continued to take it out on the surrounding area. Our triangle kept bending more obtusely until we were all standing really far apart.

I hadn't thought about it in a long time. But recently I was on my way to visit my sister-in-law in Thornhill, driving through Aurora, past Catherine Avenue, when the memory hit me in the eyes and ears and everything went dark and quiet. I practically yelled at Douglas to turn. He made a sharp right on Catherine, and decelerated, coincidentally braking directly in front of the Greys' crumbling driveway.

I don't know what I'd been expecting in those brief seconds between the turn and the house, but there it stood. Nothing had been repaired, nothing had gotten worse. It was a house encumbered by the weight of two decades worth of stagnancy—a relic.

I told Douglas the story. He kept his hands on the wheel and nodded. Perhaps it was a sad story because at the end of it he told me he loved me. Then he listened to the radio while I listened for the chime of bicycle bells being dinged in the distance. The distorted jingle of an old ice cream truck. Springs bending from boys bouncing on a trampoline. The pitter-patter of flip-flopped girls running, somewhere.

How odd would it have been to have arrived and seen us standing there. Homemade mannequins of three ten-year olds, now three-quarters of the way to middle age. Quinlynn with her new blunt bangs and apricot crochet hippy boho clothing, an eight-year-old daughter at her side, a fiancé who works security at the AGO and is not the girl's biological father, the three of them posed to the left side of the lawn with a dog and grey sedan and Parcheesi board and bed of dandelions germinating at their ankles. And me. Positioned beside my balding, beer-gutted husband to the right of the lawn under the dying honey locust. We are childless. We work for the government. We each carry a tall glass of red wine. Or perhaps I'm carrying both glasses, and have wrinkles around my mouth, and on my forehead, and at the corners of my button eyes. Me and my two empty glasses, crumple-faced and imploding, because my balding, beer-gutted husband is screwing a high school French teacher with an adorably contrived French accent and I'm pretending not to know, or mind.

Sarah? Muffin? he said. You hear me?

Then there's Sophie, set in the middle where the hole used to be. Ten. Still ten because I haven't been able to discover her online, see who she is now, place her face on adulthood. So she stands stationary as the house. A young girl sucking a cigarette, rolling her eyes at something dumb. Me, most likely.

The sign on the easel says *It's the end of the world as we know it.*

Muffin? Sarah? We good to go?

The last time a sign had been left on the Greys' lawn was two Mondays after the men disappeared. The sign read *Thank you.* For what? I wondered. For caring enough to look? I waited for Quinlynn to read the words aloud. When she didn't, I turned on my knees on my seat and looked back at her and Sophie. Neither of them was looking out the window. Sophie read a *Tiger Beat* while Quinlynn sat fixated on the back of my seat. Both of their faces were devoid of color, sanguinity bled dry.

I carved it under the bridge in the playground that week, the thing about their faces. I also carved that I missed them. I used my father's slot-headed screwdriver.

It worked better than the nail file, but a couple months after, a group of teenagers poured gasoline on the swings and slide and mulch, and burned the whole playground down.

12

Met her between the exit doors at the local hardware store. She was standing next to the gumball machine, her face practically pressed against the glass. Straight black hair and eyes dark as tar stains. I hadn't seen her eyes yet, though. Not at first, I mean. All I saw's the back her head. Hair so long it touched the top her buttocks. I'd always liked ladies with real long hair.

Tough choice? I asked.

She turned. I'm sorry?

Can't decide if a gumball's worth that price?

She smiled pretty and turned back to the machine. I looked too. There was a picture of a boy scotch-taped to the glass. The picture was printed on paper peeled at the corners. MISSING CHILD it said, words pixelated red above the boy's face.

I knew who he was. Not personally, but I'd heard stories. Soccer Beally. That was his name. He'd disappeared in ninety-one, three years prior to that day at the gumball machine, which was nineteen ninety-four. I was sixty-three and she forty-two. And the boy, well, in ninety-four he would've been thirteen. Ain't a teenager now, though. Ain't much nothing now, I'm sure. All hope for him being anything other than dead pretty much died a long time ago if we're gonna talk real about the matter.

The lady at the gumball machine was called Easter Nagasaki. She was born in Toronto, where her pa worked as a housepainter for close to forty-five years. Owned his own business with a couple Japs he'd met at the internment camps. They called themselves The Truly Good Housepainters. Easter said her pa even had it written on the side his truck, one that didn't run. He'd hit a moose with it. The truck still sat on their driveway, though. Served like a billboard with the company's digits on the side, and moose hairs still stuck out splits in the windshield.

Easter never knew her ma much growing up. She'd gotten cancer and croaked when Easter was a tot. Had a couple older siblings, though. Easter did, I mean. Victoria, and Hal, which is short for Halloween. All the Nagasaki kids were named after the holiday closest to their birthday, Easter's being mid-March. She preferred people call her East.

I married Easter less than a month after we met. The decision to do so was out the ordinary for both us, I think. We still did it, though. Tied the knot, and laughing the whole time like love had turned us into these new people, giddy as hell.

She wore the white dress I'd picked her at the outlet mall. White pearls in her ears and around her neck. She'd cut her hair shorter, the back curled at the shoulder blades. She didn't bother with no veil. Her face was round and caramel. I'd always had a thing for the Orientals. Ladies, I mean. Even mentioned it during my vows. Said they gave me the butterflies and all that corny crap. She smiled pretty and told me she'd always had a thing for bald, uneducated older men who didn't know how to dress proper for getting married. I didn't know what she meant. I wore the darkest pants I owned. And best shirt, the one with the yellow and black checkers, and button missing third from the top. It was my lucky shirt. Wore it the first time I took out an elk. It was cow-sized, honest to God, with antlers like sprawling branches. What I did, I got the elk in the shoulder. Watched its legs buckle perfect like a camping chair.

The judge declared us official and we kissed, pressing hard. Only person attended was Easter's pa, the painter, Kato. He was seventy-two, just nine years older than me, but looking worse, prehistoric-worse, a statue ready to crumble.

I shook his hand and told him I'd take damn good care his girl. Damn good care, I said. His throat burped, but lips kept shut. His hand scratched mine like splintered wood. I pulled away and pocketed my fingers. He looked at me with eyes I couldn't tell were sad or angry and nodded like a deal'd been done.

Easter moved into my cabin in the Port Woodlot woods off Leeding Road. I turned the old darts room into an office for her. She was real smart, a professional writer. Wrote columns, and helped edit some magazines, including a bi-weekly about Orientals they published in the city. She no longer needed to be there in order to perform her duties, though. In Toronto, I mean.

She worked nine to five weekdays in the office like a proper job. It gave me plenty time to be by myself. I went hunting most days, or read books. I liked reading books about hunting, then going to do it. It felt like I was being written.

I'd get home from hunting and she'd be done work and we'd kiss and make a fire and drink coffee together. Sometimes I'd cook what I'd killed, other times we'd eat canned soup or ravioli and such. She wasn't much a chef. Had other things going, though. A real people-person. She was one those people-persons you felt you knew, even when you didn't. She'd say things, and you'd get them. And she'd get you.

After about a month, I saw she'd put the MISSING CHILD picture on the wall above her desk. Soccer Beally's face in black and white and grey like he was staring out an old TV. Easter said she was planning to write an article on the boy.

What's that gotta do with being Oriental? I asked.

Asian, she said. Then pointed at the picture on the wall and told me to take a closer look. I looked closer, but didn't much like it. Like it was one those pictures where they alter the kid's face to make him look older, better match the time that's passed. It didn't seem right, though. The kid's face, I mean. It didn't look real.

He looks Japanese, she said.

He ain't, I said.

I know. But he looks it.

Computers did it.

He looks exactly like my Uncle Kaz did as a boy, my father's brother. I've seen photographs. They're in black and white, just like this one. So that adds to it too.

They botched the boy's face, I told her. Made his eyes too small.

She was typing words as I talked. I asked if she was paying attention to me. She said she was, that she was writing all what I was saying. I asked what for.

My new article, she said. It's going to be about a lot, not just Soccer Beally's face. It's going to be about you, and me as well. And my Uncle Kaz. My father. And meaning. It's going to be about the implication of all these things combined. Do you understand? I'm excited, Ronald. Really. It's going to be the culmination of everything.

Kato was sent to the internment camps when he was twenty. His family lived west then, in BC. That was during the Second World War. Japs got gathered and thrown on the exhibition grounds. A lot of them were put in horse stalls. A stall per family. Jobs got divided between them. Kato was in charge the food. By food, I mean potatoes mostly. He was the one going stall to stall handing them out every evening. He told Easter he'd give extra potatoes to the pretty girls. Girls with eyelashes so long you saw them flit all butterfly from far away.

Being in the camps wasn't much a big deal for Kato at first. Probably because he felt his family had nothing to lose. They were dirt poor. Didn't own much anything. It was a lot worse for people who had things, the richer folks. For them, well, there was stuff to get took—jobs, homes, whole lives. It happens that quick. One second you're free, the next you ain't, and it's all account your face.

Originally I thought her obsession with Soccer Beally began at the fact they both had names that weren't proper.

Is it real? she'd ask.

Course it's real.

Does it say it on his birth certificate?

It's his real name, I'd tell her. He comes from a whole family of strange names. Six kids and all them got one. A strange name, I mean.

What are they? What are the other names?

It was two and a half months into our marriage, and a month before the end. By then, you couldn't see the walls in her office. Entire spaces covered by maps and old newspaper clippings she'd found at the archives in the library out of town. Articles about Soccer Beally's disappearance tacked all over. The room reeked of lady BO and rotted, half-eaten fruit.

Easter, I'd say.

What, Ronald? What?

The boy's dead, I'd say.

She'd look at me like I was the one that killed him. Don't say what you don't know, she'd tell me. Seriously, Ronald. Don't say what you don't know is true.

It's true, though. It's what I know to be certain. I'm sure of it.

Please, Ronald. You're not. So please.

What you planning to do?

Find him, she'd say. I'm going to find him.

I wound up reading her article around that time, the one that was supposed to be about me and her and Soccer and Uncle Kaz and her pa and the meaning of everything. Wasn't much about none those things, though. It was more about being little. When she was a kid and had a doll she called Black Beauty. The doll was white, a baby girl with blond hair and blue eyes and eyelids that shut when you tilted its noggin back. Part Easter's article read:

. . . It never occurred to me I did not look like Black Beauty, that my face was different than hers, that my own daughter, assuming I were to have one in the future, would more than likely have a much darker complexion, and darker features than my doll's. I had no real concept of what it was to be Japanese back then, or white. There was no difference between black hair and blond hair. It was all just hair. We were all just people.

One of Easter's older articles mentioned her pa lived in a horse stall with his ma and brother Kaz. Kaz was thirteen, seven years younger than Kato. He had large cheeks and feathered hair that stuck rough to grime and sweat on his forehead. Easter said Kaz was Kato's favorite thing, ever. Same way I loved hunting, same way she loved writing, well, Kato loved his little brother.

Eventually they got sent to the basketball arena. That was better than the horse stalls because it was warmer and had bunks. On the first day there, though, the Mounties started calling names, called Kaz's name first. He didn't answer. Sat there on a bottom bunk beside Kato with his head down. He was scared the Mounties were gonna take him from his ma. But Kato told Kaz not to worry. Told him it'd be safe to answer, all the Mounties were doing was checking to see who was there, who wasn't, the way teachers did at school. So Kaz did what his brother said. Raised his hand, fingers outstretched like he was pointing five directions. The Mounties saw, and one them stepped forward, and he had an eye patch, the patchless eye looked real angry for having had to wait. He snatched Kaz by the unfeathered strands of his hair and hauled him off. Dragged the poor kid down the aisle between bunks and out the exit doors.

Their ma got hysterical, hollering and bawling, blinded by tears. Had to be held back by the other Mounties. Kato just sat there, though. Like his body cemented. And his face, too, sat there, cemented, cold and quiet.

Easter said the best part of getting married was adopting my last name—Kaysen. She told me her maiden name was too much a giveaway. People read Nagasaki and they know what you are, she said, but Easter Kaysen? People hear that, they're not sure what to think. They're free to imagine whatever. No particular kind of face pops into your mind. It's a name that leaves things open. Do you understand, Ronald?

Yeah, I get.

I'm still going to publish under Nagasaki, however.

Soon she stopped getting dressed most mornings. Worked and wrote and obsessed over Soccer Beally from the comfort of her PJs. Told me she had feelings in her gut, and that the gut's never wrong. Told me she was gonna find him; he was alive and she was gonna find the kid and bring him back to the Beally family. Even started packing a suitcase in preparation for her journey. A new passport. Asked about the gas mileage on my car. She'd sold hers.

I hunted more and more during then, more than ever. Went away whole weekends, and well, shot about a thousand things dead. Cooked rabbit and beans over fire and listened to the spark of it, trying to forget about the strange lady living back at my cabin. Focused on nature. The smell of oak, the sound of pine cones dropping. My bags hanging high from rope I'd tied between two trees.

It wasn't lonely being out there alone. I talked to the fire. I got kept company by the reek of whatever I'd killed.

They never found Kaz. He'd escaped the Mountie's hold and ran off. Apparently. Lost. Seemed gone as dead. Kato blamed himself. He was the one who'd told Kaz to raise his hand. He was the one who'd sat there watching.

A decade later Easter was born. Her ma died. Her siblings having reached the double-digits. So it was just her and Kato most the time, father and daughter, a team. He'd wake her sometimes, early enough it was still dark. I've got a feeling I know where my brother is, he'd tell her, only his words were a mish mash of English and Japanese and maybe sometimes neither. He'd lift Easter out the bed, carry her to the garage. He'd strap her in the front seat even though she was too small. And they'd drive. Kato and Easter in a car in the dark and a road looking too short in front of them because all they could see was what fit inside the headlights.

I forced myself to look at the collage on her wall. Mostly maps, but also a couple lists. Lists of words, or names. Some the names were scratched out.

Trigger
Sherri
Carver
Quinlynn
Minster (Monster?)
Hermia
Birdie

I recognized them as Soccer Beally's ma, pa, brothers and sisters. I asked Easter about it. She was in the kitchen.

Had Soccer Beally's picture pressed flat to the table and was measuring millimeters between his eyes. Wasn't looking at me, only him. Told me she talked to them.

Who?

The ones I crossed out, she said.

What about the ones you didn't?

They got away.

Where'd you find them?

The father works at Home Repair, which is why the poster was put up on the gumball machine. The mother works at a Wild'n'Wacky Wings in Aurora. I haven't spoken to her yet. I found most of the children at Wells St. Elementary, and the oldest boy at Dr. G.W. Williams High School. Both in Aurora as well.

I pictured Easter at a grade school, walking around in her PJs, calling kids to her. She'd crouch beside some little boy or girl and start asking, Did Soccer Beally ever talk about wanting to go here or there, this way or that? I pictured cops. Saw Easter getting grabbed by her hair, dragged out the schoolyard and tossed in a car with bright lights flashing round and round.

She'd interviewed most everyone in Port Woodlot within weeks of being there. So I knew the end was near. That her search would carry her elsewhere. To new towns and cities and fields and forests, take her to new people, more important places to be.

I kissed her one time. She was sleeping at her desk. I leaned and pecked the side her head and the whole thing felt like it wasn't real.

This is what you do, Ronald. This is how you be loving. This is marriage.

I went outside after. It was early and pitch black. The air was burnt leaves. I rubbed my eyes hard and saw ghosts floating in the dark. I stood with the taste of her hair on my mouth, listening to birds. A million birds chirping, but not one I could see. There's something special about that, I think. Feeling so close to something that feels like it ain't even there.

Kato was part an Angler's Club for Japanese fishermen who sometimes went catching bass together. Easter said fundraisers got held at Christmas to raise cash for them. For the club, I mean. She said there was always a Santa Claus, too. Usually played by one the club members. White beard, Oriental eyes. But one year the club hired a Caucasian to do the act. Kids'd been complaining the Japanese one wasn't real, saying a Japanese Santa ain't how it is in the *Miracle on 34th Street* or any those other films. So Easter got extra excited that year, finally felt like she was seated on the real thing, going on about what she wanted the elves to build her and such.

I want a magic wand that works, she said to Santa Claus. I wanna make things go blam! and appear.

Easter told me her pa looked over and saw her sitting there on the Santa Claus, and for whatever reason, got convinced the Santa Claus was actually the Mountie who'd took his brother. Made no sense, but not everything does. Some things just are as is—Kato tugging Santa Claus by the beard, and beating him senseless, punching the poor guy in the face until he blacks out. People screaming. Easter screaming. An unconscious Santa Claus drooling blood into his beard, and Kato's screaming too.

Where's Kaz? Where's Kaz? What've you done with my brother?

I'd asked her if she wanted to get coffee. That's how it started, more or less. We were standing there next to the gumball machine, the one with the picture of Soccer Beally staring at us. And she was staring, too. At me. Her brow tight, studying hard, like maybe my face was some sorta puzzle.

There's a diner two blocks down the road, I said.

Alright.

Across from the grocery store plaza. It'll be on your right.

Alright. She looked back at Soccer Beally. I feel like I know him, she said, like I know him quite well. Do you ever feel that, Ronald? Like you're already so close to someone, like you know them but you don't? You know them before you do?

No, I said. I got the opposite. I don't feel close, no matter where whoever is. Easter stepped closer. I like hunting, though. Doing it alone. I mean, well, I feel fine being far from things is what I'm saying. Hunting is, yeah. I don't know what I'm trying to say.

She laughed like what I'd been saying was a joke. Maybe it was. I laughed, too.

You're not a crazy person, are you? she asked.

Don't think so.

We were both still laughing.

I'm parked over there, she said, pointing

I'm over here, I said. I pointed too.

We were both standing there, pointing opposite ways and looking at each other, her eyelashes so long and nice-looking they could've granted every wish anybody'd ever had. Meet again soon, I said. She smiled pretty the way she always would and then we both went the direction our fingers were in.

Sometimes I'd be crouched against the cold earth and aiming. Damp knees. Rifle steady on a log. Soccer Beally on the axis of my scope, but he doesn't look like a real boy. He's got one those faces that's been altered like in the MISSING CHILD posters. He looks like something else, strange and not wholly real.

Best-case scenario's what Easter believes to be true, that he's alive, out there somewhere. Maybe he found a spot to build a fort and that's where he's been living this whole time. And maybe Easter's Uncle Kaz is there, too.

I always wake like it's been a bad dream, seeing Soccer Beally in a forest, his face scaring me worse than goblins, worse than ghouls. Either that or I don't wake at all. I just snap out of it. I'm standing with my boots stuck in mud and the wind a flute in my ears. And taking aim at something. Not a missing child, but an animal. That's all there is, really. An animal, walking around in nature. I squeeze the trigger to make it mean something.

Got back from hunting one evening and found her seated at the kitchen table surrounded by three luggage bags. She was wearing tearaways and a raincoat with a hood and the hood was tied tight around her head. A taxicab is coming to pick me up at nine, she said. I'm going to borrow my father's car from Toronto, and then I'm going to head west. I'm going to find him, Ronald.

I was standing beside the microwave oven, my rifle strapped to my shoulder, my knife buckled against my belt. I ain't gonna stop you, I said.

I know, she said.

There was silence so thick the thickness throttled me. Must've been a few seconds before either us said something new. I caught my breath. I told her I'd drive her to Toronto, that a cab would cost a fortune.

No, she said. It's fine.

More that same silence. Then I said, This marriage. What was it?

She was looking at me hard and sad, and with her hair covered and no makeup, well, she looked like a little boy. Just was, she said.

Just was. Repeated it ten times over before anything started making sense, and even still, maybe it didn't. I leaned my rifle against the counter.

She stood. She appeared so tiny. I wondered how long she'd keep in my mind before the memory of her shrunk whole. I watched her walk out. I didn't do nothing about it. Didn't help her move the luggage, neither. She had to come back for the third, wheeling it past my legs.

Wish me luck, Ronald.

She disappeared out the door and into the night. Right away I liked it better that way, the way where she was gone. The way that meant it was just me again, my rifle and knife, the animals. No nonsense outside those things. No timeline, no history. Just whatever I could see directly from wherever it was I was standing.

13

Nash was always swinging his knife when he got excited. He'd go, Oh shit oh shit oh shit, slicing the air like a madman. Telling me the Air Wick Freshmatic Mini Refills were fifty percent off or that there was a sale on cereal. Oh shit shit shit cheap Cap'n Crunch!

We worked on the night crew at Loblaws. Eleven pm until seven thirty in the morning spent breaking your ass for nothing, or less than nothing if you included deductions. Truly a bottom of the barrel bullshit fucking job. The kind of place that'll hire anyone. Illegal immigrants, basket cases, you name it. All your coworkers either foreign or fucking nuts. You're asleep in the day, awake all night, and your only interactions are with them, foreigners, nuts; it's enough to drive you fucking nuts.

I was six months in. I was stocking pesto in the pasta aisle. Nash wraps around the corner with his knife and his *oh shit* and it's about one forty-five am, a bit before first break. We got given box cutters our first day, but Nash always brought his own knife from home. A trout knife. The kid was damn proud of the thing. He'd make a big show out of using it, cutting plastic wrapped around the product on the skids the way a magician might, all theatrical and queer as hell, slicing upwards so it'd end with the blade in the air.

Oh shit oh shit Ryan man you ain't gonna believe it, you ain't gonna believe. He's coming at me like my throat is a fucking trout. He's sweating, chafing. Nash with his fat wet face and tits, the blubbery body of a big brown baby. He goes, Ya gotta see man, ya gotta come see. So I'm following him to the next aisle, the baking aisle, and he's going, It's fucked, it ain't even real it's so fucked man, and all I'm thinking is I wish he'd pocket that goddamn knife. But he's pointing at the product with it, bottles of olive and canola oil, sunflower oil, vinegar. He goes, Ya ready man, ya ready?

Nash got hired around the same time I did. I remember seeing him at the orientation wearing a clip-on tie on a golf shirt, seated at the front, nodding like a motherfucker every time the group leader said something fascinating about sanitation, or how to properly pick things up. Nash with his double chin tucked quadruple on each nod, nodding nonstop. Still nodding when he'd look back at me. He kept turning, and looking, making one of those *what the fuck you even doing here?* faces, probably because I was the only one there who wasn't a middle-aged Asian lady, or brown and dumb as hell like him.

The way I got the gig's through Quin. Her big bro Carver was night manager. He put in a good word, but I still had to bullshit my way through the usual. Answer the same questions everywhere asks—One) Have you been incarcerated? Two) Are you currently employed?—but unlike everywhere, a place like Loblaws couldn't give a fuck less if your answers go One) yes, Two) no. So I start working six nights a week. I'm pulling pump trucks, opening boxes, stocking end displays, facing product so the English side of the label's facing out, and goddamn, it's sucking soul out my ass every second. But we do what it takes.

Ya ready to shit your pants? Nash asked.

Okay.

He looked both ways down the aisle and back at me, stepping close. I smelled cough syrup on his whisper. Oh shit Ryan man, he said. Shit's about to change for us man, shit's about to get real. Shit. Dude, dude ya ready? Here goes: I found a dick in a bottle of vinegar.

I looked both ways down the aisle too. What?

I found a dick in a bottle of vinegar.

He pulled a bottle off the shelf to grab the one behind it. A tall glass bottle of red wine vinegar with something sunk to the bottom, dick-sized and dick-shaped.

It's a dick, he said.

I took the bottle and pressed my eyes against it. The thing sure did look like a dick, mushroom-headed with vein-like somethings coming out one end. It can't be, I said, holding the bottle to the light. It can't.

It can, said Nash. Ryan man, we're gonna be rich. Rich as a big-titted bitch!

The reason I was there to begin with is because I needed money ASAP, even a bullshit amount like what they offered. Quin said I could only see Kim-Claire if I started paying what I owed. So I was paying what I owed and more. Put a fraction into rebuilding myself, for real this time, but most into them, my two girls.

To build us a better life, I'd say.

Quin breathed funny into the phone whenever I did.

She'd go, Be good, Ryan. Don't let my brother down.

I was outside on break one night. I was just standing in the snow. I was looking at the footprints I'd made from the door to where I was, and I was looking at all the perfect white still in front of me. The back door opened and Carver came out. He leaned against the loading dock smoking a cigarette. Eventually he called me but it wasn't right away. You crazy? he said. Where's your coat, Ry? I was wearing jeans and a T-shirt. I walked over to him, but it wasn't right away. When I got there he asked if I was doing okay. He was already done his cigarette. He tossed it in the snow. I was looking at his boots. I told him it was a fucked up thing working nights, and he said not to worry, I'd eventually get used to it.

Carver's hair was thick, but graying. His goatee had grey in it too. He was thirty-three, only four years older than me, but the guy looked aged as crusty shit. His eyes, the way he stood. The way he walked. Like every muscle in him ached, a bag of bad bones. I wondered if those were the four years that do it to you, twenty-nine to thirty-three, or if it was something else.

Carver, I said, I'm gonna do right by your sister.

He ignored me. Told me Susan kept giving him shit in the mornings. She says we're scratching the floors, he said. She says we're probably not pumping the pump trucks high enough so the skids have been dragging. But that's not it. There are black lines everywhere, but that's not it. We didn't used to have this problem, only since the renovation. They put in those cheap orange tiles. So it's not us. And if it is us, it's not our fault.

I was still looking at his boots because I hated seeing his old-ass face blabber about shit like scratched floors. I'd known Carver since we were kids. It's a tough thing, seeing someone you knew then turn into someone you know now, especially when now's got them so beat up and tired-looking, concerned with orange tiles, for fuck's sake.

Did you hear what I said, Carver? About Quinlynn.

Yeah, I heard.

I'm gonna do right.

Sure, Ry.

I was thinking about it a lot in the baking aisle that night, imagining I'd had that same conversation but with a kid-Carver. Like him how he was, with skinny arms and legs, sprinting with water guns, ollying his banana board over pop cans and shit like that. Us in a world before his bones went bad. Me telling him I'd do right, and him believing in me.

It's not a dick, I said.

It is Ryan man, it is. Look at it.

Nash held the bottle to his crotch.

It's probably a cork, I said.

Fuck you, a cork, he said. Yeah man it's a cork, a cork wrapped in human skin, it's a cork with veins and blood and a fuckin dick hole. Fuck you, a fuckin cork. It's a cock!

It's hard to see, I said.

Fuck you, a fuckin cork.

The vinegar's dark, Nash.

He was shaking his head, his fat face sweaty, creased as an old man's balls. I could smell the sour stink of him. Fuck you, a fuckin cork, he kept saying. He was right too; if it was a cork, it was the most dick-looking cork of all time. But a dick didn't make sense. That's what I told him. I go, A dick's not logical, Nash.

Fuck you, a dick's not logical.

So we argued about it a long-ass time. Both of us touching bottles to make it look like we were still being productive. Eventually Carver came dragging his feet past the aisle. He goes, Ry, and Nash starts whispering, Oh shit oh shit he's fuckin on to us. Carver asked if I had any extra Barilla pasta. There's an empty dump bin in front of the deli, he said, so you can go dump anything extra there.

I gave him thumbs up. He didn't move. He stood there in his padded vest and Dickies, spine stooped, eyes bouncing between me and Nash and the bottles on the shelf we were pointlessly positioning, then his own boots.

Carver, I said.

He looked up.

I'm helping Nash a minute, I said.

Nash touched the dick-vinegar like it was normal vinegar, pushing it to the very back of the shelf, and half-smiled at nothing as he shifted other bottles in front.

I need you in your proper aisles, said Carver. The daytime managers are going to be inspecting everything in the morning. We need shelves fully stocked, fully faced. Susan said they'll be taking pictures of all our mistakes to show head office.

Okay, I said. Just a second.

I'm serious, Ry.

Carver was always letting me know how serious he was. I'll be literally one more second.

He didn't move right away because everything he did had to be in slow-fucking-motion. A slow-motion turn, and then right foot, left foot, right, left, gone. Shyiiiiiit, whispered Nash, patting sweat under his eyes with his shirt. That was a close one Ryan man. Too close. Ya think that dumb sonuvabitch knows what's up is up?

I'm heading back to pasta, I said.

Okay, okay Ryan man, we'll talk more on break. We'll talk.

In my aisle I thought a lot about it. Not dicks so much, but money. What money could mean to me in that moment. I was stocking ketchup and thinking what'd be like to never stock ketchup again. I could be buying ketchup. Heinz Ketchup. Not the No Name bullshit kind. I could be buying Kim-Claire tickets to go see that bratty Bieber kid at the Air Canada Center, but before we go, I could be making her grilled Black Diamond cheese and fries to dip in Heinz fucking ketchup.

I walked to Tim Hortons with Nash on first break. We ordered coffee from other overnight losers, and then headed back to the store. The snow was up to our ankles but we were wearing work boots. Nash sweated in the cold. We discussed how we'd go about it, like who'd buy the vinegar, eat it. We both agreed it wasn't enough to discover a dick; one of us had to swallow the dick-vinegar, and prove that we did.

Assuming it's a dick, I began.

It is.

Okay, yeah, so, assuming it is, what if it's got a disease?

Disease? he said. He said it like it was a new word. I swear to Christ the kid was half-retarded. I think he mispronounced it too. I think he said *decease*.

Like AIDS, I said. What if the dick's got AIDS?

Eights? he said.

The second third of the night I spent making a list of the things I'd buy. The list was in my head. I was trying to think of all the shit Quin had ever said she wanted. Didn't matter if she didn't want it anymore. Like when we were kids and she'd go on about those Lite-Brites, or when we got older in Montreal and she was dying for a pink moped. Or before I did what I did, and went away for it, she wanted to paint. All she wanted was to raise our baby right, while still being able to make art comfortably.

I had a picture of her and Kim-Claire on my shitty flip phone. It was them at the Toronto Zoo in front of the penguins, Kim-Claire's favorite. And I knew Quin liked koala bears best because of *Tommy Tricker and the Stamp Traveler*. So I'd buy a stuffed penguin and koala bear, and I'd buy my favorite animal too. An eagle maybe. A stuffed penguin, koala, and eagle, all in a row on the couch in the family room of our house. We'd be a family again, with a family room. That's what I was thinking about.

I sniffled like a pussy as I stocked bags of orzo, rotini, penne rigate, fussilli, tubetti. I knew the names of so many noodles.

Carver appeared at the end of my aisle. He asked if I was making good time. I gave him thumbs up, but he knew my thumb meant fuck all. He reminded me about the managers in the morning, and I told him okay. And I was looking at his boots again because his face reminded me of all the ways the world doesn't give two shits about you. I closed the picture on my phone. When I looked up, Carver was looking at *my* goddamn fucking boots.

Second break was five a.m. I sat with Nash in the staff room. Nash had his trout knife out. He was wiping the blade on his pants. The kid's thighs were like tree stumps. He was telling me what he was gonna get with his share—a PS4, patio furniture for his parents. Ryan man, he said,

I've read about shit like this, people finding boogers on their burgers and shit. People makin mad money for motherfuckin boogers and we've got dick, a real live human man-dick. Holy shit that dick's a motherfuckin goldmine.

We decided I'd buy the vinegar. People knew Nash worked the baking aisle, so if it was him, things might seem suspicious. I'd pick the vinegar up myself, as well as other things, buy them, go home, eat. Take it from there.

It's a miracle, said Nash, a motherfuckin dick-vinegar miracle!

Back on the floor I cleared the plastic from my aisle, brought the cardboard to the compacter, and started facing up. The final third of the night was always spent facing. I was doing a damn good job too because I kept telling myself it'd be the last time. I'd be done after tonight. I'd be gone. So I wanted to leave things good for Carver.

Around seven, Andy comes strutting in my aisle. He was assistant night manager, a real ass-clown. Pompous head the size of a medicine ball, he starts dissecting what I'd been doing, bitching about it. Standing there with his ponytail and glasses and girly fluorescent kneepads, mouth breathing, pointing at the Thousand Island dressing and saying it, Can you read, Ryan?

I waited for him to make his goddamn point. But he didn't. He stood there waiting for an answer. Waiting, waiting, the silence carrying something more brutal than anything I'd ever felt. I told him yes. He asked if I could read, and I said yes, and uttering just that one syllable made me feel shrunk to the size of a fucking orzo grain.

Yes, Andy. I can read.

The Thousand Island dressing was stocked behind a sign for Ranch. I told him it'd been a mistake made by daytime staff; one I hadn't caught, but still. The fucker didn't care though. He asked again, Can you read? Cause that's what they should make all the applicants do before they get hired. At the interview, they should sit you guys and gals down and make you prove you can read. It's a simple thing, Ryan. Place the product above the proper sign. Alrighty then? Easy-peasy. Kapeesh?

I was squeezing my box cutter. The only thing keeping me from gutting the prick was a picture I kept forcing myself to see in my head. It was of those stuffed animals on the couch like I said, the penguin, the koala and the eagle. And it was a hundred other things too. It was a Lite-Brite, a moped. It was Heinz Ketchup and tickets to see that Bieber kid. It was everything either of my girls had ever wanted all in one place at one time. It was them knowing it was me who'd brought it there.

Store opened at seven thirty.

I'd corrected the salad dressing by seven thirty-five, punched out, gone shopping, grabbing the red wine vinegar, as well as baby carrots, popcorn, a box of fish sticks, another of Bear Paws, cradled them all in my arms.

I saw Nash in the pop aisle. He winked. Only the kid couldn't wink so it was more a blink. Two litre bottle of Dr. Pepper in one hand, trout knife in the other. He was blinking like a strobe light was pointed at him. He goes, Do it Ryan man, you can do it! Cock 'n' roll, baby! Cock 'n' roll!

On my way to checkout I passed Carver. He and Andy were with the douchey daytime managers, all circled around a long black cut in the floor. I am not happy about this, Susan was saying. I am not happy about this at all, at all, at all, at all. Not. One. Bit. I stood in line at the checkout. There was only one cashier because it was still so early. Andy saw me watching and glared, the fucking twerp. Then the group of them moved on to stare at another mark on the floor. Carver hobbled behind the pack. The cashier asked if I had an employee card. I paid for the groceries and walked back into the store, to the warehouse. I tossed the vinegar in the damages bin. A lot of the daytime staffers were just arriving. They were all smiles and coffee like always. Most of them were white, and the ones who weren't spoke good English, but no one said hi or good morning. I jumped off the loading dock and felt the crunch of my body sink shin-deep into the snow.

14

When I was little, I remember asking my mother why black people have white hands. There was this black kid in my class at school, and during recess one day I noticed the palms of his hands were lighter than the rest of him. My mother explained that people's hands are almost always two-sided. Look at your own, she told me. So I looked, and my mother showed me how my palms were slightly pinker than the rest of my body. It's God's way of showing you you're not just one thing, she said. You're you, but you're also something else, Hermie. You're also something entirely different.

I sit on the curb outside St. George Station. It's late October. The moon the same orange as the leaves in the gutter. A starless sky. I smoke tobacco from a Zulu pipe I found in my father's kitchen. It's beige with a brown stem, the bowl spurred like a tortoise shell.

I'm dressed in the same clothes from yesterday—the homemade Paul Baribeau shirt, army jacket, paint-stained capris, red creepers, my hair dyed green under a black army cap. I check my cell. It's almost ten o'clock. I hear the subway screech into the station. It rings through the tunnel, up the stairs and into the street. I empty the pipe, slide it down the front pouch of my cargo knapsack. I stand up and stick my hands inside my jacket pockets and finger the canister of dog mace snug inside the right one.

A heavyset aboriginal man emerges from the tunnel. He's wearing black shorts and sandals, and his hair is black too, and his jacket, polyester and crinkled, unzipped, a slit of round belly between his waistline and the bottom of a faded Mr. Bean T-shirt.

Trigger? he says.

His daughter, I say.

He reaches his hand out to shake. I look at the marred fingernails, the missing thumb. Name's Bobby, he says. You may or may not notice I've got no thumb.

Yep, I say. I don't shake his hand. I tell him I have a cold.

Lost it when I was a kid, he says. Stuck it in my brother's bike gears.

I unclip the front of my knapsack and flip it open. Bobby comments on the tiny chains inked around my fingers, calling them spicy. I thank him. He licks his soul patch. I pull the shoebox out of my bag—sticker on the lid says size ten Converse sneakers, green. Bobby steps forward. I breathe him. He smells like a cat's fart. I step back, scuff my feet. Dead leaves scrape the pavement and I cough because I'm supposed to be sick. Bobby says, Bless you. He takes another step forward, and I hand him the box, and he smiles, and I cough again. You mind if I look inside? he asks.

That's fine.

Picture looked good, he says, but I wanna make sure.

That's fine. I don't care.

My hands are back inside my pockets. I touch the dog mace. Small and cylindrical. I flick off the safety with my thumb.

Bobby opens the shoebox. Nine tufts of hair inside—blue, red, yellow, and the colors they mix to make. Just nine? he says. Hm. The ad said there were supposed to be ten. He pulls one out, hands me back the box. The mace hangs heavy in my right pocket. I watch Bobby examine the troll doll. He runs his fingers through its hair, sniffs its feet, lifts its shirt to the chest. The ones with the diamond bellybuttons are supposed to grant wishes, he tells me.

I check the time on my phone.

I think the ad said thirty, he says.

Yep.

I also think it said ten dolls, but whatever.

I hand him back the box. He puts it on the ground. He pulls out his X-Men wallet, peels it open and fingers through a sheaf of twenties. Got change? he asks. You got a ten by chance?

Nope.

All I've got are twenties. You mind cutting a deal? Accept twenty and some change?

Can't, I say. These aren't mine. They belong to my father. He told me not to take anything less than thirty.

Fair enough, says Bobby. He shuts his eyes and begins reciting numbers. I'm not sure what they mean, but I assume he's adding—twenty, thirty, forty, twenty-seven, thirty, fifteen, no, no, it was sixteen. Sixteen, Bobby corrects himself, and now thirty. He opens his eyes, standing there, staring at the shoebox as if the sum is on the lid.

Hundred and sixty-three, I say.

He shuts his eyes again and licks his soul patch. Expensive week, he sighs. His eyes open and he starts shuffling four fingers across the top of the twenties, sifting through the bills like files in a cabinet. I watch his hand—those fingernails, that missing thumb. I want to puke. He plucks forty dollars from his wallet and mumbles, You people are sucking me dry.

His hand looks like a fat, fleshy fork. I want to tell him to keep the money, but it's too late. I'm already holding it, and folding it, shoving it inside my pocket. Bobby thanks me, saluting. I light a cigarette and watch him waddle off.

I arrived less than a week ago, after splitting with Ollie, who I'd been with since high school. It was early when I got there. Stormy clouds crept over the old building, distorted the sun. I entered the lobby. I pressed the button labeled T. BEALLY. No answer.

Rain pattered the front windows. I hung my jacket on the inside doorknob and sat on the floor. Leaned against a wall of mailboxes. There was a mirror across from me. My hair was wet and the green looked black, like sopping strands of seaweed stuck to my face. An unlit cigarette perched on my lips.

He arrived an hour later, maybe more. He wore a garbage bag and carried an axe. The axe head was wrapped in a garbage bag as well. I stood up, stuck the cigarette behind my ear. A cargo knapsack, duffle bag, and small white cardboard box rested at my feet. The box had a yarn handle and air holes punched in the top. He observed my luggage before noticing me. When he noticed, the axe head hit the floor.

Little Hermia, he said.

Hi, Dad.

He looked the same as he did three years before—brown buzz cut, beard, sharp nose, taut lips, eyes like you'd done him wrong—the features unchanged, but a bit more worn. I wrapped my arms around him. The garbage bag crackled between us. He lifted an arm to hug me back, while the other held the axe. Missed you, he said. I let go and looked at him. His eyes were wet from the rain.

My father's apartment was on the second floor of the four-story building. It had two bedrooms, a bathroom, a kitchen and a living room. The walls were painted white, wooden floors, and there was a big, brown radiator under every window. I followed as he carried my things to the spare bedroom across from the kitchen. I warned him there were rats in the box and he nodded. He carefully rested them on the mattress. I handed him back the axe and he leaned it against an empty bookshelf.

You want coffee? he asked.

Do you have tea?

No. I got coffee, water, and milk.

Water's fine, thanks.

The kitchen was a narrow space, with burnt bulbs and no windows. The tiles were stained like teeth. I stood in the doorway and watched him clear the countertop, which was buried under an assortment of things—seven inch records, hockey cards, Ziploc bags of beads, PEZ dispensers, fountain pens, VHS tapes, brooches, pornographic coasters. He spread the mess apart with his arms and made room for the coffee maker he kept in a cabinet under the sink. Pulled it out and turned it on and the machine whirred and white steam leaked out the top. He prepared my drink while waiting for his coffee to drip. Held a mug under the tap, filled it with water and handed it to me. The mug was striped wasp-like with brown semicircles staining the bottom. He poured his coffee into a second mug, which was pink and white and said *It Isn't Easy Being a Princess*, and nodded. He still drank coffee black.

I don't got chairs or a table, he said.

We sat on the musty sofa in the living room. There was a short stack of Frisbees on the cushion between us. I watched him stick his forefinger in the coffee, dipping it deep to the knuckle. It was a habit I remembered. I used to sit across from him and watch his face turn red.

I'm still not good at talking, he said.

I know, Dad.

It's good though, to be quiet. It's good for people to feel fine silent.

The sofa faced the window. The rain whipped the glass, blurring our view of outside. Bathurst Street turned liquid. The cars and buses appeared to melt.

So, how's things? he said. How's Little Minster?

He's good. He graduated college last spring. He's spent his time since then working on a manuscript. And it's good, Dad. I think writing's been really good for him.

What's he write?

Fiction. He writes short stories.

What's Little Minster write about in his short stories?

I don't know, Dad. You should call him. You should ask to read one.

He nodded, scrutinizing the items spread across the floor—cassette players, Christmas ornaments, a dog bowl, Barbies, Kens, plastic Dreamhouses, the face of a father clock, My Little Ponies and troll dolls, mandolins, two bolo ties in the shape of swastikas, three framed photographs of white men in black face, a taser gun. I needed a cigarette.

You're twenty-two, he said. You and Little Minster, twenty-two, born nineteen eighty-seven. Little Hermia and Little Minster, twenty-two years old now.

Yep.

Your birthday's October. He pointed at the calendar on the wall.

The first, I said.

October first, he said. My twins, born October first, nineteen eighty-seven, Little Hermia and Little Minster. He was looking at me, nodding, almost smiling, proud for having remembered. Then he gestured toward the room. You can take anything here. Anything you want, you take it. A present. You take something for Little Minster too, if you think he'll like. I even got a couple books he might like. One's got pictures of dinosaur bones. You take that book for Little Minster, will you.

I stood, untucked the cigarette from behind my ear and watched him cringe at the sight of it. I asked to borrow an umbrella, pointed at the dozen or so in a laundry basket next to the pile of chessboards.

That's product, he said. There's a roof extension in the alley.

Okay, I said. I turned to walk out.

Little Hermia, he said.

Yep?

He didn't say anything.

What? I said.

Nothing, he said. How's Sher?

Mom?

How's your mom?

I stood beside three metal lanterns on the floor. The same, I said.

He repeated it, The same. Then he asked, You need to live here?

No, I said. I was hoping to stay a couple days though.

His shoulders relaxed then. I hadn't noticed how tense they were until I saw them slant back down. He swigged the remainder of his coffee, swallowed and said, A couple days is good. A couple days is something we can do.

A long time ago, my brother and I found a turtle in Craddock Park. We named the turtle Whitney Houston because that was our mother's favorite singer. We made Whitney Houston a home out of an old pastry box. We filled the box with grass and clovers and raisins and a cream cheese container of water, and then we placed Whitney Houston inside the box and shut the lid and sealed the roof with Blu-Tack. After that, I punched holes in the lid with a paring knife from the kitchen.

Meanwhile Minster found a photograph of our parents to stick to the bottom of the lid. That way Whitney Houston would have something happy to look at. My father wore a black suit and a yarmulke in the photo, and my mother wore her own mother's old wedding gown. She was laughing. I'd asked my mother why she was laughing the first time I saw the photo, and she told me, Your father had just said the funniest thing. Had told me he liked my face. *I like your face, Sher. I'll like it forever* is what he said.

I couldn't understand why she found that so funny, but every time I was about to shut the pastry box lid I'd say, I like your face, Whitney Houston, and imagine the turtle laughing, the turtle happy, so I wouldn't feel so bad about shutting it in there.

I return home after selling the troll dolls. My father is in the living room sorting through hundreds, maybe thousands of stamps. He's wearing a bathrobe, which is beige and beer-stained, boxers and black socks. I hand him the money.

This is forty, he says.

Yep.

I told the guy thirty.

I got forty.

He holds a twenty in each hand, nodding at the bills and then at me. The cut on his lip moistens, spreading redder. I imagine blood running down his chin.

You're a killer, he says.

I take off my jacket, drape it over the armrest and sit down on the sofa facing him. He's on his knees atop an island of newspaper. There's a fan plugged into a power bar next to the stamp books. It's panning side to side pushing dank air in every direction. The windows are shut, radiators turned all the way up. The apartment smells toxic because earlier he painted a wooden stool. Purple paint speckles his hands and chest. I pull my jacket off the armrest, retrieve the mace from the pocket, show him the purple canister. Look, I tell him, it's the same color.

He looks at the can, and then at the stool, and then at the money.

Different shade, he says.

You sure? Looks the same to me.

Different shade, he repeats. You need to learn to tell the difference in things.

I'm looking at the canister. There's a picture of an angry dog on the front, big cartoon teardrops dripping out of its eyes. The script on the warning label is in Chinese.

Where'd you get this? I ask.

Doesn't matter, he says. It's a different shade of purple. It's important you don't assume all purple's the same.

I know, I said. Okay.

He folded the money and brought it to an empty olive jar he kept on the floor next to the rat cage. You're a killer, he said again. Little Hermia, the killer. He stuffed the bills inside the jar. The ratties poked their heads out of the bars to take a closer look.

I was ten the year my mother called the *major emergency meeting* in her bedroom at nightfall. It was December, some time close to Christmas. Silver mistletoe hung on the frame above her door. Zero presents under the tree downstairs.

I was wearing the Spice Girls T-shirt Uncle Tony and Aunt Jane had bought me, but my mother ordered me to go change. She said the *major emergency meeting* was far too major to be attended in such *vivid, floozy colors*. So I put my Nagano Olympics jacket on top, zipped up, then rushed down the upstairs hall to join the others. Quinlynn, Birdie and Monster were already seated in a row on the end of my mother's bed. Carver wasn't there though. He was eighteen, so a couple years out of town by then.

My mother wore a pastel blue sweater and violet sweatpants, pacing back and forth, cotton socks rubbing streaks across the carpet. Her blond hair was wet and looked brown and reminded me of soba noodles. She told us she loved us. Then she carried on to explain how our father did not; he didn't love us anymore and would no longer be picking us up on the occasional weekend.

The only time you'll be seeing him from now on is Hanukkah, she said.

What's Hanukkah? asked Birdie.

Our mother said, Your father's not right, loves. He's not together. He's breaking, and has been for some time, and it's unfair to you children. You shouldn't have to see him so broke.

Quinlynn got up. She gently put her hand on our mother's shoulder, held it there and then walked out of the room. She was allowed to walk out of rooms because she was a teenager. The rest of us had to stay. I looked at Birdie. She was six at the time, a pinky stuck up her nose. I looked at Monster. His eyes followed the red stain on the big toe of our mother's right sock.

What's making Dad break? I asked.

Nothing, she said. Nothing, and that's why it's so dangerous to be around him, love. Because sometimes people break, they shatter for no reason, and it becomes dangerous to be around them because pieces might fling up and hit you.

She stepped forward, reached out and held my face in her hands. I could smell flowery lotion on her wrists. It made my eyes shudder. She knew I liked it when my father touched my face that way, when he'd press my cheeks together to make them chubby. But his hands were warm. My mother's were bone cold.

I sell the Zulu pipe to an aging punker in Nathan Phillips Square. She wears a leather jacket, tattered fishnets, army boots and fingerless pink gloves. She has bleached blond dreadlocks. Her face is beaten, blemished, swamp-colored bruises peeking behind black eye shadow. Her nose is bent out of shape as well. She smokes a joint and offers me a pull and we sit together on a concrete bench facing Queen West. The sky is smoggy and damp leaves clog the sewer drains. I hand the woman the pipe. She examines it in both hands. I focus on her hands, how rough they appear, how one day my hands will appear the same, like bones shrinking underneath the skin, folded skin, wavering. I tell the woman she can have the pipe for free.

She says, The Trigger dude told me twelve bucks.

It's free, I say. He told me to give it to you for free.

The woman's smile is full of chipped teeth bent every direction but the way they're supposed to go. She unzips her breast pocket and slides the stem of the pipe inside. The bowl pokes out like a baby kangaroo head.

She points at the grey sky. Everything adds up, she says.

Her joint, my cigarette, the hiss of them, harmonizing.

You want to hear something amazing? she asks.

Sure.

I didn't bring money today.

What do you mean?

Here. Today. I arranged to meet you, to buy this shnazzy fucking pipe, but didn't bring any dough. I purposely didn't. I didn't bring the cash the Trigger dude told me to because I knew I'd get it for free. I just knew. Things add up, and they've been adding up to this moment, to me getting this pipe for nothing, man. Swear to fucking Christ.

I pretend to care. I ask if things always add up to something good.

She shakes her head and nods and tells me to watch. She slides herself closer. Her eyes are wet, discolored skin sags below the eyelids. She places her fingertips on top of her cheekbones and pulls the skin down. Her battered features smoothen. This is what I used to look like, she tells me. Then she takes her hands away, and the flesh folds back to being old and worn out and cracking. And this is what things have added up to, she says.

I look at the pink marks her fingers made on her cheeks.

You carry the hard parts with you wherever you go, she says.

I show her the lashes I'd instructed Ollie to put on my back, and tell her it's true. Tell her I already know.

I'd been there about a month when he woke me one morning and summoned me to the living room. It was five o'clock. He handed me a black mug filled with microwaved water and told me to sit down on the sofa. I sat and sipped the water and watched him crack his neck from side to side, front to back.

There were newspapers spread across the floor. Not an inch of hardwood remained visible. Empty beer bottles were arranged in groups along the walls, their labels torn. The room smelled of alcohol and paint. My eyes stung from lack of sleep. The axe leaned against the radiator. My father wore brown overalls and no shirt, and he was sweating profusely. It dripped off his nose, made tiny starbursts on the newspaper.

Can I talk to you? he said.

Okay.

I think someone's been stealing product.

I looked at his eyes, the pupils big and black, like shadows of tall buildings, stretching, reaching out. No one's stealing from you, I said.

He shook his head. I've noticed things gone missing.

Like what?

The room's been getting more empty the past few weeks.

Because we've been selling things, Dad.

He flinched, like the word was a racial slur—Dad. He bent over, picked up a piece of kindling from a pile on the floor and threw it across the room. It bounced off the wall and landed next to the rat cage. I folded my legs onto the sofa and yelled at him to be careful. There was more kindling around his feet, thirty or forty pieces. A third were painted purple. He believed any item could sell, so long as it was painted purple. He picked up another one.

Dad, I said. Don't.

He whipped it across the room. It skinned the doorframe. Bark broke off and ricocheted toward the ceiling. The ratties scurried around in their cage. We need to make a change, he said.

To what, Dad?

Quit calling me that!

He sat down on the floor with his legs straight out, bare feet pointed up. The bottoms of his feet were chalky with white lines. He stared at his toes and picked up another piece of kindling and placed it on his lap.

I was in shops the other night, he said. I was looking around for items to buy and sell, and then I saw the air conditioner in Scott's Hockshop. The air conditioner that's supposed to be ours. They were selling it for one twenty-five.

How do you know it's ours?

I know. It had the same dent. The one I put in it.

He ran his palm against the cut surface of the kindling on his thighs.

We sold it, I told him, so if it's the same one, then the guy we sold it to must've resold it to the store. That happens, Dad. No one's stealing from you.

He spread his feet apart. The wood dropped between his legs. He picked it up and tossed it underhand toward a smaller pile of unpainted pieces next to the window. You need to quit calling me that, he said. His voice quiet, like someone had turned the volume on everything almost all the way down. He bent his legs in and stood up. His face was still sweaty. No more. No more saying the word.

Dad?

Right.

Are you serious? You don't want me calling you Dad?

When money's involved, I'm not your dad. This becomes a business.

What does?

Our situation. This relationship. Our dymanic.

You mean *dynamic.*

He nodded. You start calling me sir, he said. That's what I called my pa, and that's what you call me. I showed him respect, and you show me respect.

Do you think I'm stealing from you?

You can call me Dad at night, but in the day, when we're working, when we're working on selling things, you call me sir.

I'm not stealing from you.

I didn't say you are.

I'm not.

He picked up a beer bottle.

Don't, I said.

He picked up another bottle, and another. Collecting them. I'm going to paint these, he said, and then I'm going to make profit. He gathered the bottles until his hands and arms were full, and then he looked at me and apologized for having thrown the kindling and scaring my rats. I told him it was okay. He waited. I called him Sir.

Sometimes I think about Whitney Houston. The day we decided to let her go. She'd been trying to eat her way through the box, so. Monster wept, trying not to. He pressed his chin to his chest and his body shook and I stared at the top of his head for a long time, and then he looked up. He asked me to fix it, but I wasn't sure what he meant. So I stood with the pastry box in my hands as Whitney Houston slowly inched her way back into Craddock Park. I looked at the photo taped to the bottom of the lid. My father sliding the ring onto my mother's finger, telling her he'll like her face forever. Fix it, Monster pleaded. Fix it, Hermie. Fix it. I wasn't sure if he was talking about the turtle, the punctured box, or what. Fix it. Fix it. Please, Hermie. I remember thinking the air holes in the box looked like little coin slots.

I ride the subway northbound on a Thursday afternoon. I'm wearing rain boots, jeans, my army jacket, a ladybug clip in my hair. My knapsack on the seat next to me, and I'm listening to the Misfits on my iPod—Spinal Remains—as I watch the dark tunnel pass.

A woman is seated about fifteen feet away. She's black, and elderly, with a face that needs to be ironed. I watch her sew the fuzzy ball onto a knitted winter hat. It makes me think about my mother, how she used to knit us mittens every year for Christmas. All the kids got different colors, except Monster and me. She made sure ours matched. Blue. Because it was my favorite color, and Leonardo was Monster's favorite Ninja Turtle.

The subway stops at Lawrence West. A few people get off, and a man steps on, and the doors ding and slide shut behind him. The man is tall, skinny and albino. He wears black jeans with the belt hanging loose under his flat ass, boxer briefs and a black long sleeve polo with holes in the armpits. He walks with his toes pointed in, as if aimed in conversation. I press pause on my iPod. The subway proceeds and enters the tunnel. The man stares at himself in the reflection of the window. He's about thirty, maybe thirty-five. He's wearing sunglasses with brown plastic rims and has thick white eyebrows, a white goatee, and several blemishes, like rosy drops of watercolor on his ashen cheeks. He says, Hello? He stares at himself, making faces. His reflection is dark. Hello? he says. Are you there? Will someone help me?

I pull my knapsack closer to me. Bottles clink inside it. The man walks over to the old woman sewing. Hello? he says. Cracker? Dirty cracker? The woman keeps her eyes on the fuzzy ball. Dirty cracker, the man keeps saying.

He leans closer. The woman holds up a threading needle as if that'll protect her.

Leave me alone, she says.

Spare change for a burger? he says. He drops to his knees and places his hands around the heels of her orange crocs, begins whispering, Please, please, please. The woman is shaking her head. She tries to kick him away, but his grip is strong. Please, dirty cracker? Please? Everyone is watching from behind newspapers, books, scarves, their hands.

Please?

I press play on my iPod. The song Angelfuck thrashes through the earphones. My heart accelerates. I shut my eyes. I see lightning. I hear him saying, Please, please, please, over the music because he's yelling now. I stand, slide my hands deep inside my pockets.

Click.

I spray dog mace in the man's face. His screams are like a kettle, blood leaking out his eyes instead of smoke. I look for an expiry date on the can, but everything's in Chinese. The man rolls on the ground, flailing, flapping his arms, his wrists, his hands are white on both sides. I stand over him. The old woman is trying to give me the threading needle in case he gets back up.

The subway stops at Yorkdale Station. The light brightens above the doors. They ding and slide open and the man crawls out, blood dripping like a trail of bread-crumbs, and everyone is looking at the old woman, and me.

I give the woman the dog mace. She says I'm her hero.

H-E-R-O, she spells.

The subway arrives at Downsview. I step off the car wearing the white winter hat with a pink ball on top. My hands slide inside empty pockets. My knapsack clinking with bottles. I meet a man upstairs, inside the bus terminal. He's wearing a blue bandana like he said he'd be—middle-aged, hairless, fanny pack, acne on his chin. He walks with a cane. The handle is carved into a horse's head.

I open the knapsack and pull out the first bottle. It's clear blue, shaped like a stork. I hand it to him. He twists off the cap, holds it under his nose and sniffs.

Smells like nothing, he says.

My dad cleaned it.

My girlfriend loves blue liquor bottles, he says. They're for her.

I pull out the second bottle, which is also blue, shaped like a standard wine bottle. I hand him the third bottle. It's plump, crystalline, blue glass as well. He holds it under his armpit, the others in each hand. Seventy? he says.

Seventy-three's what my dad told me, but seventy's fine.

D'you guys have more? he asks.

I stand outside the terminal watching buses come in and out. I smoke a joint, and a cigarette. I watch five o'clock people pack the buses in droves. They all look miserable. It's getting dark and starting to snow. The first snowfall of the season. The flakes are big as potato chips. I pull out my cell and dial my brother's number.

Hello.

Oh hi there. Is this Mr. Monster?

Long time, Hermie.

Yep. You ready? I've been living with Dad.
. . .
Monster?
No you haven't.
Yep.
Why? How long?
Bit over a month.
. . .
Monster?
What?
You okay?
Is he okay?
Dad? Sure.
Did he act like a dick?
He sold my rats.
Why'd you let him do that?
I didn't.
Dick. Does Ollie know?
Ollie and I split.
When did that happen?
I don't know. It doesn't matter. He's back to the same old, like pills, and selling. I want to apply to grad school soon. I need to get my life back on track, away from that.
Sorry, Herm.
It's fine. I'm fine. Are you?
Yeah, I'm fine.
You're taking good care of your craziness I hope.
Think so.
Monster.
I am. How is he, how's Dad?
Fine. I can tell you about it.
Did he talk in the voice?

It's Little Hermia, folks!

Yeah. *Look at her go, folks. Little Hermia. Being coot as a bag of boots!*

Not really.

Did he say anything about me? I don't care if he didn't.

He said he wants to read one of your stories.

No he didn't.

Yep. You want to grab coffee? I can tell you all about it. I need to tell you.

Okay. When?

Tonight?

Where are you?

Toronto, but I'm going to bus it north. Are you still at Kate's parents?

Yeah. We're saving for Toronto, but for now, yeah, we're here.

Okay. Well perfect. I'm going to bus it up to you. I'll see you in an hour, or less. Probably forty-five, fifty minutes tops. Does that work?

Just text when you're at Aurora Go Station.

I have a belated birthday present for you, from Dad.

No you don't. What is it?

It's nothing. You'll see. I'll see you when I get there. Tell Kate I'm dropping by. Ask her if I can crash on the basement couch a few days. Cool?

She won't care.

Okay. Ask her though. I'll see you soon.

I hang up. Walk farther down the bus loop and step onto the thirty-two northbound. The ticket's seven fifty. I use the bottle money to pay the driver. He tells me he likes my hair, my hat, my style. I take a seat near the back. The floor is sticky. My window's fogged. I watch snow melt on the glass. The fog glisters. I slide in my earphones and turn on my iPod and listen to Whitney Houston, what used to be my mother's favorite song—I'm Your Baby Tonight. Their wedding song. It's corny, but makes me smile. *Feel I can, feel I can do any, do anything.* I smell pot. It's me. I take off my jacket and fold it in a square. I shove it inside my knapsack next to the troll doll, the one with the diamond bellybutton. Then I shut my eyes and I keep them closed and I think about Monster. I think, Maybe one wish can be enough to fix everything.

15

Trigger decided he'd resurrect Hanukkah a few years after our split. So aligned eight tea lights along the windowsill with a book of matches on a pincushion in the middle. He hadn't purchased any yarmulkes yet, so got our children to place their hands flat atop their heads. And told them about the oil, and the Maccabees. And told them not to believe everything their *bitch* mother says. After that, he sang a prayer. It was the first time any of our children had heard Hebrew. Birdie explained afterwards it had sounded very very extremely funny. So imagined dead kittens to prevent herself from laughing, then started crying because she'd imagined dead kittens. Trigger assumed his voice had moved our daughter to tears. In falsetto, he sang louder.

Earlier that evening, over a home-cooked meal of undercooked pirogues and butter on toasted rye, Trigger had apparently informed our children of the details regarding our first date. We were high school freshmen. We went to a hamburger place in Bush Flats called Weir's Grill. I remember him in a shiny sharkskin suit with a peaked lapel, and carrying a lifeless bouquet of garden tulips with the roots still sticking out the bottom. His tie had been tied incorrectly, a failed attempt at a Windsor knot. And hair, inelegantly flattened and weirdly white, as if he'd tried to wring his curls straight with egg yolk. A checked ivy cap could not hide the error.

Thanks for coming, he said nervously, repositioning a spoon.

Ordered us two Cherry Cokes, no ice. Rubbed his boots on my heeled loafers under the table. I told him the bruises on his face made him look tough, and he said my hair was the blond of corned beef fat. I don't remember eating, or too much of the conversation we shared, but what stays with me most is the end of the meal. The server collecting our plates. I'd finished most of my Caesar salad, but not the celery they'd included on the side. Trigger asked the server to put it in a doggy bag so he could take it home. An entire bag for a single celery. Maybe it's not such an odd thing, but that's what sticks with me, or to me. Fixed so firmly against my skin I could almost start stripping bare, down to blood, bone and muscle, purely to relieve my insides of the load that memory carries with it, day to day, year to year.

He had them all hold hands—Birdie to Minster to Hermia to Quinlynn—the four of them with palms pressed sweaty around the workbench Trigger had been using as a kitchen table, their fingers clasped and greasy from pirogues and melted butter because he did not own forks, nor napkins or paper towels.

I chose your mom over my religion, he said. But that was wrong. Cause love's not real. When you're young and dumb as shit you think it is, but no. Only thing is, is God, what God made you. Me, I let it float—Judaism. I let it float like a carcass in a gully, but I'm getting it out. I'm pulling it out the gully. Cause your Judaism's not some carcass in a gully. Say it. Say, *My Judaism's not some carcass in a gully.*

They said it, then stood, gathered under the window-sill, as Trigger pontificated, praying what he prayed, in falsetto, while Birdie envisioned dead kittens, causing herself to cry, hence having to dry her eyes on Quinlynn's broomstick skirt because again: no napkins, no paper towels. Trigger lit a match with his teeth. The tea lights had unusually long wicks extending off-center out of the wax. Or so I heard.

Happy Hanukkah, he said.

Happy Hanukkah, they repeated.

And cleaned and cleared the workbench.

Trigger put Birdie's leftover bread crusts in a container in the freezer. Hermia and Minster scrubbed dishes. Quinlynn took apart the Hanukkah Bush, which was in fact an empty urn wrapped with silver tinsel, and positioned on a hamper Trigger had been using as a TV tray. The radio played Eddy Arnold. Frost on the windows. There were no gifts given or received that evening, other than the misshapen dreidel Trigger had folded for Birdie out of cut pieces of an old pizza box.

Nes gadol hayah sham, he said.

Looking back on our first date, I guess I'd been the one who'd dropped him off at home, considering his house came first. We walked together to the door. Trigger's little brother Tony's eyes peeping through blinds in the window until Trigger punched the glass. I told him I'd had a very nice time, and thanked him once again for the tulips. He told me I was pretty as the ocean, pretty as the stars, pretty as a horse, but not an ugly horse that smells like *shit*, more a pretty, good-smelling horse, like how some people thought horses were real real pretty and even good-smelling sometimes.

Don't they? he said, red in the face. Don't people?

He was in the bedroom by the time I arrived to pick our children up. Hello Trigger, I called from the front hall, but no answer. The basement apartment smelled of cigarettes and feet. Our children put on their boots and coats, and Birdie said something about a carcass in a gully that was quite literally the craziest thing I'd ever heard. Goodbye Trigger, I called. It wasn't until we were all squeezed inside the car I noticed the tea lights burning on the windowsill. He'd lit all eight even though it was only the first night.

16

First Tony's arms gave out. They hung off his shoulders like damp towels. I can't move them, he said. Honey, I can't move my arms. I drove him to the walk-in clinic. Then to the hospital. It was early, somewhere between breakfast and brunch. I fed him spoonfuls of applesauce in the ER. He breathed wet breaths, his sighs sounded like a spit valve. We fell asleep to their faint crackle and woke later between dinner and dark. That's when the doctor told us nothing was wrong. The situation was entirely psychological and, therefore, not much of a situation at all. We nodded coolly as if we knew that was coming. Tony didn't shake the doctor's hand.

On the ride home I asked, What does it feel like?

Nothing, he said.

But what does the nothingness feel like?

He took a moment to think, or pretend to think. I was used to waiting. The road turned to gravel. The radio stammered and the moon appeared smoky behind black clouds. He turned his head to the smoke and said, I guess I feel choked, sick, like you do when you ram a raccoon with your car. I feel numb. But I also feel everything.

I pulled to the side of the road, turned off the radio and squeezed his fingers in my hand like a bundle of sticks. I told him that I loved him, and that the kids were waiting at home. He kept his eyes on the moon. I told him to think about the kids.

I'd dated Tony the second half of high school into college. He still looked like a Tony then, with cauliflower ears and tanned calves and five o'clock shadow and hair like John Travolta in *Welcome Back, Kotter*. I used to go watch him wrestle. He was good, and his bulge looked like a bent sub sandwich bun inside that uniform. I used to joke about his penis being whole wheat, and he'd christen me his shiksa, and we'd both smile because back then it was impossible not to. He'd press his smile to my face. I liked how his lips touched my temple, then crept toward my ear. We made love on Tuesdays and Thursdays and every other Sunday when his parents were at Bagel Boon. He said you couldn't get pregnant if you urinated immediately afterward. I gave birth to our first child on a Monday during *The Cosby Show*. I was twenty-one, and Tony was twenty-three, and the baby was a boy, and we named the boy Kirby.

It's noon on a Saturday and I'm wearing mom jeans. I pull into my sister Sally's driveway. She recently painted her garage doors fuchsia because that's the kind of person she is. Her garden in bloom with batches of periwinkle flowers. I remain seated in my car for a few minutes, pretend the song on the radio needs to be listened to in its entirety.

Then knock on the front door, which is also fuchsia. I hear M. Night Shyamalan barking from the laundry room downstairs. My nephew Maxwell answers the door. He's seventeen and shirtless, and smoking one of those smokeless cigarettes, the kind that release water vapor. Aunt Jane, he says. Then screams at M. Night Shyamalan to shut the fudge up! I hear the rascal whimper through the vents. Its sadness sounds tinny.

Maxwell, I say, is Kelsey here?

Don't think, he says.

What about your mother?

He turns toward the hall and yells, Ma! Ma, it's Aunt Jane!

I'm in the kitchen!

She's in the kitchen, he says.

I step inside, take my shoes off and place them next to Kelsey's slippers on the bottom tier of the shoe rack. Maxwell watches with glazed eyes, cigarette between fingers in front of his face. I know it's gay to smoke these, he admits, but it's supposed to help me quit. Ma says she'll buy me a Milbro slingshot catapult if I do.

I ruffle his bushy head and say, Good luck. Then walk to the kitchen to find Sally, who's humming Donny Osmond's Puppy Love while crushing avocado on the bottom of a peach plastic basin. The avocado's gone bad, browning, and smells similar to the inside of a pumpkin. I kiss Sally's rawboned shoulder. She sighs with unblinking eyes. Max loves guacamole, she says.

My boys too, I tell her. But not Kelsey.

Your girl's picky, she says. I had to make her pizza with vegan cheese. What kind of girl will still eat the pepperoni, but insists her cheese be vegan? She's wild!

I sit at the table. I ask Sally if Kelsey's out with Tom, my brother-in-law.

No, she says, chopping red onion. Tom got called in to work today. Kelsey went to her boyfriend's. Federico?

François.

François. Bingo. Knew it was something exotic.

Sally recently turned forty-two, which is three years older than me. She looks younger though, or happier. Her hair curled and cut short, dyed the red of rare steak. And she does Zumba—every day with the Zumba, never giving it a rest: You really *should* try it, Janey. Makes your buns burn like a pyro at a bakery! And it's made her body start to curve like a college kid's. Plus, the front of her neck looks gorgeous. Since she quit smoking, everything seems to have smoothed out.

I tell her Tony is in a wheelchair now.

She turns from the counter with tears in her eyes. I'm touched, then remember she's chopping onions.

It's getting bad, I say. I mean it's getting worse.

She's touching her lips with her fingertips and nodding.

I need Kelsey to come home, I say.

She's licking brown avocado off her fingertips and nodding more.

I need Kelsey to come home, I say again, this time to myself. Then sit and stare at my lap, the faded blue of my jeans. I hold my thighs like bags of frozen vegetables.

Maxwell enters. Ma, he groans, M. Night Shyamalan's being a little slut-nugget.

Inappropriate, says Sally.

Maxwell fingers a mess of chopped onion, then drops them in his mouth like raisins. Then pushes himself onto the counter, seated next to the sink, and faces me. Kelsey snores, he says. I can hear her through the wall. She sounds like a mastodon.

Sally playfully slaps Maxwell's bicep. Don't be a goofball, she says, giggling the way a mother does when she wants you to know how well she gets on with her son. As if you know what a mastodon sounds like. You're wild and crazy, Maxwell!

A mastodon sounds like Kelsey, he says, and both of them start making snoring sounds that sound more like donkey sounds. Then Sally joins me at the table. She sits, and blows breadcrumbs away from her. They gather at the base of a vase overfilled with lilacs and baby's feet. She's crying, either from the onion or laughter. Pats the tears with a strap from her apron. I tell Max all the time, she says, family first. It's more important than anything in this world—more so than girls, or the Maple Leafs—and when Kelsey showed up at our door, Max welcomed her with open arms, and even made her fries. He used the oven instead of the George Foreman Grill, which takes longer but tastes better. He's a good boy, my Max. And so's your Kelsey, a real good girl. I get it, Janey. All we want is for our children to be safe and sound and good.

One of my nephews, Tony's side of the family, went missing in the early nineties. Tony and I moved to a motel in Port Woodlot for the subsequent three months. Tony partook in the search parties with his brother Trigger (though each searched alongside a separate party as the brothers had had a falling out some weeks before), while I spent most days lending a hand to my sister-in-law Sherri and her other five children.

They lived in a basement apartment made to accommodate a couple of college kids, not The Disadvantaged Brady Bunch. The rooms were cramped and had a perpetual odor of burnt challah. The children seemed tired and confused, and afraid, and Sherri did what she could to shield the younger ones from the reality of what had happened, and what was going to happen, the inevitable disintegration of their family, happening.

To make matters worse, or more absurd, or extra problematical, or heartbreaking to a further extent, the reason my nephew went missing is because he ran away. And he ran away because he'd fortuitously killed another boy. And that boy's parents happened to be the people uncomfortably living above Trigger and Sherri's basement apartment.

Because quote: Sometimes life hits you in the head with a brick.

One evening I stepped outside to get some fresh air. Circled around to the backyard of the semi-detached. It was snowing, and I thought about Tony and Trigger and others still out there, searching through the dark and snow. And I thought about my nephew, Soccer, ten, who'd left without a coat, in the dark and snow.

The sound of a sliding glass door startled me. Sylvia came out to say hello. She was the mother of the boy who'd died. The bags under her eyes were so puffed-up it was a struggle to keep my own eyes on her face. They repelled my attention with the reminder of her wakeful nightmare, and I kept pretending to check my nails for dirt. When I'd look up, she'd blink, extensively, like there was sweat stinging her sight.

I knew she and her husband Harry were going to want to file a lawsuit. I also knew, because my sister Sally is married to a lawyer, that the details of their situation would not carry them further than a preliminary hearing.

Do you have children? is the first thing Sylvia said to me.

A two year old boy, I said.

What's his name? she said.

Kirby, I said. He's at my sister Sally's right now.

What was his first word? she said.

Ball, I said

My Eddie's was onomatopoeia, she said.

By then we were holding hands, and the snow felt lighter on my shoulders, not quite so cold. We didn't speak again. Not even to say goodnight. We stood, and listened to the sounds in the night, and the quietness of the night, and let go. When I went back inside I called my sister and got her to hold a colicky Kirby to the phone.

I never returned to the backyard.

My son Kirby is a back catcher now. He describes the position as paramount. Before he left for school on a baseball scholarship, I'd find inspirational sports quotes scribbled on Post-its around his room—*Champions aren't made in gyms. Champions are made from something they have deep inside them—a desire, a dream, a vision - Muhammad Ali*—so began leaving my own Post-its in response to his—*Desire + Dream + Vision = my Kirby! (I love you) - Mom.*

Tony had already gotten bad by the time Kirby had packed to go. His arms, hands, legs, feet had all failed him.

On his last day home, Kirby sat beside his father's bed. He held his father's hand. I'm leaving, Dad, he said.

Tony wore gold pajamas. He looked like a paralyzed pimp. He told Kirby to come close, and Kirby came close, and Tony kissed Kirby between the eyebrows. You're going to be a Jay one day, my boy. A Blue Jay. I can't wait to see you soar.

Kirby turned to make sure I was still in the doorway. Then turned back to his father.

Now listen. You don't go telling people you're a Jew, said Tony. Understand?

What do you mean, Dad? Who would I tell?

They don't like the Jews over at that university. A lot of anti-Semitism in the world, Kirby. A lot of hate. For no good reason, a lot of hate exists. Especially in that area of the city. There's still a lot of hate out there.

Okay, Dad. I know.

But not everyone hates, Kirby. Remember that. Only some. But some is enough. You should be proud of who you are, but you should also stay safe.

I know.

Tony had grown a beard. The hairs were wiry, graying the same as his teeth. His mouth looked like a nest, his tongue a pallid pink egg. But you speak up, he told Kirby. You don't go broadcasting you're a Jew, but if you witness hate, you speak up. You sock intolerance in the jaw, Kirby. You understand me? Kirby turned to me again. His eyes asked for help. I stepped inside the room. You see a swastika on the bathroom wall, continued Tony, and you piss and you shit all over it. You whip out your circumcised schlong and you piss, Kirby. You piss and shit like a true MVP.

Tony, I yelled.

Jane? he said. Janey, I didn't know you were there.

Kirby kissed his father's head and said goodbye, and went downstairs to start loading his things in the van. I sat next to Tony. He turned his head away. His hair was feathered and grey, like John Travolta's in *Primary Colors*. I told him to look at me.

I can feel it, he said. It's crawling up my spine. It's lifting inside my neck.

Tony. You look at me.

He turned to look. I kissed his lips. They were uneven and greasy as tempura. I looked at him, into him. He smiled, and his eyes turned to tiny crescents. Whenever Tony smiled, you could tell exactly what he must've looked like as a small child. It was one of those smiles. It was because of the curve in his eyes.

I'm on lunch duty at school. It's autumn, and the trees are the color of fire bells. I'm next to the playground drinking eggnog from a thermos. A little girl approaches, grade one or two. Her hair is brown and pigtailed. Mrs. Beally, she says.

Good morning, I say. Fun recess?

My big brother's in your class, she says. Trevor Kean. He's bald. He shaved his head cause our mommy's got chemo.

Trevor's a character, I tell her. He did his book report on a joke book. He said he liked it because it was funny. I gave him an A.

The little girl gives me her best blank expression, looking middle-aged and unimpressed. She wears a purple sweater with a tap-dancing ferret on the chest. What'd you do on the weekend, Mrs. Beally?

I visited my sister. What'd you do?

You've got a sister? she says, her head perking like a Whac-A-Mole. Me too, Mrs. Beally! I've got two sisters, but both them are gerbils. Their names are Squish and Playful. They're not gonna be alive long cause gerbils don't be alive long, just like my mommy's not gonna be alive long, right?

I don't know what to say, so I say, I don't know.

My mommy's gonna die-die-go-bye banana-nana-fo-fi! sings the little girl, grabbing hold of her pigtails like two ends of a jump rope.

Go play, sweetie, I say. Recess is almost over.

Okay, she says. She runs back toward the playground, climbs a ladder onto the bridge and starts doing jumping jacks—one, two, twenty, thirty. She doesn't stop until the bell rings. Then leans over the railing and yells, Did you see, Mrs. Beally?

I give her a thumbs up.

It's important to be healthy so you don't die, she tells me.

I keep my thumb pointed, smiling like I'm in a Mentos commercial. The little girl slides down the pole and starts running toward the school. I watch her merge with the swarm of other students, leaving me with my thumb and my thermos, and dead gerbils and mothers on the brain.

Sally answers the door this time. She's wearing a bathrobe and slippers and holding a cheese grater. Janey, she says. Kelsey's here. She's doing homework in the backyard.

I step inside. It smells like a chocolate factory.

Keep your shoes on, she says. I follow her through the house. Her husband Tom is seated on a couch in the living room, feet kicked atop a leather footrest. The top of his head nods behind a Toronto Star. We enter the kitchen. Chocolate chips and bars and morsels of cookie dough cover the countertop. I ask Sally if she remembers taking care of Kirby in the early nineties when Tony and I went to help Port Woodlot to help search for Soccer. She's always had a lousy memory. Soccer, she says, as in football?

I step back outside. Kelsey is seated at a picnic table on the deck. She's using someone's laptop, and is surrounded by textbooks. Her hair is long, sunkissed brown. I smell day lilies when I kiss the top of her head. We miss you, I say.

Miss you too, Mom.

I sit on the opposite side of the table and take her in for a moment. It's almost been a month, I say. Come home.

She doesn't answer. She's watching Maxwell roll around on the lawn with M. Night Shyamalan, tickling his belly. I tell her to look at me. She does. She says, How's he?

He used to sleep in a chair beside your crib, I tell her. He was afraid something might happen to you in your sleep. I'd tell him not to worry, but he did. There was no stopping his worrying. He'd fall asleep in our bed, and wake next to yours. I'd find him in your room every morning, on guard. All your father ever wanted was to keep you safe, Kelsey.

She listens, chewing her thumbnail. Okay.

Kirby had colic, I say. He cried and cried for those first couple months. Never seemed to stop. Our neighbors pounded the walls, the ceiling below. But you never cried. I think that's what made your father so nervous. He was used to crying babies. The silence threw him off. And on top of that, it had only been a year since your cousin went missing. And you know how much your father cares for those kids. So there were many things throwing him off, Kelsey, and, perhaps, maybe, in more ways than one, he's still a bit thrown. But he's recuperating. Always. Your father is a good man.

Kelsey nods, then shifts her attention back to the laptop. She presses keys so fast they sound like Tic Tacs spilling. You seen Kirbs's new girlfriend? she asks.

No, I say. We've spoken about her on the phone, briefly.

She turns the screen toward me. There's a picture of Kirby in his catcher's helmet and chest protector, eye black applied under each eye. He stands next to a Muslim girl wearing a white burka. Aren't her eyes gorgeous, says Kelsey, and blue, so blue. She clicks the keyboard. Another picture, Kirby sans helmet, kissing the girl's veil now, right where her lips would be. I originally thought this was some kind of weird offensive joke, says Kelsey, but it's real, Mom. I was Skyping with him. He said her name's Nazneen and she teaches voice lessons to kids. She's helping him learn how to sing, so he can sing the anthem more confidently. Oh Canada before games and stuff. That's how I know it's real, Mom, because she's teaching Kirbs to sing.

On the night before Tony's problems began, I baked a pie. I could tell something was wrong by the way he ate it—quick, angry bites—and raspberry was his favorite. After dessert Kirby helped clean the dishes. And Tony disappeared. It wasn't until later I found him seated in the garage holding a golf club. He had our daughter's laptop shut atop a barstool beside him. I asked what he was doing, and he replied, Waiting for Kelsey. So I waited too, asking questions he refused to answer. Then we heard a vehicle pull into our driveway. Tony opened the garage door with the clicker and we saw Kelsey climb off of her boyfriend François's motorcycle. Tony called her. She stepped inside the garage and Tony clicked the door closed behind her. Open the laptop, he said. Kelsey looked at me, and I looked at Tony's club, and Tony looked at the laptop. Kelsey lifted it open. There was a high-resolution image of my daughter and three other girls onscreen, all with their shirts lifted to their chins, bare chests exposed. Kelsey's eyes were crossed, and she had her tongue curled bow-like at the camera. Tony stood. He smashed the laptop with the club. It fell to the ground. Tony continued smashing it and Kelsey was screaming and crying and so was I. Tony kept yelling, Your tits? Your tits? and I kept yelling at him to stop calling our daughter's breasts *tits*. She's fifteen, he said back at me. He looked at me with hope eradicated from his eyes.

I wrote a Harlequin novel once. It's the only thing I ever published. The book came out when I was thirty-four, the week Kelsey turned ten. We celebrated both occasions on the same day. Tony even baked a couple of cakes. One had a dolphin, and the other, a rack of washboard abs. Tony kissed my temple and said he was proud of me. So did Kelsey, though she didn't know what a Harlequin was. When it was time for her to blow out the candles, she asked, Why don't you got candles, Mom?

Because it's not my birthday, I said.

She pulled one from her cake. I'll share one of my wishes with you, she said, and stuck the candle inside the bellybutton of the torso cake.

What should I wish for? I asked her.

An aquarium, she said.

I shut my eyes and blew out the flame and wished for my family's everlasting health and happiness. White smoke pirouetted like the ghost of a ballerina. Tony and Kelsey applauded, but Kirby was too cool, hands in pockets, looking bored, a phase. Then Kelsey started blowing her own candles as Tony took pictures with our new Polaroid. I wondered how much money I'd make off my new novel. The camera flashed, hummed, and I wondered how much an aquarium might cost.

Sometimes Tony got me to read him the sexy parts of the novel, and we'd laugh together, but it was serious when I wrote it.

Other times I'd catch him in bed reading the novel, and he wouldn't be laughing. He'd be seated against the bed rest, holding the book like a wounded animal. He handled it with great concern, or love, careful not to crease the spine. I'd watch him from the doorway to our washroom. He was the kind to lick his fingers before turning a page, tongue touching thumb like stamp, then on to the next.

Tony took me to a bowling alley on our first date. He was a first-year York University student, and I was in high school, grade eleven. It was winter. Snow melted off our shoes and gathered in puddles on the entrance mats where we left them. Tony told me he felt nervous about losing because I looked *coot as a boot* in my flutter sleeve top and he feared it might distract him from rolling a perfect game, and I melted as well.

We shared a poutine and sipped hot cocoa as we bowled. We discussed wrestling, and poetry, and politics, and debated over who was the better actor, John Travolta or Harvey Keitel. Tony talked a little about his brother Trigger, and Trigger's three children, Carver, Soccer, and Quinlynn. I asked what the story was behind the name Soccer, and Tony said, Trigger played soccer in high school. He's a simple-minded man.

Later on the car ride home, Tony told me about his sister-in-law Sherri. She was devout, fair-haired, meek and pretty, but seemed to be visibly aging by the day. He said she'd called him recently in tears to tell Tony something Trigger'd done. Sherri had taken Carver and Quinlynn to church one Sunday, and left Soccer (who'd been misbe-having) with Trigger at home. That afternoon she returned to find three year old Soccer crushed into a corner of their furnace room, held in place by Trigger's foot. The poor child wept with his face squished under his father's sole, and Sherri screamed, What are you doing! What are you doing! and Trigger said, Not gonna let the shit go til he quits the waterworks.

Tony had to pull the car over then. He parked in a court next to a Zellers. He told me I needed to know. I can be good, he said, but sometimes it's hard to be good. I told him I know. He said he was sorry for being weak, and I told him he wasn't.

My pa was born in Poland, he said. A boy during the Holocaust. Watched his family get killed in front of him, and I can't even stand up to my own brother.

He kept apologizing. I told him not to. He told me he'd seen Trigger quietly hum Que Sera Sera to Quinlynn, and pile letter blocks with Soccer, and put cream on Carver's face once when the little guy decided he wanted to learn how to shave like his old man.

Trigger broke the blade off a razor, Tony explained, so Carve could shave the plastic to his cheeks without cutting himself. Trigger sliced his own fingers doing it but didn't care. So I know my brother can be good. That's just one example. I know he can be good, and I can be good, too. I know nothing is ever too late for us. Right, Janey?

Not yet, I said. It's not too late yet.

Now I sit beside him in the dark. The curtains are drawn. His eyes are grey spots on blackness. He can't talk. He can't move his jaw, or tongue. He is only forty-one years old. I touch his arm. It's so lean, I can almost wrap my fingers around his wrist. I recite passages from my novel to him, the sexy parts. He breathes faltering breaths, like air escaping a leather couch cushion. The room is heavy and damp and reminds me of August rain. I touch his neck. I touch his cheek. I touch the bloated contours of his cauliflower ear. He breathes, still breathing, slowly, slower. It's not until I whisper Kelsey is coming home that anything about this scene can alter. Those two grey spots curve into crescents. They appear as orange slices, or moons tipped over in the darkness.

17

Kim-Claire. That's your name. Kim-Claire, like Sara-Jane or Nancy-Jo. Kim because that was your daddy's sister's name and Claire because that was your daddy's mother's name. They were both gone by the time you got here. A Dodge Caravan that tried to dodge a train. It was your daddy's job to identify the bodies, which he described to me in great detail. The colors, the mangled shapes. They were the kinds of things I knew he'd never shake, so who was I to object to giving you those names?

You were born June third, two thousand and four. Six pounds, exactly. Ten fingers and ten toes, and legs kicking air like you were trying to escape.

I held you in a blanket and loved you. It's true what they say, how the universe is transformed, owing to this thing in your arms, no bigger than a paper towel roll. I couldn't stop kissing your head, the smell. You smelled of earth. Your daddy took pictures. A disposable camera from the gift shop, the clickety-click of it winding. He told us to look. Quin, he said. Kim-Claire, he said. Look. But my eyes stuck to you, as if peeling them away might mean you'd— Say fromage, he said. I smiled against your ear and whispered the most delicate words I could muster.

Told you your daddy steals. I wanted you to know a secret because I wanted us to be best friends.

Seven months earlier I'd turned twenty-one, practically a baby myself. I was in art school. A painter, a barista. My hair dyed auburn. My bangs straight to the top of my eyebrows. It was early autumn. I remember how the trees looked, or how I saw them, like luxuriant scabs, how I planned to paint them later.

I called your daddy. We arranged to meet at a coffee place close to the university. He was there when I arrived, seated at a table on the patio, wearing jeans and a fitted hoodie with Che Guevara on the back. I leaned to kiss him. I touched his face. He didn't touch back because his hands were in his pockets because of eczema on his knuckles.

I ordered you coffee, he said.

Decaf?

No. Since when the fuck you drink decaf?

A girl brought our coffees. She looked at me and winked, as if she knew, the world was about to go down. I lifted my mug off the saucer. It left a goldenrod ring. The girl walked back inside, and it was us again, he and I and the beginning of you. Chitter-chatter. Small talk about the fifty-fifth Emmy Awards, the smell of tooth decay, our horoscopes. I looked at his face, the acne scars on his cheeks. He'd ordered a hazelnut macchiato with extra whipped cream and chocolate shavings sprinkled all over and the cream stuck to his lips and nose and then I told him.

Told him I'd been sitting on the toilet at school on break between classes. I also told him which classes they were, though it didn't matter. Life Drawing, I said, and Figurative Photography. My way of making the story last longer, move slower. Life Drawing and Figurative Photography, and then I told him I was sitting on the toilet at school when I noticed something written on the backside of the stall door. *shit ping-pong look to your left.* I looked to my left and it said *look to your right.* I did. *look to your left.* And so I kept looking back and forth, faster and faster and it felt as though my head might eventually unscrew. I threw up on the floor. It hit tiles, and the toes of my shoes. It was yellow, orange, red like the scabs in the trees.

I like to think I threw up before I saw the pink lines, I said.

Pink lines? he said.

It got colder out then. I held the coffee under my nose, let the steam slink up my face. He shook his head, right, left, back and forth. Fuck, he said. Goddammit, Quin. Fuck. He looked at me, my eyes, then belly blocked by table. I placed my coffee back on the saucer and we watched how the sun fragmented on its black surface.

I first meet your daddy at the start of grade school.

Ryan Mior, but the kids call him Cryin Ryan. His mother Claire—the Claire from your name—tries dropping him off at school in the mornings, but your daddy doesn't like it, and starts crying as soon as she turns to leave. Arms wrapped around her waist, he refuses to let go. And this happens every day. Your daddy tossing a tantrum in the doorway to our class. The other kids laughing, they find it hilarious. I never laugh, however. Your daddy knows I never laugh.

We're seven the first time we exchange words. It's middle recess, and I'm drawing flowers on the ground with colored chalk your Uncle Soccer swiped from the Hendersons' shed. Red roses, yellow daffodils and mimosas, or floral arrangements of my own invention. Your daddy says, Quinlynn Beally. I look up and say hi and call him Ryan, not Cryin Ryan. He's holding an eight-pack of AA batteries.

What'cha drawing? he says.

A garden, I say.

Garden, he says, g-g-g-gardennn, g-g-garrrrrden. Feeling the word on the bend of his tongue like it's got a strange taste. I think he's being funny.

What are those for? I ask, pointing chalk at the batteries.

He looks side to side and over each shoulder, and crouches closer in my garden. His chubby face a litter of freckles you can only see from so close. His breath nothing but peanut butter. I remember his sociopathic plan: to break the batteries and pour acid on Heather Klein's head. She's his worst tormenter, who wears lipstick and is the one who started Cryin Ryan.

I'm not sure what acid is. I back away as your daddy whips batteries against the ground, grinds them on the pavement, or along the edges of sharp rocks, uses a house key to try and cut one open. One minute, two minutes pass, and three. Your daddy beginning to break, the batteries still refusing to. A glint in his eyes as he shrieks at the portables, the playground, and the tetherball poles. Yowling at the batteries as well. I stop backing. I move forward as he throws them to the sky. His face gone cherry. No more freckles.

Heather Klein and friends take notice. They walk over to watch, and others watch too, even your Uncles Carver and Soccer are there, both slack-jawed, everyone watching but no one making fun. No one name-calling Cryin Ryan. We can't look away.

Your daddy sobs so heavily he can't breathe.

I'm beside him. His eyes beg as he punches his knees. I tell him to stop. He picks a battery off the ground, sticks it in his mouth and tries chewing, he wants to swallow the acid to make it all end.

A teacher on duty has to shove her hand in your daddy's mouth to claw it out. But he bites her fingers. He's rabid. Your Uncle Soccer belly laughs. The teacher chucks the battery and grabs your daddy by the neckband, shaking him fiercely, shakes as if to stir the bad behavior out of him.

A bit over a decade later and he started working at a sporting goods store called Athlete's Foot. It was massive, one of the biggest in Montreal. He worked in the back warehouse because his French wasn't strong enough for the front. *Bonjour*, he'd say. *Je ne sais pas. Pourquoi. Puis-je aller aux toilettes? Au revoir* was the extent of it.

I stayed in school. Kept painting. Compositions that bled off canvas and onto my hands and wrists. Seeped through my pores, located the bloodstream, ran up and down my body until they found you, and entered you. You ingesting paint. I imagined how it might appear, this poisoned baby inside me. That's mostly all I made during the pregnancy—paintings of poisoned babies. I remember asking your daddy if it was crazy.

It feels crazy, I told him. Is crazy even allowed anymore? Too cliché?

He shrugged, but barely. He was tired. He'd spent the past nine and a half hours unloading trucks at the store, heavy boxes of basketball rims and backboards, hockey nets, kayaks, hunting rifles, bicycles and fishing poles. He sipped an iced mocha at the kitchen table as I stood behind rubbing knots out of his back. And kissing his hair. It smelled of sweat and cardboard. Your daddy was working so hard because he knew you were on the way. He wanted us to have a cushion. I failed to contribute. All I did during that time was paint pictures like I said. People and places and poisoned babies, as if such things carried weight, or could help us in some way.

I remember the day the story became a love story. A couple of years after your daddy tries eating the battery. His ninth birthday. The year after your Uncle Soccer disappears. Your daddy has a party at an indoor swimming pool in a town between Aurora, where I now resided, and Port Woodlot, where he still lived.

Not a lot of kids show. Me and a few others, but the others are family, a crop of blond-haired, green-eyed, freckled cousins. Your daddy doesn't have many friends. He's a good boy, but that doesn't always mean as much as it should.

We're looking at each other underwater. He's wearing white briefs. He tickles his tummy and shouts bubbles out of his mouth. It's the first time I've seen him shirtless. His nipples are unusually small and his bellybutton pokes out like a thumb with no nail. He kicks back to the surface.

I'm wearing a plain black one-piece fit too tightly. I hate the feel of the bottom of the pool against my feet, so hang to the lip with my legs kicked up. An hour, and then two hours pass, and I begin to wonder how long people normally go swimming for. I doggy paddle in circles then hang to the side some more.

Your daddy wears neon orange goggles. He dives for lost coins and jewelry. He discovers Band-Aids, hangnails, crumbs of sock and strands of hair. Occasionally he calls my name from the deep end. Quin, he yells, Quinlynn, Quin, and it echoes. Syllables that sound like exhilaration and smell of chlorine.

Ryan, I yell back.

We're standing in line at the water slide. I don't know how I got here, but here it is, the beginning, like I said. Your daddy's pinkened eyes, and blond hair soaked a darker shade. It's so friggin fun, he says, referring to the slide. We climb the stairs leading up to it, me in front, and turning, and seeing his face, the fervor, the snot. Whitish-green like soap in the washrooms at school. It dangles from his right nostril, and I want to wipe it, brush his upper lip and your daddy wouldn't ever know it'd been there. This is something I'd keep for myself.

A view of the pool from the top platform. The lifeguard seated beside the railing. I look at his toes, knees, chest, a Smartie of callous on his fingertip, forefinger pointed like a pistol. He tells me to sit in the puddle at the top of the slide. It makes me sick, the soft plopping sound of my bum pressing into it. Water on my groin and buttocks. Feet out in front. The color of the slide, the exact color, bitter lime, like the blemish on an old potato.

I hit bottom and doggy paddle to the side. Pull myself up, turn and sit, kicking water, waiting for your daddy to drop. I want to see the snot one last time before it washes. So he's coming. I narrow my eyes and look and see him smiling. This is the year before the gap in his teeth will start to close on its own. I don't see snot. It might be there, but I don't see it. All I see is that gap. See it like it's something perfect. He splashes, sinks, and surfaces, and spits water my way.

Your daddy steals things, I whispered.

It was early morning. The sun a ginger cut on the horizon. You reached for the window, tried to grab hold of this new, natural light.

Your daddy with his face behind that cheap camera, calling your name.

Kim-Claire, Kim-Claire.

My lips on your ear.

Quin, he said. Kim-Claire, he said. Look.

The first item he took was a hockey puck. He didn't play hockey, never did. It wasn't about that. I'm not entirely sure what it was about in the beginning.

I took this, he said, and held the puck in both hands as if cupping water.

This was a few days after we heard you were on the way. He slid the puck in his back pocket. Walked to me, went on one knee and lifted my shirt. His hot breath on my belly. I wasn't showing yet, far from it, but he still pressed his ear and listened, and claimed to have heard your voice.

Next he stole a dozen three-packs of propane cylinders. He said there were hundreds at the store, and throughout the day, your daddy stashed them, one pack at a time every twenty minutes or so, filling a garbage bag kept in a corner of the warehouse he knew couldn't get captured on surveillance.

End of the day, it was your daddy's job to take the garbage out. Two dumpsters were behind the store. His manager would turn off the alarm system and let your daddy out the back where he'd toss the trash.

I threw the propane last so it landed on a bunch of soft shit, he said.

I'd made spaghetti that night. His eyes watered from too many red pepper flakes. He said he was going back at midnight to salvage the bag, that he was going to sell the propane cylinders, that he was going to continue to take things and sell them until we had a cushion soft enough to fall back on, a cushion that included a crib in our apartment and a closet full of diapers and baby food and Fisher Price toys, a set-up that helped our nerves settle, and enabled me to keep painting, and made sure rent wouldn't become an issue for us, at least not for a *long, long-ass time.*

I didn't respond, never acknowledged it. Not until you were born. Breathing your scent, whispering those words. Telling the truth, and you yawned. You stretched your arms. You snatched at scraps of dawn.

As your daddy wound his camera and waited for the nurse to walk in. There's only one picture left, he told her, so make it count. He handed her the camera. She was young like us. Your daddy spat in his hand to slick his hair back. Joined us at the bed. You and me and him, together. He told you to look, and smile, and babies don't smile, but you did.

Now this next part happens the year your daddy's face thins. Thirteen, and his baby fat burns away, is replaced by chin, brow, cheekbones, prominently defined, and a swarm of pimples budding coarsely on top of them all.

We take separate buses and meet in Richmond Hill, where his granny lives, your great-granny Bonnie, in a condo close to Lake Wilcox. She feeds us bread and chili and half a grapefruit dipped in sugar and gives your daddy his granddaddy's fishing pole and then the two of us make our way to the water.

It's July, the sting of sun on the dock, my bare feet, ducks and mosquitoes, your daddy with his face scrunched, his hand to his head like a visor. He wears a Toronto Argonauts hat backwards with blond hair protruding over the adjustable strap. His T-shirt looks like mine. Discounted and baggy, some tacky logo flaking off the front.

You look pretty, he says.

I know I don't, dressed in your Uncle Carver's hand-me-downs. An old Umbro shirt, and shorts that were once jeans, my hair greasy and knotted in a lopsided tail, scars on my forehead accentuated by the early afternoon light.

So do you, I say.

He slides a worm along the groove of his hook. Fingers speckled with dirt and blood. The worm wiggles, a ringlet. Your daddy casts it to the water. Bob bouncing on the lake and bugs leaping off the ripples, and a canoe gliding in the distance.

Your daddy is seated on the end of the dock, dipping the toes of his Reeboks. I remain ten feet behind. I pull a pencil from my pocket. I draw a picture on the dock, of the dock, and your daddy's backside, the knobs of spine showing through his shirt, his bum crack because he isn't wearing underwear, the fishing pole, the fishing line snaking its way back in.

The pole doesn't bend, but your daddy stands, winding. As if he's caught something. He says things that aren't words. I press the pencil so hard it snaps against the wood. He drops the fishing pole then. He points at the lake. Quin, Quin, Quinlynn! he says. Sweet fucking jesus! It's a body! A body! A dead fucking body!

My instinct is to make a dash for the shore, so I do.

A child, he cries. It's a dead kid. I recognize him, Quin.

It's then reality sinks in. Your daddy's shifty look, and mendacious manner. He knows what he's doing is wrong. That's what stays. His awareness of it, the shameful look in his eyes, even as he carries his lie to the next plateau.

It's Soccer, he says.

I left after that. Took the bus back to Aurora. I got off at Yonge and walked down Catherine, past the Greys' place, past Maple and Mark and all the half-opened windows, the barbeque air, the neighbors, a toddler tied by leash to a tree. It was dinner when I arrived home. Your aunts and uncle were eating rice and chicken on the floor in the television room, paper plates in front of their folded legs on the vermillion carpet.

Where's Mom? I asked.

Doing a double, said your Aunt Hermia, who was nine then, blue Kool-Aid in her hair.

Where's Grandma? I asked.

Backyard with a headache.

I looked at the three of them on the floor. Your Aunt Birdie was a kindergartener, cross-legged in smelly socks and underwear. Eating with her hands. Rice on her lips, the carpet, some on her shoulders. Your Aunt Hermia wore pajamas and your Uncle Minster was dressed in a Flaming Carrot long sleeve and a pair of blue sweat shorts with holes in the thighs. *Hook* was on TV and I screamed for no good reason. Told them I hated them and that I wanted them all to die and scorch in hell.

Your Aunt Birdie tossed the converter at a glass frame on the wall and started crying.

Your Aunt Hermia leapt to gather the shards.

Your Uncle Minster said, Wha?

I ran to the basement, to the bookshelf where your grandmother kept the photo albums. I knew there was a picture of your daddy and me somewhere. Us at your daddy's tenth birthday, a mini putt course, the fourth hole, the one with the gorilla statue stood tall beside a winding slope. It was big, black, with seething nostrils. Me and your daddy posed on either side of the statue, holding golf balls over its eyes. A blue ball and an orange ball and the gorilla's tongue was grey because whoever made the statue had forgotten to color it in. I peeled the picture from the album. Ripped your daddy out. Tore him to pieces, and tossed them in the recycling bin.

After you were born, your daddy continued to steal. He stole and sold and he was making up to five hundred dollars a week on top of his regular pay and it was all going to you. To build a better life for Kim-Claire, he'd say.

I dropped out of school the week you arrived, and began painting on my own time. Painted variations of you, fixed and broken. I painted you with eyes so large and green they folded over your sockets, stretched across your face and body. I painted your eyes with skinny red chinks in the white. I painted you as one gigantic blood-shot eyeball.

I remember sitting down to dinner with his family. It was your Auntie Kim, your Grandma Claire, your daddy on one side of the table and me on the other. We were eighteen. Your daddy with his hair buzzed short and flipped in the front. He wore a blazer, a brown tie, black pants and socks, dressed nice because he knew he had bad news to break. We were moving. Montreal, Quebec. Six hours by train, more by car. Your Grandma Claire shut her eyes as if the dark might eclipse the reality of what was being said. She shook her head.

Your Grandma Beally had done the same, sat shaking with hands balled.

Your Great-Uncle Tony and Aunt Jane had been the only ones who'd congratulated me, with a hundred dollars cash, and a goodbye dinner at Mandarin.

I never told your Grandpa Beally I was going.

Concordia University had accepted me to their art program. Your daddy tagged along. He got a job at the sporting goods store and I learned French and worked at a coffee shop and a week into my first semester those planes hit the World Trade Center, adequately setting the tone for years to come. We sat in front of the television in our rundown apartment and watched. Footage on loop. A sunburst explosion that generated infinite black clouds, and every single person, in every respect, scrambling, lost and alone, as your daddy's eczema worsened, and I ran brushstrokes over water stained walls to come to terms with it, try to understand.

He'd brought it up again after I'd told him you were on the way.

There's so much bad shit in the world, he said.

But we can make it good.

We're far from home, Quin.

Ryan. Please. Help me make our baby's world good.

The next part I see inexact. Like connect-the-dots, but before you know your numbers right. Certain dots get skipped over. Something exists, it's just not the whole picture.

It's your daddy past midnight on a Tuesday. He parks his car beside the dumpster behind Athlete's Foot. He climbs inside the dumpster. He starts tossing bags out and onto the pavement. Three green garbage bags, hunting rifles in each. A couple rifles per bag. Six rifles. Your daddy stealing six rifles.

Here's what he tells me, that he saw brightness before he heard sound.

Standing in the dark and then the dark is flashing red. A siren like a flying saucer spinning. Your daddy with a flare gun in hand, pointed at the lights.

Orange fire shot like a puck across the night.

I try to make sense of it, but there are too many dots missing. That flare gun for one. I remember your daddy standing in the doorway, but I don't see a gun. No bulge in his pocket, or orange grip sticking out the waist of his jeans. Only him, there, dressed in black and kissing me goodbye. It's always almost midnight when he leaves. There's no gun. You're already asleep.

In days following, the city seemed smaller. Even the winter season felt enclosed in some tight, illusory place, like we were trapped inside a snow globe and everything real was taking place outside of it.

The phone rang sharper than normal. It cut the apartment in two, and I stood separate from all else. Picked up. Hello.

Your daddy cried. He cried loud and he cried hard and I could feel his tears, they leaked through the receiver, moisturized my hearing to make things more clear.

Quin, he tried to say.

Ryan, I said.

Quinlynn. It's not looking good for me. Shit's not looking good.

I listened to his voice crack, break, scatter and then regather, and swell into static. It's not looking good, it's not looking good. He kept repeating the line, until, finally, he asked how you were. How's KC? he said. He'd never called you that before.

KC? I said.

Yeah. How's she?

Why'd you call her that?

KC? Kim-Claire, Kim-Claire.

Why'd you call her KC?

Fuck. I don't know, Quin. I thought it'd be faster. I don't got forever. Fucking assholes are gonna cut me off. I'll say Kim-Claire if it makes you happy, okay? Kim-Claire. How the fuck's Kim-Claire doing without me there?

I thought about what he'd said, KC being quicker. Both were two syllables. Both are two syllables, I wanted to say. But didn't. I told him you were fine, good, great.

I told him you were seated in the high chair at the kitchen table, which was true, and then I told him you were drawing a picture of us three, which was not. I told him the picture was us, our family, inside of a house, one big square under a triangle roof. Your daddy asked if I was painting on the walls inside the house and I told him yes. I told him you'd drawn me with a brush in hand.

That's my girl, he said.

I nodded at the lights in the street. A full moon like it was closer, falling toward earth. I stood next to the window and watched it and all the other lights collapse, and burn bright as predators' eyes in proximity to the ground, staying put in order to pounce.

An uneasy feeling lifted inside my chest. My breasts felt sick and strange. The moon kept approaching, got closer and closer. It blocked the sky. I hung up the phone, walked over to you and smelled your hair. Your daddy used to complain working at the warehouse made his hair dry and his mouth parched. All that fucking cardboard, he used to say. It's funny, because that's how I imagined him. I pictured him in a cell with his hair like hay and a plain, thirsty tongue. It dangled from his mouth, grey and empty, until I pressed your tiny hands into my palette and together we colored the whole thing in.

18

I'm turning onto Eccles Avenue, driving past the playground, the one with the missing tire swing, just three limp chains on a piss-yellow pole, when there's this thick sounding thud on the back windshield of my brand new 90 BMW M5. So I know it's gotta be some little dumbass kid throwing snowballs, and I should probably keep driving, just ignore it, but I don't keep driving, I can't, cause the situation's just one of those things, the kind of thing you don't realize is gonna happen til it's happening, and what's happening is I'm pulling to the side of the road, opening my glove box, and grabbing hold of the pocketknife I've got under all the crumpled highway maps. The knife's name is Sean Vortex cause my pop used to say a good knife needs a good-sounding name, and Sean Vortex just seemed to fit. So I slide my winter glove on top of the knife in my hand, open the door, and step out into the freezing cold. My car's still running, tailpipe blowing smoke, but I look past it, across the street, gazing right at them. Of course they're still standing there, couple little kids, both boys, a redhead and then a darker haired one who's maybe a bit smaller. They're eight-ish, or nine, not sure, it's hard to tell with kids these days. They're standing next to the road, hoodless and hatless and wearing these puffy black coats that make their arms stick out like charred gingerbread men, with lower halves hidden behind a barricade of snow. Me, I'm standing beside my car still, motor chugging, and the kids are looking at me like they've got no clue what's gonna happen, but what happens is this, I start walking towards them, kicking through the brown slush on the street, a knife in my hand inside my glove, and the kids are looking at each other now, and then back at me, and then they're running. Like I said, it's just one of those things, the kind of thing that catches you running too, a grown-ass man chasing two little dumbass kids, and it's something you don't quite get, even as it's happening, but even still, you can bet your ass it's somehow happening. So the kids cut through the playground first, pushing past those dangling chains, over the seesaw and under the monkey bars, hopping out the sandbox and then onto the diamond, not much a diamond now on account its shape's been buried under all the knee-deep snow. The cold air's making my eyes water, but I can still see them, the redheaded one about five feet in front of the littler one, then ten feet, fifteen feet now cause the littler one's so little he can't trudge two feet without falling flat on his little face. So I slow down. I'm catching up without effort, taking these big steps, and each time the littler one looks back he probably sees me bigger, like Frankenstein's monster, gaining on him in spite of my leisurely stride. But the kid's got these little turquoise mittens, and he starts taking them off and tossing them at me, like maybe they'll knock me down, but they don't, so he's panicking now, little dumbass, packing snow, forming a ball in his shiny pink hands til I smack it out of them. Hey! I look up then, and the redheaded one's standing in the outfield with his hands held to his face and he's yelling, Don't touch my friend, you stupid butthole fart! I wave the kid over, but he doesn't come, just stands there half-sunk in snow, and he's watching me handle the littler one, who's turning wild now, trying to punch me in the balls so I gotta grab him by the back of his coat collar just to hold him away. The redheaded one starts running then, tracing the backwards path of his footprints, and he's yelling again, Don't touch my friend, butthole fart! and the littler one kinda laughs. The sky's darker now, darker than a minute ago, and there aren't any lights over the diamond, just the moon bouncing off the snow, making everything blackish-blue, including the redheaded kid, a blackish-blue shadow til he's standing right in front of me. I notice he's got fear in his eyes though, a fear the littler one seems to lack, but when I'm expecting something cheeky to come out of his mouth, what the kid says instead is, We're sorry, okay? Sorry, mister. Please don't tell Mr. Beally. He says it like every single person in the world must know who this Mr. Beally is, and I'm letting go of the littler one now, watching him dawdle to his friend, and then the two of them are just standing there looking at me again, the same way they did before, from across the street, only up close I can see how rosy their cheeks and ears are, and instead of staying mad at them I start wondering why they aren't wearing hats and scarves and snow pants instead. It's cold, I tell them. The redheaded one nods, takes off his black mittens like I'd been hinting him to do so, and hands them to the littler one, who pulls them over his own hands without even saying thanks. I ask the boys what their names are, and the redheaded one says Eddie, then immediately changes his mind to Joe, so I know that's a lie, and the littler one says soccer cause I'm pretty sure he wasn't listening to the question. I try explaining to them that throwing snowballs is dangerous, that they could've seriously messed up my driving and caused an accident. The redheaded one nods like he knows the spiel, while the littler one just stares blankly at his new mittens, the ends flopped over with nothing inside them, too big for his small hands, and all a gosh damn sudden I start feeling kinda bad for these two little dumbasses, the way you do for kids sometimes, the way you want them to know everything's gonna be just fine. So I tell them I'm not mad, not gonna hurt them, not gonna tell their teacher or whoever Mr. Beally is the things they did, and then I take off my glove to show them the knife, Sean Vortex, pulling the blade out all the way. It dazzles in the dark under the moon, and the littler one stares at the knife like it might be magic, so I hand it to him, tell him to keep it, cause for some reason, whatever reason, I want these kids to like me now, remember me as the man who gave them that really neat-looking knife that one time rather than the man who chased them down. I turn to leave then, following my tracks back to the playground and regretting about a million things at once, when suddenly there's another thud, different from the one before, much denser, bringing a welt to the backside of my head and dropping cold down my spine. When I look back, I see the littler one's running again, or trying to, his little legs too short to properly tackle the snow and so he's still falling every couple feet, but keeps Sean Vortex held high above his head, as if not to get the blade wet, and he's yelling, I'm Peter Pan! I'm Pan the Man! The redheaded one's not running though. He's looking back and forth between me and his stupid friend, and waiting to see if there's gonna be another chase. And in the end it's just one of those things, the kind of thing that happens, the kind of thing that's got your car running back at the street, key in the ignition, but even still, you're taking steps in the other direction, either for something important, or maybe you've just got some little dumbass kid to catch. The redheaded one sees I'm about to run down the littler one, so what he does is he catches up to him first, and lifts him, piggybacking the littler one over all the high snow. But I don't end up chasing after them. Instead I stand shivering, lost in some thought about Sean Vortex, how sharp he was, cutting rope, cutting squirrel, the gum off my boots, and how I won't ever pocket him again, or feel my thumb against the cold carbon steel. Hey! I look up. The little dumbasses are in the outfield now, two blackish-blue blurs in the distance. You're one stupid asshole fart! the redheaded one yells, and then there's laughter, and then they're both just standing there, waiting to see what my next move is, and it's on repeat now, inside my head, the little dumbass kid disrespecting me like that, calling me a stupid asshole fart even though I gave them Sean Vortex, and it's just one of those things, the kind of thing that gets you thinking, the kind of thing that leaves you feeling empty, a new kind of lightness in your pocket, and you're wondering if maybe the little dumbass kid's got a point.

19

There were mice in the ceiling. We'd listened to them scratch around up there for days. Finally the old man couldn't take any more. He bought a dozen or so traps and spread them across the living room floor. Then he took a steel bat to the ceiling and knocked out a hole the size of a hamburger patty. The mice must've been drawn to the light because they immediately began dropping like hairy figs onto the carpet. Babies, said the old man. He loaded the traps with small cubes of cheddar cheese. The springs screeched as he pulled the hammers back and placed the bait on top of the metal catches.

I joined him the following morning to see if anything had been caught. But there was nothing. Only traps and cheese. The old man got pissed at the sight of the bait still being there. He punched the doorjamb with the base of his fist and stomped the floor hard in his moccasin sheepskins. Then he kneeled down and cursed God under his coffee breath until there were no more bad words left to say.

Sylvia visited around that time. She wore a baggy sweater even though it was summer because she hated the shape her new breasts made. I could still see the outline of her bum in violet bellbottoms though. She walked with her hips. She asked why the old man had begun wearing a rawhide hammer in the belt loop of his jeans. I told her it was because the mousetraps hadn't worked. She said she wanted to see the mice. I told her they hid during the day but she insisted. We waited in the kitchen until the old man left for work.

I poured us a couple cups of water and we brought them in the living room. She held the cup under her nose and sniffed the way the old man did with whisky. Her nose crinkled and made sharp lines along the bridge. I sat down at the upright piano. It was mahogany and stood taller than either of us. She told me to play something to attract the mice. I played Ode to Joy because that's all I knew. She told me to play the Pied Piper song but I wasn't sure what that was. I played Ode to Joy a second time.

She explored the room. Examined tight spaces between the walls and cabinets. She fingered the lampshade. She toed the floor vent. She lifted the old man's fishing trophies from the rustic mantel. She put them back. Then she stood and stared at the oil painting of the bad lady hung behind the black wing chair. Sylvia always liked looking at the painting because she knew the bad lady was my mother and she said we shared the same lips and earlobes and eyes. She touched my mother's pupils and ran her fingers across the canvas even though I'd told her to please not touch it many times before. She said the painting felt like her father's face.

I stopped playing piano. She put her cup on the mantel beside the trophies and we looked at each other and neither of us spoke for a long time. We listened to the mice move inside the walls. I sipped water. Mice and sipping sounds and silence. Carrying a conversation had become more difficult since she'd grown breasts.

I asked Sylvia to marry me in the spring of nineteen seventy-three. We were in our final year of high school and it was a couple hours after prom. I drove us to the town park where we sat on the aluminum bleachers overlooking a small tee-ball field. She wore a light blue dress and white stockings and silvery shoes and there was a plastic magnolia clipped to her hair. The straps on her dress were patterned with pieces of fabric cut in the shape of rose petals. I put my jacket on top of her legs and my arm over her shoulders and kissed the mole on her neck. She complained about my stubble. I kissed her mouth. The taste of cigarettes and spiked fruit punch. I touched between her legs but she swatted me away. Too cold, she complained.

The moon was white. Not a single blue blemish. Not a single star. Sylvia looked at me and asked what was in the duffel bag. I told her to wait. I carried the bag out to the middle of the tee-ball field and dropped it on top of the mound. I looked back at the bleachers but it was too dark. I unzipped the bag and pulled out a half dozen fireworks and dug each one into the crusher dust. I looked again at the darkness and wondered if she could see. I pulled a matchbook out of my sock. Struck a match and lit the fuses and ran. I was halfway back to the bleachers when things started exploding. The field brightened under all kinds of pretty colors.

I ran up the bleachers until I arrived at the row in front of Sylvia. She was wearing my jacket. She was watching the sky. I said her name. She looked down at me. Her red hair hung coiled over her shoulders. I pulled my mother's ring from the side pocket of my tuxedo pants. It was gold and engraved with butterflies. The fireworks fizzled and Sylvia's skin turned grey under the night. I didn't have a box so I held my hands like a clam and parted my fingers with the ring rested on my palm.

I'd first met Sylvia in nineteen sixty-two. The old man and I had moved into the house across the street from hers in North York. It was a square bungalow with two square windows and a square driveway that sloped toward the beaten street.

We were seven. I was invited to play with Sylvia one day while the old man was at work. Our date began in her backyard. She showed me the croquet wickets and the cilantro garden and the hole in the fence where she sometimes spied on her Taiwanese neighbors. She showed me the red oak tree. Climbed the wooden planks nailed to its trunk and entered a fort built atop the branches. She grabbed a soup can from inside the fort and let it drop. The can landed on the grass in front of my sneakers. It was attached to yarn. She told me to walk as far as possible. I walked until the yarn tugged. I was standing about ten feet away. She told me to press the can against my ear and I did and she asked if I could hear her and I could hear her fine but it probably wasn't because of the can.

My dad invented this, she said.

I held the can up to my nose. It smelled like clam chowder. Sylvia asked me if my mother was dead because she'd noticed I didn't live with one. I shook my head at the grass and then looked up at her. She's helping end the war, I said.

Sylvia's house was square the same as mine. But the inside looked different. The walls were yellow and the rugs were orange and the lampshades and curtains and picture frames were all red. It was like living inside of autumn.

We took our shoes off and shuffled down the front hall. A picture of an old man's hands hung low on one of the walls. It was a pencil drawing. The hands were grey and covered in veins like worms under the skin. They were pressed flat against one another like someone praying. Sylvia said her father used to be an artist but now he sold cars.

I told her the old man drove a taxi.

That's supposed to be really dangerous, she said.

In the kitchen her mother kissed our foreheads and poured us each a glass of skim milk. She told Sylvia to give me a tour of the house. Sylvia started by showing me the collection of cuckoo clocks on the wall in the dining room and then the plastic bags of clothing kept in the garage. She showed me the mildew on the shower curtain and the dark hairs gathered at the base of the toilet. She showed me the automobile books on the coffee table. She showed me the birdcage. She showed me the cat dish. She showed me the storage bin in the basement where her father kept his cigars and photographs of naked black women. She showed me the cupboard under the stairs. She showed me the step where she'd carved her initials with tin snips. She showed me my milk. She asked if she could please drink the rest.

Sylvia's bedroom was painted pale yellow. The carpet was brown and scribbled with vacuum lines. Her bed was low to the ground. She sat down on it. This is the desk to my office, she said. She patted the comforter. I touched it too. Then I circled the room and examined the walls. All were bare but one. There was a photograph hanging at its center. A boy about our age. He had buzzed blond hair and a monobrow and big lips smiling with only a bit of teeth showing. His face was held in place by a tack.

Who's this? I asked.

Clinton, she said. He's dead. He died. I thought maybe if your mom was dead then we'd both be people who know dead people, but your mom's still here.

Clinton's shirt was white with a neckband and his head was tilted to the side slightly. He sat with his hands on his lap in front of a bookshelf backdrop.

My mom's a bad lady, I said.

How come?

She's not even my mom, I said. The old man says she's my mom cause she had me so that makes her my mom, but she's not my mom.

Sylvia slid off the bed. Her dress looked like a pink rectangular box covering her body. Her socks were tall and striped scarlet. She walked over and stood beside me and her hair was a mess of red spiraled like springs in every direction. She touched the photograph of Clinton with her ring finger. He was gonna be my husband, she said, but something inside his head went wrong.

What did?

It exploded.

Like bombs? I said.

It's called *aneurysm*, she said. It's already inside your brain. It blows up and your head fills with blood and you die. Clinton wasn't sick. It just happened.

I looked back at Clinton and tried picturing him as a ghost or a skeleton or an angel but couldn't. He looked too young to not be living. I felt lightheaded. I sat down with my back against the wall. Sylvia ran over to her closet and opened it and pulled out a vinyl lunchbox from the top shelf and brought it back over to me and sat down. The box was a quarter full of chewed gum. The pieces were hardened and in a variety of shapes and colors. I collect these, she said, and sometimes when I'm sad I look at the gum and it makes me feel better.

I looked at the gum. There was hair stuck to some of it.

So if you find gum, can I have it? she asked

Okay.

It's under lots of things. And in drinking fountains.

Okay. I know.

She looked at me with mint green eyes. Don't worry, she said. Kids almost never die, ever. The inside of Clinton's head exploding was a really strange thing. Don't be scared, Harry.

I'm not, I said.

Sylvia held the box of gum under my chin and told me to sniff. It smelled like sugar and salt and fruit and garbage. You can come over and look at it whenever you want, she said, but promise never to put it in your mouth. It's not cause I don't like sharing, it's cause I don't want you to choke or get sick.

The second time I asked Sylvia to marry me was in the fall of nineteen eighty-one. She and I were twenty-six and it'd been almost a decade since I'd last seen her. I'd recently begun teaching eighth grade in the small town of Port Woodlot sixty-five kilometers north of Toronto. I was up late marking quizzes when the call came in.

She'd just returned home from Alberta where she'd worked customer service at various hotels for the past seven years. She asked me how I'd been. I told her the old man was dead. She said she was sorry. I said, Fuck the old bastard to hell. She tried laughing but it was forced. I told her I was sorry for saying fuck. She said it was fine. We arranged to meet that Saturday at a restaurant in Aurora which was halfway between us.

After I hung up I thought about what I'd said. It made me want to lift the phone and slam it down. *Fuck the old bastard to hell. Fuck the old bastard.* I repeated it out loud about a dozen times. It was such a stupid thing to say.

The next day she showed up thirty minutes late. I was already on my third beer. She slid inside the booth across from me and blamed her timing on the traffic. She wore a denim jacket over a billowy white dress that went down to her ankles. Her fingers and toes were painted red. Her red hair had turned brown. She had a belly. It bulged like a globe under her dress.

Your hair, I said. And you're expecting.

Her face looked a lot rougher but still pretty. I asked how far along she was. Seven months. I asked who the father was. Not in the picture. She drank half a pint of water in one gulp. The ice cubes clattered against her teeth. I asked if she was scared and she said she was and I told her I was scared too.

Of what? she said.

Huh?

What do you have to be afraid of, Harry?

No. I'm not.

She plucked the lemon off the rim of her glass and dropped it on the ice. I slid my foot under hers under the table. The waitress came and took our orders. Sylvia stared longingly at the people in the smoking section. I reached my hand across the table and held it there and eventually she touched my fingers. I asked if she was in love with the father of her baby. She shook her head. I told her I loved her and that I wanted to try again. She pulled her hand away like I'd burned it. I pulled out my wallet and spread it open and my heart was beating so hard I could feel it press against my ribcage. A couple loonies and my mother's ring fell to the table. The ring twirled to a stop. Sylvia held her belly like a basketball player gripping the ball on the foul line. The waitress returned and refilled Sylvia's water and we both watched the lemon wedge float back to the top. Then the waitress left and we were alone once more. A white seed slipped out of the lemon and sank slowly to the bottom of the glass.

Harry, she said. Harry. Are you listening?

It was my mother who'd named me Harry. The old man never liked it. He started calling me Edward after she left.

Harry ain't sturdy, he said. Ain't a proper man's name. A proper man's name gotta be sturdy, like Edward. Now there's a proper, sturdy name for ya.

The old man had always been an old man for real. Fifty-six the year my mother gave birth to me and sixty-two the year she split and seventy-seven the year he split himself. His heart attacked him in the washroom at a Dairy Queen. He'd been sitting on the toilet dipping fries in an Oreo Blizzard when a blood clot clogged a coronary artery. The cops contacted me at college three days after. They asked to speak to Harry. I didn't know what to say.

Sylvia went through a pregnancy phase around the time we were in the third grade. She wore baggy shirts so she could fit a balloon underneath. Her mother worked at a party store and would bring home bunches of balloons already filled with helium. Sylvia used to draw faces on the balloons with permanent marker and then give birth to them. We'd sit and watch the newborns float to the ceiling and pop against the stucco.

Once Sylvia and I were playing checkers on her bed. She sat with her gut inflated on her lap. There was a bowl of BBQ chips beside the checkerboard. Sylvia kept rubbing the orange powder from her fingers on the comforter and it made smears that looked like little flames.

She was better at checkers than me. She had three kings on her side of the board. She asked if I wanted to feel the baby kick. I touched the balloon. Her older sister Marsha walked by the door and saw me and laughed and asked when the wedding was going to be. Sylvia hopped a red checker over two of my blacks and asked if I would.

Would what?

Marry me if we were grownups.

I said I would. She asked what we'd name the baby if the baby were real. I told her Edward. Edward's a good name, I said, a good, sturdy name. She lay back and looked up at the ceiling with her legs bent and her knees pointed in the air. She lifted her shirt and the balloon rose. It was indigo and attached to curling ribbon like an umbilical cord. The ribbon was tied to the zipper of her pants. The face on the balloon had buckteeth and crossed eyes and I snipped the cord with nail clippers and it floated and bounced against the ceiling fan.

Edward sounds too old, she said. That's an old man's name.

No, I said. It's proper. It's a proper, sturdy name.

How about Eddie? she said. That's proper too, but not so old sounding.

Is it actually proper?

It is, she said. Sure is.

I pulled Eddie down and tied him to the bedpost. Sylvia walked over to the picture of Clinton. She took out the tack and Clinton slid down the wall and fell face forward on the carpet. Sylvia brought the tack over and told me it was boring playing checkers with me because I was so bad. She pressed the tack against the balloon. Scraps of Eddie exploded everywhere.

I don't like this one, she said. Let's make another. We need to draw Eddie a better face. I wanna make him smiling. I wanna make him the happiest baby in the world.

It was a quiet Friday in late November in nineteen ninety-one. Sylvia nestled under a blanket on the recliner reading a James A. Michener. I did a crossword in a cheap book I'd picked out of a bargain bin at Giant Tiger. We'd amuse ourselves by joking about the answers never quite matching the clues.

Very Loosely, I said. A six-letter word for Very Loosely.

And? she said.

And the back of the book says the answer is Openly.

She quarter-smiled shaking her head and turned back to her novel.

Not too long after we heard the kitchen door slide open and someone's sneakers skitter inside. The oldest Beally boy Carver ran past the living room entryway. Evening, Carver, Sylvia called to him. Then she lowered her voice and said if Sherri didn't buckle down and start teaching her kids manners they were all going to end up in jail or worse. Except Birdie, she added frivolously. I like Birdie. And winked.

It was the last time we laughed together. Then she turned back to her novel and me my book of crosswords. I wrote O-P-E-N-L-Y. I thought I heard the wind. I asked Sylvia if she could hear the wind and she said she could and it was because Carver hadn't shut the kitchen door. So I stood. She turned back to her book a third and final time and I watched her eyes move along the lines. I don't know how long I stood there. Her eyes going side to side to side to side to side and then up at me. Sylvia smiled.

Carver sprinted past the entryway yelling, Eddie's hurt in the backyard!

Sometimes I dream about the day I'll ask again. It won't be for another couple decades. I'll find her living in a retirement home in northwestern Alberta in a town called Peace River. She'll be seventy-eight and so will I and together we'll be old and shrinking. I'll stand on one knee. Hold her hand in mine. It'll be cold and covered in spots and wrinkles and I'll kiss her knuckles and slide the bad lady's ring on top of her brittle tobacco-stained finger and turn the bad into something good.

Sylvia, I'll say.

And I'll touch her face and look at her eyes and see the little girl who lived across the street from me. The girl with red hair that turned brown that turned white and I'll tell her that she and her baby were the two best things that ever happened to me. I'll walk over to the closet. I'll pull out the lunchbox and open it and find the picture of Eddie glued to the backside of the lid because the shoebox is where Sylvia kept her treasures. And I'll spit my gum inside the box. Breathe in and out and shut the lid and hold the box tight against my soft sagging body and keep it safe forever and keep her safe forever and that's how things will end for us.

There was a baby mouse on the floor. It trembled in the shadow between two coffee table legs. I'm not sure how long it'd been there before Sylvia saw it and pointed and hopped on top of the couch with her black socks sunk in the bronze-yellow cushion. I thought she was scared at first but realized she'd only jumped to avoid hurting it. She told me to jump too. I hopped on top of the piano bench.

The mouse was the size of a golf ball. It had a pink wormy tail. I told Sylvia the old man wanted the mice dead but she said we needed to save it. I stepped down from the piano bench.

I'll catch it so we can bring it outside, I said.

It's so cute, she said.

I told her I'd trap the mouse under a cereal bowl. Then I could slide it across the carpet and kitchen tiles and wooden floor in the hall until I got to the front door and released it. Sylvia told me to hurry. I ran to get a bowl.

When I returned I saw she'd unfastened the bun from behind her head and stretched the elastic band over her wrist. Her red hair sprang to life like blood exploding off her scalp. I dropped to my hands and knees and crawled across the floor toward the mouse. It shivered in its spot. I got close enough so that my shadow came together with the one from the table. The mouse inched forward. Sylvia told me to be careful. She was on her knees on the couch leaning forward to get a better look. I held my breath and cupped the bottom of the bowl in my right hand and held it back behind my head like I was about to throw a football. The mouse stopped and moved and stopped again. I counted to five in my head and brought down the bowl. Sylvia squeezed her eyes shut. I was looking at her instead of the mouse.

When the old man returned home from work I was waiting for him on the steps outside. It was getting late. The sun had already set over Sylvia's house across the street and the light in her kitchen was on but the blinds were pulled shut. The old man asked what I was doing. I told him I'd made a mess inside.

What sorta mess?

I showed him the mouse on the living room floor. It'd been split almost in two by the rim of the bowl. Its insides blotted the carpet. The old man put his hand on my shoulder. It was big and hairy and calloused and I could smell the crud under his nails. You got one, he said. And there was delight in his voice. He told me to go grab the broom and dustpan from the front closet.

When I returned the old man was standing with his hands on his hips and he was looking at the painting of the bad lady. Then he turned to me. You got one, he said again. His smile was wide and his eyebrows were high up on his head. I swept the mouse onto the dustpan. Now we know it's possible, he said. You got one, Edward.

20

Mom's finally lost it. She's been crying a lot lately, and praying. And wearing her pajamas everywhere. Pajamas at the bank, pajamas at the grocery store, pajamas on dates with sadsacks she met online. I try telling her to wear pants like a normal person, but she won't listen. Jammies feel good, she says, and I mean honestly, Birdie, shouldn't I be allowed to feel good every once in the bluest of moons?

I'm secretly seeing this girl Tess Gardener. She's got armpit hair, face freckles, a pierced septum, sundresses in the spring. Seventeen, which makes her a year older than me. And we've done things with each other, but nothing too intense or sexy. I mean it's not like we've worn nipple-clamps and finger-banged each other's buttholes or anything. We do take our shirts off though. And bras. And sometimes I'll stick an ice cube in my mouth and suck her nipples awhile. She says she likes the slippery coldness of it, and breathes hard, makes sounds that remind me of pterodactyls.

I told her I loved her once. It was over the phone, but that still counts. She was carrying on about this goth girl at school who gets off on cutting her own ribs with broken guitar strings or something, and I was listening, trying my best to keep the words in my mouth, but failed. Tess, I go, like a total tool, I love you.

She didn't respond. I could hear the TV on in the background. I think she was watching *The Apprentice*. I said it again.

No you don't, she said.

I think I do, I said.

No, she said.

Casey Lynch is a boy in my co-ed gym class. Today he wore shorts under his pants so he wouldn't have to change in front of anyone. Franco said guys have been giving him a hard time for having this brown birthmark on his thigh that apparently looks like diarrhea running down his leg. So people were laughing about it during stretches this morning, calling Casey Colonel Bum Sauce, and Poo Thighs, and Attack of the Shit-Legged Homo. Even some of the girls joined in. I thought he was going to start crying because his lip trembled and he kept looking at the lines on the floor. It was pretty funny, even though it was really sad.

I wake to the sound of these high-pitched giggles. It's nine in the morning on a Sunday. Downstairs smells like a butthole. I find Mom in the TV room on the floor in her pajamas with about a half-dozen bunny rabbits crawling around her.

Mom? I say.

Look, she says.

They're shitting everywhere, I tell her.

Watch it!

They're crapping, Mom.

It's fine. I'll clean it. Watch your mouth.

Where'd you get all these?

Mrs. Romios from church.

She rolls across the floor, steamrolling turds, lifting bunnies above her head and nuzzling their crotches. It's pretty much the most fucked up thing ever. I sit on the couch and try to think.

Aren't they cute? she asks.

I guess.

They're so innocent, she says. Their feet will bring us luck.

You need to clean up all this crap, I tell her.

Tess says I need to start talking more to her parents. My mom and dad think you're, like, anti-social, she says. You never say anything to them.

What am I supposed to say?

Uh, anything? Like literally anything is better than nothing.

I try.

Well try harder please, cause they're starting to think you're a little weird, and I mean, like, telling them their daughter's a rug muncher's going to be a bitch enough, you know, let alone the fact I'm seeing you, like, uh, some mute creepy weirdo. Kidding. But seriously, if they're talking about the weather, say something about the weather; if they're talking about a show they like, say something about television; if my mom gets a haircut, compliment her titties. Kidding. But okay? Seriously. It's not that difficult.

I get invited to the Gardeners' for dinner. The food is served in small portions. A slice of chicken breast, some string beans, half a baked potato. Drink options include water, water with lemon, or milk. All signs point to a bowl of fruit for dessert.

Tess is dressed conservatively in a cashmere sweater with horizontal stripes and black skirt. She's seated beside her kid sister Macy on the other side of the table. Macy is a tomboy. Cute kid. The same orange hair and green eyes as Tess. Makes me wish I'd known Tess when we were little, like elementary school age. I picture us cracking up on a playground, throwing sand at each other and not caring if it got in our hair.

Mr. Gardener is seated to my left, Mrs. Gardener to my right. They pray before they eat. Amen. I'm about to put a string bean in my mouth when Mr. Gardener starts telling this story about a coworker of his who recently gave him several jars of homemade jam.

That's lovely, says Mrs. Gardener. I've actually given a lot of thought to that myself, making homemade jams and all. The idea intrigues me.

I tried some of Bob's jam during lunch, says Mr. Gardener. Orange jam. I spread it across a toasted Tim Hortons biscuit.

Mmm sounds good, says Mrs. Gardener.

Tess toe punts me under the table. I try to think of something brilliant to contribute to this already brilliant conversation. Options include a) My dad likes to put jam on Matzo, b) Do you prefer jam chunky or smooth? c) Peanut butter and jam sandwiches are good, although some people are allergic to peanuts, or d) Jam spelt backwards is *maj*.

Maj? says Mr. Gardener. What exactly is maj, Birdie?

I don't know, I say.

Mrs. Gardener looks at Tess. Tess looks at me. I look at my plate.

Later I'm on the back patio with Tess's sister Macy. She shows me a Styrofoam food container she's stored with pictures of teenyboppers she's cut from magazines. And there's a kettle in Macy's hands. And she's pouring hot water on the pictures. And in a demonic voice goes, Burn! Bleed! Die! And it all happens so fast. And Macy's totally laughing her ass off like a sadistic little shit. And to be honest, so am I.

Tess opens the door to tell us our fruit bowls are ready.

I'm partnered with Casey Lynch during warm-up. We toss a fitness ball back and forth. I can tell he's queer by the way he throws it. Thin, flimsy wrists, and long blond hair he keeps curling behind his ears. The foot of the birthmark pokes out the bottom of his shorts and it does look like shit. I throw him the ball. It slips through his fingers. He has difficulty picking it up. When he bends his hair hangs in his face and he looks like a flat-chested girl. He yells. His yell sounds like, GRRRRAH!

What the hell? I say. You okay?

Why?

I don't know. You just yelled like an idiot.

I'm in a mood, he says.

How come?

He tries rolling the ball, but it only moves a couple feet.

I got fired from my job last night, he says.

I didn't know you had a job.

How would you?

I don't know. Where'd you work?

Staples.

Why'd you get fired?

He puts his hands on his hips. Your friend Franco's a dildo, he says.

Franco's clinically retarded, I tell him. How come you got fired?

Do you ever do things that don't make sense? he asks.

No, I say.

Sometimes I shut my eyes and run, he says.

Where?

Nowhere. I run until I run into something.

Why'd you get fired? I ask for like the billionth time.

I did it at work. I was mopping the floor because this kid spilled slushie in one of the aisles. I don't know why, but at one point I stop mopping, shut my eyes, and start running. I ran right into a display of electronic equipment cleaner, like canisters and canisters of the stuff, and made a bigger mess than the one I was already cleaning. It'll take them forever to rebuild that display.

I step forward and lift the ball off the ground.

Do you think that's weird? he asks.

Who knows, I say.

It's late when I walk past Mom's bedroom. The TV is still on. An infomercial for a Bowflex. Mom is sleeping. The lights are turned off. The nightstand is covered with pill bottles and pictures of my brothers and sisters and me. There's a pillow beside Mom's head, the corner of a picture of Dad sticking out underneath as if The Trigger Fairy might come exchange it for money. I enter the room.

I look at Dad's face in the picture, and then at Mom's right there. I see myself in both of them. I turn the TV off so I can't see shit.

I tell Tess about Uncle Tony. How he used to take us camping in the Port Woodlot woods. We'd fish and roast beans, swim in the lake. My sister Quinlynn's an artist, so she'd bring a sketchbook and draw the whole time. She drew snakes, the dock, squirrels, trees, fire, us, everything. One picture was of Uncle Tony and my cousin Kelsey with melted marshmallow lips and Mr. Stay Puft bodies, and another was of Minster and Hermia sword fighting with sticks on the rocks near the canoe. But my favorite was of the toad. It was humungous. Quinlynn found it by the fire pit. It just sat there not moving because it was totally comfortable and didn't care much about anything. I was pretty obsessed with it. I asked Quinlynn if I could have the drawing, but she gave it to Uncle Tony as a thank you for taking us camping again.

It was a Fowler's toad, I say.

I don't think Tess cares because she changes the topic to her own uncle all of a sudden. She says he molested her when she was five. She woke dizzy in a bathtub, her pussy hurting. There was blood in the water. Her uncle sat outside the tub, naked and smoking a cigarette with blood on his fingers.

Jesus, I say. Jesus Christ, Tess. Oh my God.

And she starts laughing. Naw, naw, she says. I'm totally bullshitting you, dummy.

Casey invites me over after school. He lives on Avondale Crescent, only a few blocks from Spruce. The inside of his house smells like dogs and lemons, and the walls and the carpets are different shades of yellow and brown.

I meet his mom. Her name is Edna. She's nice, but dumb. She keeps asking me questions without listening to the answers. She looks and sounds like Frenchy from *Grease*. She bakes us cookies and burns them. The kitchen fills with smoke. She hands us each a butter knife to scrape the burnt bottoms.

Casey's bedroom is in the basement. Walls the color of honey mustard. There's a bed, a computer, a stack of skateboarding magazines, socks, hand sanitizer, a mini fridge and a construction helmet.

We sit on the bed, flip through his magazines and eat the burnt cookies. Then Casey turns on his computer. Come here, he says. I walk up behind him. He's wearing a white T-shirt and tight navy jeans. There's a picture of Bruce Lee as his desktop background. He clicks a folder labeled Geography Notes that has a lot of video files inside. You want to see something fucked up? he says.

Okay.

This actually happened, he says.

A man is on his knees, hands tied behind his back. There are four other men standing behind him. They have turbans wrapped around their faces. Three of them hold guns, and one carries a chainsaw. The man on his knees is crying. He says the date. One of the other men holds a newspaper in front of the crying man's face and the crying man reads a couple of the headlines. Then they cut off the crying man's head with the chainsaw and hold it in front of the camera.

Did you hear the gargling? Casey asks.

Yeah, I say.

You think it's disturbing?

Why'd you show me that?

I wish it wasn't so blurry, he says.

Casey goes upstairs to get a pizza his mom made us. I sit at the computer and go on Facebook. He comes back a few minutes later, carrying the smell of burnt crust and cheese down with him. He puts the pizza on the bed and stands behind me a minute, watching me click through photos. There's one of my cousin Kelsey and a few other girls flashing their boobs. It hasn't been flagged yet. Grade ten sluts, Casey laughs. I click Like. Casey asks if he can show me something. He reaches one arm over my shoulder and starts working the mouse, then reaches his other arm over my other shoulder, works the keyboard. He's practically hugging me. I can feel his lips against the back of my head. He's kissing me. Another fucked up terrorist video pops up on screen. His mouth opens. I can feel him eating my hair. Then his face lowers. He's kissing the back of my neck. He starts squeezing my chest.

What are you doing? I ask him.

Nothing, he says, pushing away. He calls me a bitch. He asks me to leave. He says he has a lot of homework to do, gesturing towards the screen. The man in the video is in a state of shock as he is dismembered with a hatchet.

The garbage in the garage is full of bunny shit. I think Mom's trying to be clean and normal again. I'm not sure what did it. Maybe someone threatened to fire her from Boston Pizza, because she's back to wearing daytime clothes, finally, and bathing on a regular basis. She even cleaned the house and gave away most of the bunnies. Only kept two—Love and Hope.

Are you going shopping this weekend? I ask her.

I plan to, yes. What can I get you?

I need someone to Febreze the hell out of this place because it stinks.

Language, Birdie.

Stinks?

Hell.

Oh. Sorry.

Anyways, I can do that, she says. I can get us some scented candles from Walmart.

Okay. Thank you.

We're eating dinner in front of the TV, but the TV's turned off. Mom made tuna melts and fries. She also started buying Fruitopia, which I'm pretty obsessed with. Mom drinks a glass of cream soda with a bit of milk in it.

I heard from your father, she says.

Really?

Yes. He mailed me a handwritten letter because apparently we're still living in the eighteen hundreds. He said he's moving out of the basement in Port Woodlot.

Really?

Yes, Birdie. Really. And it's about time if you ask me.

Where's he going to live?

He says he's moving downtown in the fall.

Toronto?

Yes.

Cool.

Yes, she says. Cool. Then she says, Would you like to hear something, love?

Okay.

She nibbles a small piece of tuna melt, then swallows as if it'd been a big one.

I found a wallet, she says.

Where?

In the parking lot at work.

Was there money in it?

Yes there was.

How much?

A lot. A foolish amount. More money than you or I have ever seen, that's for sure. It truly was a foolish amount.

What did you do?

There was a Health Card, so I looked the person up and contacted him. That's what I did. I returned the property to its rightful owner, who by the way, happened to be a man in a wheelchair. He had a normal sized head, but an extremely small body, and very odd-looking clubbed feet, not that that's important.

Was he thankful?

Of course he was. Wouldn't you be?

Tell me how much money was in the wallet, please.

Mom dabs her lips with a crumpled napkin.

It's important to do the right thing, she says.

I know.

You're my baby, she says. You'll always be the baby, Birdie. You know that? Promise me you'll always try your very best to do the right thing. Can you promise me, love?

I tell her I promise.

She keeps dabbing her lips. They're clean, but she's dabbing.

We've had a rough run, she says.

I know, Mom.

It's good to know my baby is going to do right.

I'm on top of Tess. My waist between her thighs, she's biting my shoulders. The couch in her basement is a grey futon. It feels like we're dry humping on a patch of stormy clouds. She's wearing a Slipknot tank, black leggings, her hair so orange and pretty it tightens everything inside me when I look at it. I pull the collar of her shirt, stretch it out, pull her bra down, start sucking her nipples. She smells like cherry candy. My guts twist like pretzels. She tells me to take off her leggings and panties, and I do, and she's hairier than I expected. Her legs spread, my hands on her knees. Her pussy looks like a Venus flytrap.

Talk dirty, she moans. Call me something disgusting.

No thanks.

Birdie.

I don't want to.

C'mon, ya fucking cunt.

Stop.

Stank-ass, big-nosed cunt.

No! Bitch! Don't be mean to me you stupid bitch!

Ha! That it?

You're the cunt. Bitch-cunt. I'll bunt you in your big, bushy cunt.

You'll bunt me?

With a bat.

We don't have sex because she says I ruined it like I ruin everything. We sit up. I just love her so much, it makes me feel completely crazy and incredibly sad, especially since she won't love me back. I reach for a hug but she pushes away. We sit on opposite sides of the couch. I try my best to think of something important to say. I need her to know I'm not as simple as she thinks. I ask if she believes in God. She laughs and tells me not to be so dramatic.

A bunch of us are standing along the end of Casey Lynch's driveway. It's two in the morning. We're dressed in black shirts, pants, and ski masks. I feel like a ninja. Each of us holds a carton of eggs. Franco points to the window above the garage and asks if that's where Casey sleeps.

No, I say. His room's in the basement. Just aim wherever.

Franco counts up.

One . . . two . . .

Sixty eggs lasts ten to twelve seconds.

After that we're running down the street as fast as we can. I'm the only one who keeps her ski mask on. It's hard to breathe inside it, but I don't care. I like it. I run faster. My muscles ache and I feel completely reckless right now. Sprinting like I did playing Cops and Robbers as a kid. My legs unable to keep up with me. I stumble, scrape my arms against the pavement. I start screaming. Not because I'm hurt, but because I can. Screaming, and soon the guys are screaming with me. It's like we're the only people left on earth, and maybe we're screaming for help, from God, or the aliens, or whatever else stupid fucking assholes believe in.

The phone rings early on a Saturday morning.

Hello?

Hey. I need to talk to you.

Tess.

I need to talk to you, like, right now, like in person. You dressed?

Do you need to tell me something bad?

Yeah, it's bad.

Tell me now, I say.

I really think we should meet up in person.

No. Just tell me.

She says she doesn't know how to say it. Then does. I cheated on you.

My eyeballs feel paper cut. I squeeze them shut. There's something gelling inside my throat, like wet packs of sand blocking my voice. Breathe in. My stomach feels like I'm about to shit it out of me. Breathe out. Ask, With a dude?

Birdie, what's it matter?

Tell me.

Yeah. A dude.

Did you have sex with him?

No. God. What am I, a fucking porn star? We only made out.

For how long?

I don't know. A long time, maybe. Like an hour, maybe.

I hang up. I sit on the edge of my bed, try my best to keep together. Sit. Just sit. I stand, run towards the wall and smash my forehead into it. My neck is sore. I start slapping the wall with an open hand, but it feels more like I'm giving it a bunch of high-fives.

I call Tess back.

Hello? Birdie?

Yeah. Maybe we should meet up.

Good. Can you come here? I can't leave my house right now.

Are your parents home?

Naw. Only Macy. That's why I can't leave. I'm like, watching her.

I'll be there in fifteen.

The air smells like sand. No clouds. Dead grass in front of all the houses. I walk, think about Mom. I remember when I was little and she wore her hair in a blond beehive. I'd pick at it, stab the tresses with my fingers. She'd look at me with mascara running down sallow cheeks and warn me my hands better be clean.

I also remember waking in the middle of the night with growing pains in my ankles. I'd call for help. Mommy! She'd be there in seconds, rubbing my legs and singing Rainbow Connection until the pain went away. And the pain always went away because Mom was magic.

Dad wasn't. He'd have me on the odd weekend and try the same, rubbing my legs. But his hands were so large, so warm, they made the pain feel worse. I'd have to pretend to fall back asleep. Fight the tears until he went back to bed.

Mom told me he proposed to her when they were eighteen. He drove them from Bush Flats to Port Wood-lot. He parked beside the lake. Carver was a baby in the back seat. Dad told Mom the lake connected to another body of water through an underground tunnel. That mobsters used to dump bodies there. The current dragged the bodies under and they got jammed inside the tunnel, never to be found.

Dad pulled out a ring he'd been hiding in a pill bottle. Sher, he said, you're the best thing that's happened to me, ever. And I wanna take care of you and Little Carve here, the rest of my life, forever.

Carver goo gooed and gaa gaaed, and Mom accepted, wondering what the tunnel had to do with her and Dad's now looming marriage.

I arrive at Tess's house. I knock on the door. There are bruises on my hand and forehead, but the only thing that hurts is my stomach. She opens the door and steps outside. We're standing on the front patio. Her arms are wrapped around herself.

Hi, she says.

I don't say hi back.

Her hair is flat, how I like it. She's wearing a white tank and sweatpants, and there are fluffy pink slippers on her feet with googly eyes and heart nostrils. If I wanted to kiss her she'd probably let me.

Who did you cheat with?

Why?

Who?

Philip McFoster.

Who the hell is that?

I don't know. He's in my Media Studies class. He has a fohawk.

I try to imagine what he looks like but all I can picture is a puckered anus.

I don't even like him, she says. And we were, like, high as fuck, if that makes a difference. I know it doesn't though. Like, I know there are no excuses.

Children play road hockey on the street in front of the house. Their rollerblades purr against the pavement. It reminds me of being young and dumb and oblivious, back when I'd eat ants on a log and Mom was infallible.

Tess can't even look at me.

Look at me!

What?

You're a miserable cunt, I say. A slut. A fucking germ farm. And you were never nice to me. Go choke on Philip's dick and die and get raped by a million dicks in hell, you bitch.

I turn, start marching towards the sidewalk. The front door slams behind me. Then I hear screams. I run back up the steps and start pounding on the door. I can hear her smashing something inside. Tess, I yell.

The door opens a couple inches. Macy is crying in the background.

Tess. What the hell. Are you okay?

Fuck off, she says.

I tell her to open the door. It opens. I can see she's thrown a candle pot through the TV screen. The door closes. She's standing in front of me. Her skin is white and she's totally winded.

Tess, I say.

What, she gasps, do you want?

Try to calm down.

Just go.

I can't leave if you can't breathe.

I fuck—everything—I fuck everything up, she says.

Me too, I say. Everyone does. Everyone fucks everything up.

She walks into me and waits for my arms to wrap around her. She dries her eyes on my neck and kisses it. I tell her I'm sorry for what I said. She's not a germ farm. She tells me to never let her go, but I do. I let go. Her hair doesn't smell good to me anymore. She enters the house, something else smashes. I walk home. I enter the house and pick up the phone and hold it for ten or fifteen minutes. I want to dial Quinlynn's number but she's in Montreal and it's long distance so I don't. I call Uncle Tony. I ask if Quinlynn's drawing of the toad is still hung above the scanner in his home office. He says it is. Cool, I say. I want to ask him if I can have it, but instead I tell him about the picture of Kelsey flashing her boobs on Facebook. He hangs up.

I visit Dad in Port Woodlot that weekend. He's grilling sausages on the barbeque out back. He's wearing work pants and a wife-beater, and he's shaved his beard since the last time I saw him, so now he looks about ten years younger.

You look good, Dad.

Yeah?

Yeah. You look like Minster.

Sher used to say me and Little Minster got the same mouth.

I'm seated on a deckchair near the door that leads into Harry's place. There are ants on the brick patio at my feet. I'm wearing shorts and the sun feels perfect on my shins. I try not to wonder what Tess is eating for dinner.

Dad saunters across the lawn. He stands beside the vegetable garden. There's a stone engraved in memory of Eddie in the soil. I can't tell if Dad's looking at it or the tomatoes. He calls me over. I take off my socks and walk to him.

Look, he says.

The stone says:

EDDIE

OUR SUPERHERO
1981-1991
WE WILL LOVE AND MISS YOU FOREVER
- MOM & DAD

What about it? I say.

Where's Soccer? he says.

Soccer doesn't have one.

No, he says. Where's Soccer?

Dad? I say.

He nods. He scrapes dirt from his boot sole against the memorial.

Stop it! I yell.

Dirt collects in the inscribed *DAD*. I check to see if Harry is watching from an upstairs window. Then walk back to the barbeque and check the food. The meat looks ready. I call Dad. One minute, he says. He's scraping his other boot. I sit down on the deckchair and cry. Dad asks what's wrong. I don't answer, so he asks again. He asks again and again, and each time presses on me more and more, until I can't even keep my back straight. I'm hunched, drooling on the ants.

Hi, Casey.

Hey.

I egged your house.

I know.

Did it take long to clean?

Not really. My mom did it.

I'm sorry.

. . .

Do you hate me?

. . .

Casey?

What?

I said I was sorry.

You're ugly. On the inside and out, you're pure shit.

Do you hate me?

. . .

Do you want to hang out after school?

. . .

Casey.

I do hate you.

Do you want to hang after school? I'm sorry.

. . .

Casey. I'm sorry.

Fine.

A month later Tess shows up at my door. It's past dinnertime. She's wearing a red tank, a black skirt and flip-flops. She's eating a granola bar. She asks if I want to go to the park. She says she has something important to tell me. I put on my shoes and ask if she's got another granola bar.

We walk down Batson. Chalk drawings on the sidewalk. The backs of our hands touch, knuckles scrape. She asks me how I've been doing. I tell her fine.

We arrive at the Lester B. Pearson playground. We sit on the swings. There are a couple of kids playing on the playground with their mother. A boy and a girl. Both of them are little orange-haired things like Tess. They're laughing loud. I laugh too. Tess asks what's so funny, and

I tell her it's nothing. She smiles, but barely. Points at the sky, both hands in opposite directions. Look, she says. I look. The sun is on one end, moon on the other. Both unclear under evening grey. I toss my granola bar wrapper on the sand. Tess pulls out a mint tin of cigarettes. She lights a cigarette and says, I miss you, Birdie.

Same.

Her toes are painted blue. She keeps cracking them. There's a tattoo on her ankle.

A tattoo, I say.

Yeah. My parents let me get it like a week ago, for passing my G1.

What is it?

An outline of a bell jar.

I like it. It's simple. I like simple tattoos.

She flicks her cigarette and scratches her head. I, like, really miss you, she says again.

Same.

Can I put my head on your shoulder?

Okay.

We sidestep towards each other until our swings touch. She puts her head on my shoulder. Her hair smells like Altoid-scented cigarette smoke. I don't know what to do, she says.

About what?

Everything.

Like what?

Philip, mostly. Philip McFoster.

I push her off me. What about him? I ask.

I don't know what to do about that crazy asshole, she says.

I look at her face. She took out her septum ring. It makes her look different. Older, better. She looks like a woman. Suddenly I feel small, like a child in comparison. I stand. I start to pace. She holds the cigarette up to me. I take it and take a drag, and cough.

Stop seeing him, I say.

It's not that easy.

Why?

It's just not.

It is.

He said he'd kill himself.

You're fucking with me.

He's very intense.

So let him kill himself. Good riddance, cock.

I, like, actually think he would though. You don't know him like I do, Birdie. He's troubled. His family really sucks.

So? My family sucks too. What does that have to do with anything?

The little boy on the playground slides down a pole. He lands awkwardly on his ankle, and falls, and cries. The mother runs to him. She examines the boy's leg, bending it gently. The little girl builds a sandcastle at the bottom of the slide, oblivious. Her castle looks more like an elephant took a huge dump.

Tess, I say. Listen. I want you to leave me alone, okay? From now on. Please. Just leave me alone.

I do leave you alone, she says.

You don't, I say. You came to my house. You put your head on my shoulder.

So what?

So stop it!

No.

Tess. Please.

Oh God you're pathetic. No one even likes you. I'm, like, your only real friend.

Don't be mean to me.

Your only other friends are Franco and Casey, she says. A sped, and Poo Thighs.

I try throwing her cigarette, but it slips through my fingers and falls on the ground behind me. I spit at her feet.

Don't you spit at me.

I spit again.

Cut it out! she screams. Cunt! You're pathetic. Your parents are both basically retarded and no one in your family, in the world, even gives a shit about you. I'm like, the only person who loves you, and I fucking hate you!

I'm walking away. I walk until I can no longer hear the little boy crying. Then I start running. Then start scream-ing. I'm running and I'm screaming and cars are honking at me and I don't give a shit. I shut my eyes. I wait for something to block me, to stand in my way. When nothing does, I open them. I stop running. I walk. I turn back around, towards the school, and I walk, and I run. I run back to the playground and the kids are gone and Tess is still sitting on the swing. I walk up to her. She's got earphones in her ears. She cracks her toes. I love her face. The sun's setting and the moon's rising and I love Tess's face. I want to bash it to pieces. Make her as ugly as I feel.

Hi, I say.

She takes the earphones out of her ears and says, Pardon?

Hi.

Oh. Hey.

What are you listening to?

A singer-songwriter. You wouldn't like her.

Why?

She's corny.

Can I hear?

I sit on the swing next to her. She hands me the earphones. Hot pink buds. I stick them in my ears and listen. Hiss. Lo-fi acoustic recordings. I shut my eyes. It's still warm out, but I'm shaking. I bite the inside of my cheeks so my teeth don't chatter. A woman sings about birds and squirrels. I take the earphones out.

Sounds like Tiny Tim, I tell her.

Ew, she says. I guess.

But better, I say.

We sit for a little while longer. A warm breeze sweeps over the sand. Tess stands, moves in front of me. She bends forward and wraps her arms around me. She presses her face on the side of my neck. She breathes into my neck. She lets go. She sits back down on her swing. I knew you'd come back running, she says. She's laughing when she says it, but not in a mean way. She puts her head on my shoulder again. Then says, Summer's already sucking balls.

But winter was cold, I say.

Aurora sucks dick, she says. I'm always bored. Bored all the time. Nothing to do in Aurora but be bored and bullshit around, and like, do nothing. I can't wait until college.

I kiss the top of her head.

She sighs. I love you so much, she says.

Tess can't see me, but I nod. Then stand, rub my hands together and blow air into them. The moon is clearer than before. I pick up the granola bar wrapper off the sand. I also pick up the cigarette. Where's the garbage? I ask.

I love you, she repeats.

Is there a garbage can somewhere?

Hey, what the fuck's your problem?

I raise my voice. I say, Where can I throw these things out?

Wow. Birdie, you're being a total bitch. I just, like, I just said I love you.

I'm walking away. She asks if I'm coming back, but I don't answer. She tells me my clothes are tacky and I have a big nose. I pretend not to hear her until I actually can't hear her. I'm standing too far away, over by the school next to the garbage. But I don't throw anything out. I walk home with it. I enter the house and search inside my room for all the things Tess has ever given me—the miniature Buddha, photocopied journal entries, a bouncy ball. I weigh these items in one hand, cigarette and granola bar wrapper in the other. I can hear Mom talking to someone in the next room. I leave everything in a pile on my desk, walk into the hall, into her bedroom, and find her sitting on the end of her bed with Love and Hope, and pictures of our family spread all across the carpet. Birdie, she says, come sit. And I do. I sit beside her even though it's totally fucked up and weird, and she's talking to the pictures, apologizing to them, to us, carrying on about how she wishes we hadn't ended up so *scattered*, and I'm nodding along, as if I agree and am in sync with every batshit crazy word she has to say, telling her it's okay.

It's okay, Mom. I'm still here.

21

I want to write a poem about my dying cat, but I also don't want to be someone who writes poems about dying cats. Minster tells me not to worry about being what I am.

What am I? I ask.

Someone who's about to write a poem about a dying cat, he says.

He's standing half-naked in front of the air conditioner with his arms spread like Jesus, like he's getting frisked. His black T-shirt's laid flat under Sugar-Nips on the floor. In the sunlight I can see the white scars on Minster's belly, zigzagged from when he used to cut himself with a drawing compass. For a moment I consider being someone who writes about that instead. Or perhaps cuts are no less sentimental than cats.

Sometimes stuff happens on cold, stormy nights, Minster says.

I know.

So just say it, he says. Say it was a cold and stormy night if that's what it was.

What are you trying to say? I say.

I'm saying write about the cat if that's what's true.

Sugar-Nips is a shorthaired British tortoiseshell. We adopted her when she was eleven. Now she's thirteen, which is sixty-nine in human years. That's the same age Saddam Hussein was when he died. I really, really hope Sugar-Nips lives longer than Saddam Hussein did, but she hasn't been eating her food. She won't even touch the salmon, or venison. Whenever she hears the can opener, she scurries under the couch and throws up on top of all the board games.

Lately I've been thinking a lot about *what if.* Like what if death could be something tangible? Maybe I'd lather it in food and medicine, and watch Sugar-Nips come back to life as she dies, her entire existence revolving in and around itself until she's both living and dying at once. Or I suppose we're all already doing that.

The only thing I know for certain is my cat's neck seems to be shrinking. I can almost wrap my fingers around it now, and I have very small hands.

Minster says my main problem is I haven't lost enough, which is mostly untrue. I've lost plenty. I've lost the key to our apartment six times, for example. I've also lost a pair of earmuffs on the subway. I've lost my temper, my mother's phone number. Final year of high school I lost the volleyball match that would've taken my team to the semi-finals. I lost my father that day, too. Not literally, but figuratively. He stood and stomped off the bleachers, slammed the gymnasium door behind him. And he was supposed to be my ride home. I never saw him again after that, in many ways.

You've never lost someone you loved, says Minster, accusingly. He thinks death is a competition, but only because he knows he's winning. He lost his beloved uncle three years ago. He's also lost three grandparents, and in all likelihood, a brother. Not figuratively, but literally. It's strange how closely death can cling to some and not others. I can't compete with that. It's difficult to compare a person to a pair of earmuffs.

Minster spoons Sugar-Nips on the air mattress on the floor. Her golden-green eyes half shut as I take a photograph of my fingers wrapped almost all the way around her neck. I show Minster the photo, the fingers, the neck. I need us both to understand the weight of what's coming. This isn't just a dying cat. After seven strong years, this is the first thing we're about to lose *together*.

I work at a design firm called Passion Couture. I hate telling people where I work because I hate saying the word *couture*. I also hate passion.

I just tell people I'm the creative assistant at a design firm. It's another way of saying I water plants and wipe crumbs off the kitchen counter. Occasionally I'll mount a poster, replace the mouthwash in the washrooms, but mostly just watering, crumb cleaning, making a difference.

I call Minster in the afternoon. I ask if Sugar-Nips has been taking her pain killer.

No, he says.

Have you tried giving it to her?

Yeah.

She still won't take it?

No.

Okay, well. Well—

Well what, Kate?

Well, I don't know. Can you keep trying?

Fine, he says, and after a short pause, I did something you're not going to like.

Okay?

Don't be mad.

Minster. What happened?

Don't be angry, but I sort of gave myself a fat lip today. Don't be worried, because I'm fine. I just thought I'd tell you so you don't come home and go, Where'd you get that fat lip? I'm telling you now so we don't have to talk about it later. I'm fine. Don't be disappointed in me, please. I love you. I know we'll get through this just fine. It's just sad sometimes because I love you and Sugar-Nips so much, and we're a little family, and it hurts to think about, but everything's going to be fine. I love you, Kate.

Minster, I say.

He hangs up. He can be rather abrupt. If I was watering a plant right now, I'd probably kill it, out of anger, melancholia, whatever, but I'm not watering a plant, I'm dusting the ping-pong table in The Imagination Room because that's the kind of place this is. It's the kind of place with ping-pong tables and Imagination Rooms, and in the fluorescent light of everything, it all adds up to be a bit much.

Sugar-Nips's examination, including hospitalization and X-rays, cost four hundred and fifty dollars, sixty cents. The medicine cost sixty-two dollars. I took the day off work, which cost me an additional ninety-six dollars. This evening Sugar-Nips had diarrhea on my pillow. It's cost us six hundred and eight dollars and sixty cents total to get to where we are, six hundred and twenty-three sixty if you include the cost of a new pillowcase.

Minster reminds me I can't afford to quit my job, but it's been done. I've always hated working there, and hatred grows when your cat's got a mass in her belly, it grows like a mass in my own belly, ballooning until I find myself in the CEO's office, slapping his desk with a dirty cloth to watch the dust envelop him.

Sugar-Nips sleeps on the black luggage beside the red IKEA couch. She looks like one of those Ethiopian children on television, if only those children were a lot smaller, and had tails, and were cats. I sit on the floor beside her, put my hand on her left front paw, the beige one, my favorite. The grey fur around it, graying. A new shade of grey. A deader, darker kind. But that one paw's remained the same beige, almost yellow, like the inside of an autumn red peach.

I tell Minster we can't afford option one, which is surgery, which is not guaranteed to work and may even make things worse. I tell him option one is no longer an option.

Minster tells me to touch myself. I am. I am for a really, really long time because I know he likes watching. I'm on my back on the air mattress touching myself, but every time I open my eyes, he's looking elsewhere. He's looking everywhere but where I am.

You too, I tell him.

Huh?

Touch yourself, too.

It's dark, but I can see he's soft, I can see his fat lip, I can see he's distracted by whatever's not there. I tell him to touch himself, I want him. I tell him to fuck me.

Fruit flies, he whispers.

What?

Fruit flies.

Fuck me, I say.

Kate. Do you see them?

I sit up and turn on the Christmas lights we have strung in a half-moon on the wall above our mattress. He stands, his pale, wounded body lit rainbow, his hands cupped over his genitals, blisters on his knuckles.

Do you see them? he repeats, but I don't answer. I try not to encourage these things, the him-seeing-things kind of things. I ignore it. I tell him it's late. I ask if he wants to carry Sugar-Nips to the bedroom so she can sleep between us tonight.

We have to put her down, he says.

I know, I say.

Remember when she was scared of the balloons? he says.

Yes, I say.

I wish I hadn't kept kicking them at her, he says.

Minster is gone by the time I wake up. I'm not entirely certain where to. He doesn't have a normal job, like a butcher, or a junior sales associate. He's a writer, which means he could be almost anywhere. He's what my grandmother might call a free spirit, or a nonconformist, or a no-good lazy bum, a busted flush.

The air in the room is biting, a stench other than Sugar-Nips. It's coming from a Tupperware container on the floor at the end of the mattress. The top of the container has been sealed with plastic wrap, pricked with tiny slits to let the stink escape. A half-inch of golden-brown liquid rests at the bottom. My tummy turns at first with a fear it might be Minster's urine, but it's not, it's actually apple cider vinegar. I start to recognize the smell from the last time I made cranberry chutney. I turn to Sugar-Nips, her emaciated face and the ribs showing through fur, and ask her, What's your pappi up to this time?

I find another container of apple cider vinegar on the back of the toilet, and about two-dozen more spread throughout the main living area and kitchen.

Fruit fly traps.

Sugar-Nips is still lying on the floor in the bedroom, her body spread to catch the coolness of the wood. I can tell she knows she's dying, but I begin to wonder if she knows what dying is. I wonder if I even know.

When I was thirteen, my best friend Lindsey returned home from Hawaii with a puka shell necklace she'd bought for me at a hotel gift shop. She gave me the necklace on the first day of grade eight. I wore it every single day for that entire year, up until graduation. I was standing in the shower an hour before the ceremony when the necklace broke. I hadn't touched it or anything, but the band snapped as if it'd been swiped and all the tiny puka shells twirled down the drain.

Sometimes I think maybe that's what dying is in a way. It's graduation day. It's something significant triggered to coincide with something else, something smaller that's breaking in the world.

I call the clinic and arrange to have Sugar-Nips put down. She meows, as if to say *thank you.* Either that or *bitch, don't you be putting me down.* I hang up the phone and wonder aloud, the way people do in movies sometimes. Sugar-Nips listens to the wonder.

I'm standing outside Passion Couture. I didn't mean to be here, but I am. I'm standing outside the front door wearing pajama pants because I'm unemployed and unemployed people do such things. We wear pajama pants in public and stare pensively at places we used to work.

Eventually the front door clicks open and Ocean Burns comes strolling out. Ocean Burns is a girl I used to work with. She wears a straw hat, a brown vest and leather boots with pointed toes because she's not only employed, but employed at a design firm, where people are often encouraged to dress like really, really fancy cowboys.

Kate, she says. Hi. What are you doing here?

I was just passing by, I say.

She pulls out a long, pretentious cigarette, and takes an equally showy drag.

Ocean Burns tells me, I totally heard what happened. God, girl, you've got balls.

I'm not entirely certain what Ocean Burns does at Passion Couture, other than that it requires a lot of ping-pong playing. One time she asked me to fetch her some coffee, however. I started barking, but she didn't get it. She was like, Whoah, what the fuck are you doing? and I was like, Arf-arf-arf-arf.

I remember her mug had SOCA MUSIC written down the handle. Other than that, the mug was blank. I brought it to the boardroom, the one with the glass table and swivel chairs, and placed the coffee in front of her. Ocean Burns was facing a projection screen set up at the end of the table, positioned behind the creative director. The word IDEAS was in all caps across the screen and there was a picture of a falcon eating a mouse underneath. I think the carrion was supposed to represent IDEAS, and the falcon, people like Ocean Burns, but I'm not entirely certain because I'm not a creative type.

Someone said, Can we help you?

I looked at everyone looking at me from behind thick-rimmed glasses and lens-less glasses and even sunglasses, and I told them I had an IDEA.

The creative director was one of the ones wearing sunglasses. They were hexagonal and tinted violet. He also wore a scarf with frills on both ends. It was summer. He said, Please do share.

I had no idea what they'd been talking about, but I shared nonetheless. I told them I had an idea for a restaurant where the waiters massage you as you eat. They stand behind you and massage your shoulders. It'd be optional, of course.

Ocean Burns spoke first. She said, Ew. I would literally throw up if some stranger touched me while I was trying to eat. That's literally disgusting, Kate.

Standing outside Passion Couture and my bum's all sweaty because it's hot and I'm wearing these flannel pajama pants. I ask her to take a picture of me beside the PASSION COUTURE sign, for the memories. She holds my camera phone as if it's infectious, like if she touches what I've touched then maybe she'll turn into a girl in pajama pants, too.

I'm posing for her. I'm flipping off the sign.

I'm seriously not taking a picture of that, she says. She hands me back the phone. God, she says, I swear to God, Kate. Seriously. You're so immature. You don't have the passion it takes to flourish at a place like Passion Couture.

Next morning I put on daytime clothes and meet my dad in the Annex neighborhood. He's wearing a black flannel suit and pink tie, and he asks me how Passion Couture's been, and I tell him *couturific*. He doesn't ever ask about Minster.

We're seated on the patio outside Futures. My dad talks at length about the department store he manages, and the price of leather belts and men's underwear. He uses clichés that aren't real clichés. Style's an unseen leaf in a smoldering tree, he says. I never know what the hell he's talking about. His lips move too fast, too frequently. He tells me my mom's grown *pudgy* and is beginning to look *rather dyke-like*. I ask him what I'm supposed to do with that.

I don't tell him about Sugar-Nips, that there's a mass growing inside of her, that her belly feels like a furry sack of pool balls. He probably doesn't even know I own a cat. All he knows for certain is I lost a volleyball match when I was seventeen, and now I'm twenty-five, and I live with a boy named Minster, who's a moderately successful young writer, who my dad once caught trying to burn himself over the fire at our cottage.

I ask to borrow my dad's cell phone because mine is cheap and doesn't get Internet. He hands it to me, and checks his watch. He points at the homeless woman across the street, the one strumming acoustic guitar and singing Joni Mitchell, and he says that's where artists end up, they all end up singing in the sun. He says it like it's a bad thing, singing in the sun, but the sun sounds good to me right now.

He asks what I'm doing. I tell him I need to look up an address, which is a lie. What I really do is Google *cliché finder*, then type *cat* into the search engine. I'm not entirely certain why. Perhaps I'm looking for a way to sum up the situation, oversimplify what I'm feeling and tie it in a nice bow. A list of about twenty cat clichés appears on the OLED screen and I'm scrolling through them. I look at my dad, and he looks back at me like he finally, finally sees me. Asks if I'm okay.

I tell him I'm as nervous as a long tailed cat in a living room full of rocking chairs.

He smirks, chuckles, calls me a cuckoo and looks past my face to fixate on the woman across the street, singing away in the sun.

You know what? he tells me. She ain't half bad.

I sit on a hill in Trinity Bellwoods Park under a tree in the shade. I pick the grass. That's what my mom taught me as a child, to pick the grass slowly, pull it from the ground without tearing the blade. I love the feel of the end popping out, the white tip.

I pile the grass on the ground in front of my legs. Every strand is green fading to white, our favorite colors; mine's green, Minster's is white. That should be the first red flag, when a boy tells you his favorite color is white.

I call his mother, Sherri. She told me I can call whenever I want. She told me she knows how hard it can be sometimes, but it's getting better, Minster's always getting better. But it's still something that'll never go away. She told me to call whenever the getting better seems to stop for a moment. I decide this is that moment.

She answers the phone after one ring. Hello?

I need her to know her son's not the only one. I'm sad too, I'm weird too, everything's just as hard for me as it is for him. The pile of grass is growing as I tell Sherri I don't want to see myself this way, the way I've been. I want to see myself different, creating things, turning straight lines into cartoon lightning. I see myself as someone who may go braless one day. I see myself happy, and unafraid.

Sugar is dying, I say.

Oh dear, she says. I'm so sorry, Kate. Are you guys okay?

Maybe, I tell her. We're okay, yeah. I don't know where Minster is.

She doesn't speak for a really, really long time. Perhaps she's waiting for me to add something, a *just kidding* to end the joke. I allow the silence to pile the grass even higher, until the bugs have a green and white mountain to protect their food under.

I need her to tell me Minster's fine. He doesn't need me.

Minster's fine. He doesn't need you. He's better now, he's always getting better. He'll be there for you when you need him. You don't need to worry. It's okay to cry now, Kate. It's your turn. It's your turn to cry. He's there for you. Cry.

I stand.

Sherri says it's taken her a long time to know what to do, how to be. She says some of us spend our entire lives learning how to be good people. But I'm already there. She tells me not to worry, I'm already standing right here.

Minster arrives home a quarter past midnight. It's been two days. He smells of alcohol. He tells me he's been writing. He doesn't have his notebook or laptop, but he tells me he's been writing in his head. The fruit flies were too distracting. He says he needed space.

I want to tell him never again.

He asks if I want to do it. That's how he says it, *do it*.

I've always wanted him to act more passionately in the bedroom, and I can tell he's trying more and more. He's sucking my tongue, pulling my hair and panting beer breath in my ear. He's touching my throat, barely. He tells me I look sexy, though it's dark and I've got hives on my belly. He rolls onto his back. I know he doesn't like being on the bottom, having compelled a number of exes to be sadistic with him under there. I make certain to be gentle, but he's got a look on his face like he's expecting a clout any second.

Do you want me to stop?

No, he says.

You sure?

They're everywhere, he says.

What's everywhere?

The flies.

Minster—

Kate, he chokes. There are flies everywhere.

Please, I say.

He doesn't say anything.

Love. Are you crying?

No.

But he is. He covers his face with his hands and sobs into them.

He says he's sorry, he's so, so, so, so sorry.

Love, I say.

He says, I don't know why I do these things.

He says, I promise I'll stop.

He says, Please don't leave me. I love you so much. We're a family.

I hold his head against my chest in the dark. I tell him I'm not going anywhere. He keeps saying he's sorry, and his tears are cold, and his hair smells the same as the city. I wonder what we'd look like in the light, him naked, sobbing on top of me, his penis shriveled inside the condom and a self-inflicted bump on his bottom lip. None of it turns me off. It makes me hold him closer, tighter, like maybe if I just squeeze hard enough, it'll bring everything and everyone he's ever lost back to him.

I finally wrote a poem about a dying cat. I wrote it in my head in bed. The poem rhymes *cat* with *fat, rat, spat, shat* and *bathmat*. It's a really, really bad poem, but I had to make it bad in order to make it memorable, my means to recall the lines come morning. That's when I'll make it better. I'll have a pen and paper, and the sun, splitting the curtains and shining light on everything, so I can spot and Wite-Out the weaker parts.

Minster woke up early this morning so he'd have time to write before we take Sugar-Nips to the clinic. I ask what he's working on, and he intones, *The caller called him Trigsly, so he knew who it was.* His answers are always elusive when he wants to shut me up.

I try to get Sugar-Nips to enter the travel cage, but she's not budging. Perhaps she knows what's coming and doesn't believe we're ready yet.

I lean close to her ear and whisper, I promise I'll take good care of your pappi.

She stands, wobbles, steps, but not in the direction of the cage. She turns toward the coat rack, to where Minster's set up one of the fruit fly traps. Sugar-Nips sniffs the trap, pressing her speckled nose against the punctured plastic wrap, and I see something inside. A small fruit fly bouncing between the apple cider vinegar and the plastic wrap enclosing it.

Minster! I say. Oh my god, Minster!

There's the clickety-click of him finishing whatever line he's on. Then silence.

What? he says.

There's a fruit fly in one of your traps!

Really?

Yeah, I tell him.

Holy shit. Really?

Yes, love. Check the others.

Together we scour the apartment, checking the others, calling out what we find. One more over here! Three in this one! Over a dozen in the trap under the kitchen sink! And I purposely don't look at Sugar-Nips the entire time. I want to give her enough minutes to make her way back to the travel cage and crawl inside, so by the time we're finished counting flies, she'll be ready, to go, to leave us, she'll meow as if to say *my job here is done*, as if to say *I love you*. And I know it's sentimental, love, more so than cuts and dying cats, but fuck it. That's just how I want things to end.

22

WHOLE FAMILIES
a short story by Minster Beally

The caller called him Trigsly, so he knew who it was. Whose syllables crepitated: Trigsly? That you, boychick? Trigger put four fingers in the holes of the rotary dial on the cabinet made of rift oak and considered it—*Trigsly*, what Dustin called him as a boy. He'd stand shirtless in the basement saying, Hit me, Trigsly. Hit me.

Trigger in the room his own sons used to sleep in. A room that was theirs, but now: the phone room, or: the room with the phone in it. And with phone in fist, Trigger pondered. He moved as he pondered (pondered himself to the doorway, then down the decrepit hall), with coiled phone cord stretching straight, receiver at hip, the caller still there: Trigsly? Hellooooo? Hello hello hello?

Trigger reentered the phone room (or: the room with the phone in it (again)). Sat on the mattress on the floor. Considered the doorframe, the growth of his sons still etched in the wood, considered his hands, contusions from a brawl with an electrical pole. He stretched his fingers out, bent them back in, then answered: (a guttural grunt).

Ah! Dustin exclaimed. Then: Ah-ha-ha! Saying (by way of shouting): My boy! Trigsly! You're there! Your mother's dead! Adding (rather gratuitously): Kaput! Poof! Buh-bye! (Clears throat.) I'm actually having a very very hard time with it if you wanna know the God's honest truth.

Hm, said Trigger. Then shut his eyes to conjure her: an image of his ma making porridge at the counter, in an apron cut from an old tablecloth, while humming Bing Crosby's Swinging On a Star. Trigger opened his eyes and punched a hole in the wall next to the Dumbo poster he'd purchased and placed to cover other, prior hollow points in the plaster. He punched Dumbo in the trunk.

Trigsly, Dustin continued (either ignoring the crush of elephant, or not hearing it), I'd like to show you where she'll be buried. It's important a boy sees where his mother'll be put to rest, boychick. Y'understand? You get what your abba's telling you?

(No.) It didn't matter. Trigger admiring the hole he'd just put in the wall, then shutting his eyes to see her again: his ma extracting a splinter from his heel. *Hold still, Coots McGoots. It's almost over.* Trigger held still. Lit a match to light a cigarette, still. And in that state, agreed to do the one thing he swore he never would.

It took two buses and a train to get there. He arrived midday, when the sun bounces so bright off the loam Bush Flats becomes blinding. Dustin waited in a handicap spot, seated on the front bumper of his Pinto, with arms folded, a still-corpulent frame squeezed inside a russet jacket with no pockets, its zipper missing, a shearling collar spotted with Dijon from whatever salami-included concoction he'd managed that morning. The two men shook hands. Dustin wore latex gloves on his.

In the car it was the same old thing. Like no time had passed. It hadn't been two decades, and Trigger was sixteen not thirty-six, and Dustin was as haggard and unhinged as always, still suffering. Couldn't make it past two intersections before he had to stop: cue left blinker, right turn, a quiet prayer that sounded Hebrew but could be gibberish (or vice versa). He circles the block, comes back around, counts to eighteen in his head and says amen before warily coasting through (no German cars in sight).

And in regard to German vehicles (and such things): Trigger was still affected too. This patchwork of pictures in his head, only his were malformed, mere interpretations of horror because he hadn't been there to see it for real. Like Dustin had told him the Nazis hung babies from barbed wire. They put the poor things up on a fence, Trigsly. Took turns shooting them down down down! So that's what Trigger saw sometimes. He saw it like he was there, but choppy—light-dark-light-dark-light—lit under some nebulous glow. Because the babies resembled his own. They looked like his youngest, a dozen baby Birdies suspended in a row.

Dustin parked on the lawn in front of the house on Haldoupis. From the Pinto it appeared the same. The front steps still missing, a 4" aluminum stepladder propped outside the door. Trigger breathed: (a guttural breath), as Dustin tugged the brake with a gloved hand, but kept the motor running, heat cranked, and uttered the first four words he'd said to his son in person in twenty years: You like hotdogs, Trigsly?

(Guttural breaths.)

Dustin informed him of the wallet in the glove box, asking Trigger to please grab it, which he did. It was

Velcro with a half-peeled Velcro strip. A patch of a wolf on the front, howling at a smaller patch of a crescent moon, and about thirty carnival tokens bulked inside the buttoned pouch. Trigger handed it over. Watched Dustin thumb through cash, receipts, old business cards, before reaching a terracotta-colored coupon folded in a square at the end of the stack. This coupon's for a free hotdog or sausage, he said, and you can have it, Trigsly. I want you to take it as a present from your abba. It's a present!

Trigger didn't bother asking where it could be redeemed. All he knew is it was the first thing Dustin had ever given him. So stuck the coupon in the slot where his license used to be and admitted it: I do like hotdogs.

And Dustin beamed, Good good! Of course you do! You're my boy. You're my son so we like the same things, Trigsly. We're family. We like the same things.

He was born in 1929: the year Popeye was created. Dustin liked Popeye a lot growing up. It's how he explained who he was to his sons. Trigger and Tony seated on their knees on the shag rug in the Gun Room, asking Dustin to tell them what he was like as a boy, and Dustin responding, I've told you already. I liked the Popeye cartoons. Haven't I already says that?

Dustin was born in Poland, but lived in Italy and Israel as well, before immigrating to Bush Flats, Toronto in 1951. But before that: WWII. He was ten at the start, sixteen by the end of it. Said it was the reason his body never grew the correct height. He broadened, but failed to reach *real man's stature*. His peak: 5'5 (or 5'8 on his toes with his chin held high.) Because the war occurred before-during-after his teens, through pre-pubescence and post. The lack of nutrition stunted him.

But by 1945 it was over. Dustin moved to Italy. Met older(ish) women. Slept with them. Kept believing in God. Considered God to be everywhere in Italy, in every woman with crow's feet trying to catch him. Sometimes he'd snatch back for varying amounts of money, booze, or both. He worked as a busboy, too. Fucked, and cleared tables. Made a living. He swore he'd never leave.

Then left to go help Israel fight for their independence in 1948. He was nineteen, 5'8 on his toes with his chin held high, a yarmulke clipped to his hair under his helmet, but by the end of fighting, he'd burned it with a blow-torch. Perforated the helmet with bullet holes.

You think Pa ever killed people? Tony asked Trigger when they were kids.

Trigger stabbed an ice pick through their neighbor's tire and shrugged.

I bet Pa killed lots of people, said Tony, but they were all bad people.

Dustin spoke of Israel even less than the Holocaust. He claimed he couldn't remember. Everyone's got a few grey years in them that keep too hazy to see, he'd say, and my haze is Israel, and always will be Israel. I swear I can't see a thing. It's too hazy, too hazy to see. Dunking his sons' heads under water as he said it. I can't see!

Pictures existed, though. They were sepia-toned with dye flaking at the edges. Fastened loosely inside dollar store frames and stood on the middle shelf of the curio cabinet in the front room at the house on Haldoupis. Dustin during the grey years (a.k.a. his haze): stood on one knee, rifle in hands. Or another picture: posturing beside a beaten soldier, whose body is battered on the gravel, as he (Dustin) stands over him (body) with fists flaunted at camera, a cigar bit between molars, and he's gloating, with bloodied-black knuckles.

Trigger and Tony had asked who the body belonged to.

Faggot wood, said Dustin.

You're just like Popeye! said Tony.

There was the sound of him washing his hands in the kitchen for thirteen minutes, exactly. Turning the tap on off on off on off on off before returning to the front room with wet, tenderized knuckles. He said, Sit, boychick. Make yourself at home, will ya?

Trigger stood beside the curio cabinet, where the photographs remained, but were barely visible, encrusted in cobwebs, lost time. He lit a match, lit a cigarette. Watched Dustin slump on the faux-leather recliner where the rocking chair once was. Dustin asking Trigger to please please please not smoke indoors.

Trigger nodded, but continued to smoke. And took a moment to take Dustin in: grey hair thinned and slicked, and rash on forehead, and skin tags like Braille around thickset neck. Dustin pointed at the couch. His hand dripping. Always adamant about the *fact* towels *cling to too much bacteria.* His breath: (crackling). The two men adrift in its phlegm-filled cadence. Trigger pinched his cigarette out, and pocketed it. He could tell by Dustin's fingers the water had been burning.

Why we here?

Sit, Trigsly. Sit sit. Sit down first.

What're we doing here, Dust?

C'mon. Dust? You're killing your father calling him Dust!

Trigger checked his watch. It had stopped ticking back at 10:16 a.m.

Sit. Please, just sit.

Trigger stayed standing, tapping knuckles on the curio door. A deliberate rhythm, while waiting for a proper reply. But Dustin kept his lips pressed, and head turned toward his own feet: raggedy slippers, white ankles, a pair of too-small sweatpants Trigger could smell from where he stood. Knocking a fist on the glass now, he wondered if Dustin's hands still hurt, or if his flesh had finally tailored itself to the sanitary burn.

Please, begged Dustin. It's important other things happen before we talk your mother.

Don't got time.

You do got the time! So sit sit. Just sit first. It's important we know each other again. So sit. And enough with the Dust! You're killing your father calling him Dust! So enough. Please. Tell me who you are as you sit.

Trigger had grown estranged from his own kids in recent years. His ex Sherri's word, not his: *estranged*. He had to look it up whenever she said it. Already knew what it meant, but still looked into it. Just one those words you look up to see exactly what the bitch is getting at, he'd explain to no one. Or to holes in the wall.

They'd been divorced six years. Her: with the kids in Aurora, and Him: still stuck in Port Woodlot where they all used to be. But things had changed. The walls, ceilings, such surfaces seemed haunted. As if his kids were dead. Had become ghosts, and Trigger, awake at night, might walk down the hall and think he sees one: a specter. One of his kids in flight in the murk. Either that or they'd be there for real. Given custody on an every other weekend, Trigger will find himself waking to the resonance of his Little Minster causing a ruckus in the kitchen. That same brand of clatter Trigger heard as a boy. Of dishes clanking. Of tap water running on and off, on off on.

He plugs his ears in bed and hums a monotone to drown it, the water splashing enameled steel, as either Dustin or his Little Minster (depending on the decade) scrubs endlessly, with bubbles overflowing, and their tears being shed scared and softly to the sound of the stuttering stream. (Hmmmmmmmmm.)

A tour of the house. Dustin presenting Trigger with pipes, timber, insulation, the spots things were and now weren't. He pointed at the Gun Room where guns once stood on stands made of poplar. Also: the living room table, the Seder plate. The transistor radio on a carpet of paper towel unrolled across the teak sideboard. And here's where Tony spilled the cranberry juice like a shmuck, said Dustin, and that's where my Audrey found the pigeon bones under the parquet. You remember that one, Trigsly? Your mother finding those bones?

It took Dustin several seconds to get a grasp of the string in the basement. He pulled too hard, and light swung their silhouettes over approximately fifty piled pairs of footwear. Trigger kicked through them to move. Moved to the center of the room.

Still doing this? he said.

Huh? said Dustin. (Louder.) What exactly am I still doing, Trigsly?

He'd hid in a Russian woman's attic from 1942 until 1945, but before that: shoes. They're how else he subsisted. Said they were protection. Dustin traded shoes for safety.

Trigger noticed a pair he'd worn himself as a boy. Black leather with brown toe caps, desert fawn laces. He remembered his ma winding those laces into bow knots as he'd kick his feet off the kitchen counter. Her: a pursed smile and berry-stained fingertips. Dustin showed Trigger where she died. On the floor in the basement bathroom without a door, no mirror. Just the putrefied sink she'd laid under, her gob opened so wide it was like the jawbone had broken loose. She was a protuberance of veins, tongue and dead eyeballs. Her face planted in soapsuds.

My poor poor Audrey, said Dustin. She was my muscle, my little matzo ball.

Trigger, having kicked enough shoes away, now stood on a circle of blank floor. He struck a match, he lit a cigarette, he shook the flame out and ordered Dustin to hit him.

What was that? said Dustin. I don't think I heard you right, boychick. (But undoing top button of pajama shirt as if he did.) Come again?

Hit me, Dust.

Dustin with his hands clenched, asking Trigger to please please repeat it.

Hit me.

Dustin stood in the washroom looking out, looking old, looking straight at his firstborn son, and burbled, I asked you to please not smoke in the house, boychick. Did I not ask you to please not smoke in the house? Did I not? Did I? Did I or not? Huh? What are you doing to me,

Trigsly? What's happening right now? Where's my son? Who are you? I can't even see you, my own son, I can't even see a thing past all the smoke in the room, in the air. It's choking me.

Trigger took a pull and said it a fourth and final time, and then the two men stood, breathing smoke and the stink of all those shabby shoes, the only sound being that of the heater, or the sizzle of Dustin's breath, slithering past mucus in his throat, the in and out of it, in out, gaining momentum, in out in.

His oldest had stopped joining the others on the random weekend. Carver, who Trigger called Carve, was nineteen that year Trigger returned to Bush Flats. A tall boy. Would've made Dustin ecstatic, seeing he had such a tall grandson. Size was important to him. Trigger and Tony's heights had been of a constant concern. Also: their calves. Dustin believed skinny legs were meant for pansies, queens, and fairy princess pansy queens, so drove his sons to the apartment buildings east of Bush Flats on weekends to have them run the stairwell. Fifteen flights, up, down, again, again, and after up and down and again, he'd wrap measuring tape around their legs and mark any difference on the back of a recycled legal pad.

A real man's muscles don't need much time to grow, he'd say.

Trigger told Carver about the stairwell. It was after he (Carver) got arrested three years before for having been caught squatting with his friend Daniel in the basement of an old lady's ramshackle home. Police called Trigger to come pick up his son from the station. It was two in the morning. Carver wore jeans and an undershirt, running shoes. Sat in the back like Trigger's car was a taxi. Lit a cigarette. They both did. Trigger drove fast. He turned onto Leeding Road, past the Port Woodlot woods, and drove faster. Your Grandpa used to make me and Tony run stairs, he said, for hours on hours. Wanted our calves bigger. You know how crazy that is?

(…)

Trigger pulled the car to the roadside, got out and ran around back. He jerked Carver's door open and repeated it: You understand how goddamn crazy that is, Carve?

Carver kept seated, belt fastened, and stared straight at the back of the headrest. He was sixteen then, same age Dustin was at the end of the war. Trigger palmed Carver's face, shot put his head across the seat. Unbuckled his belt and yanked him from the car by his feet. Carver hit pavement. When he got up, Trigger seized the back of his son's neck and shoved him over the guardrail so he'd fall face first into the shrubs.

You gotta quit blaming me for all the bad things that've happened, Trigger pleaded.

Carver in tears and bristles, yelling at his father to fuck off.

So he did: fucked right off. Slid back inside his car and drove. The speedometer rose to a tremor as he shifted gears and kept going and never looked back once to see if Carver had gotten up off the ground. Gaze forward, Trigger broke his hand on the dash. And drove on. Only seeing what lay in front. As if there were no alternatives. No such thing as a rearview mirror.

Dustin pulled out of the driveway, counted to eighteen and turned left. Shouldn't take too too long, he said. Kept his hands (in latex gloves) on ten and two. He used to be a bus driver, but that couldn't last, more than one psychiatrist deeming him too unfit to work, so from age forty-three on, was jobless, and at home, accepting a modest monthly compensation from the German government. Trigger's ma educated part-time at a nearby Toronto nursery school.

You're driving too slow, said Trigger.

Gah! Mind your business, will you?

Bush Flats waned in the side mirror. There was the fire crackle of Dustin's breathing, mixed with mid-afternoon traffic, and birds. They drove past the smoking patch, Mean Street and Holy Man Way, the lot in front of Coen Convenience. Trigger not speaking, until he did: Little Hermia's favorite number's eight, he began, cause the Charlotte Web book. So when she's young, she got taught times tables, but only bothered learning eights cause she liked eight so much. Put all herself into that. (Chuckles, straight-faced.) Didn't know much cause she was a kid, but when it came to eight, my Little Hermia was a goddamn genius.

Dustin's hands had slid to nine and three. He squeezed the wheel so hard his gloves ripped at the knuckles. He had big hands, especially for a man his size. Hairy hands, too. Used to spout diatribes on the importance of having hair on your hands and feet. He believed it meant good circulation. A true believer in the value of blood flow.

Trigger (stammering the question): So you got a story like that? (Looking at own hands.) About me or Tony? Or Ma? (Thumbing bruises on his fingers.) A story like the one I just told about Little Hermia and the number eight? Story like that about me?

What in the hell's a little hermia? said Dustin.

Trigger had called Tony the day before. Jane answered. Trigger? she said. She hadn't heard her brother-in-law's voice in seven years. Not since the Quinlynn incident: Tony hearing about it through the grapevine (a.k.a. Sherri), and showing at Trigger's place in Port Woodlot, pointing fingers, curling fingers into fists.

Tony there?

Trigger. How are you? said Jane.

Fine. You? Is Tony there?

Yes. One moment please.

(Whispers that sounded like psss psss psss.)

Trigger?

Ma's dead.

Yeah. I know.

I'm going to Bush Flats tomorrow.

Pa said.

You?

I can't tomorrow. I think I'll be there Monday but we'll see.

I work Monday.

Okay. Still at Home Repair?

When you see Ma last?

A couple weeks. Maybe two weeks ago.

She sick?

I saw her at your daughter's art show. Quinlynn had an art show at the Aurora Public Library. That's where I saw Ma last. And no. She seemed fine.

Dust didn't say how she croaked.

Jesus Trigger.

How'd she go?

We were at Quinlynn's art show, Trigger.

Yeah. Fine, I heard you, I get it. It good? They let kids do art shows?

I said it was at the Aurora Public Library. They do stuff like that. Showcase the talented young people in town. She's fifteen, Trigger.

I know her goddamn age. Stop saying my name.

Hardly a *kid*.

Okay. Fifteen's a kid. But okay.

So are you going to ask how she is? How your kids are? Ask about mine?

(The Quinlynn incident: Trigger hadn't gone about it his usual way. Was about to, but stopped himself. Put his belt back on, and buckled up. Then sat Quinlynn in the corner of the furnace room and told her to wait while he went and got something that *suited her better*. Returned with a blanket, and towel. And tossed the blanket on top of her to soften the blows. And hit her with the towel. Which was rolled. A bit wet.)

Why'd you call me?

Cause Ma died. Cause we're—I don't know—Ma died. That's why. And I saw the kids lots. Used to. Saw the twins, sometimes Birdie, lots. But the bitch won't let me see them hardly ever anymore. So how's that my fault, Tony?

You're right, Trigger. Nothing's your fault.

You're right, Trigger. Nothing's your fault. Fucking asshole.

I'm hanging up.

Hang up, fucking Baloney asshole.

After six detours (each featuring varying degrees of German car-induced meltdown) Dustin parked in the lot in front of a strip mall. Stepped out of the Pinto and started walking purposefully with hands in sweatpants pockets. Trigger followed, his eyes on shreds of baldness showing through the back of Dustin's comb over. They stopped in front of a hotdog cart outside a key cutter's shop.

This is it, Trigsly. The spot. Here's where you use the coupon I gave you.

Trigger scanned condiments along the front of the cart: coagulated ketchup, mustard, relish, Worcestershire sauce, horseradish, all scabbed around the edges of the caps. Dustin grinned bad teeth and tongue, an exhibition of lines under each eye. You go on and eat, he said. You're too skinny, boychick. Eat eat.

I don't got time.

C'mon Trigsly.

I got no time for this.

Time for what, huh? I try doing something nice for my boy who I love and he don't got the time? (Air quotes.) *No time*, he goes. (More air quotes.) *No time no time!* (Slaps own head.) Oy-a-gevalt, Trigsly! You get a hotdog and you enjoy it. (Hands together like begging, praying.) That coupon's a present for you from your abba. I'm your father, Trigsly, and a good boy does what his father tells him, no?

Trigger with his wallet flopped open, the coupon in the clear plastic slot. One Free Hotdog/Sausage (no drinks included!!!). He snapped the wallet shut.

Dustin had been his hero. His ma made sure. She'd sit by Trigger's bed at night, petting his shins through the covers and whispering stories until he slept. About how strong, brave, and handsome his father was. How one day he'd grow to be the same. She told Trigger he and his father had the same heart, and it was a good heart.

She said they'd been walking on Bathurst in the early 50s, a couple twenty-somethings new to the city, when this hulking man started following them down the sidewalk. Tossing words: anti-Semitic slurs. Telling the couple to go back where they came from. Get out of his country. Calling them yids, heebs, dirty no-good kikes. So it's Dustin with a fist for a hand, turning around and beating the hell out of the man (who stood nearly a foot taller), leaving the man's head looking twice the size it was, like a second head grown on top of the first. Trigger's ma said a police officer arrived on the scene, but they explained what had happened, and rather than arrest Dustin, the officer turned to the man on the ground and said, You know where you are right now, sir? What city, what country this is? Canada. Right here belongs to everyone. Right here's where all the people are good and free and belonging to be.

Trigger's ma said Dustin had protected her. He protected *us*.

It's important to fight back, she said.

The vendor handed Trigger an overdone wiener in a sesame bun grilled golden. Trigger held it to Dustin, in both hands: an offering.

No no no. It's yours, Trigsly.

Trigger forcing the hotdog into his father's gloved hands.

Trigsly, please.

This can't happen.

But I wanted to see you. I've missed you, boychick.

Bury Ma good. She was good.

It's important a son sees his abba, Trigsly. I'm alone. I'm done.

Trigsly—

Name's Trigger y'old fuck!

Gah! (Bites hotdog, mouth full.) You're breaking my heart!

Trigger burned a match and lit a cigarette and wanted to punch something but didn't punch anything.

You're my son. (Swallows, raps on chest.) It's good for a son to see his father.

Trigger thought: I see you. Trigger said: See you in all them.

What? See me what? See me in (Another bite, chewing) wha?

Trigger nodded, and spoke his father's full name, before turning toward the lot. He started walking, though he had no vehicle, no place to go. He checked his watch: 10:16 a.m., still. He kept his eyes straight. He didn't turn around. Didn't want to know if he was being followed. Or if Dustin had stepped inside a store yet. Or if he was still standing there, beside the cart, concentrated on his son's feet, counting the steps until they equaled a number that felt right, or right enough, for now, to carry on.

Time to time Trigger saw something else. He saw it the same as all those other things, like a memory that belonged to him.

Dustin had said the Nazis dumped bodies in the ground. They dug pits and piled people into them. And he saw the piles moving more than once. Men, women, and children, whole families, alive, buried breathing under the dead. This described to Trigger and Tony when they were still small boys, in the dark at night so there'd be nothing else to see. But whatever Dustin said: a nebulous glow.

He called his son Trigsly. It was meant to be mean, to belittle him. Forced Trigger down to the basement and said: Hit me, Trigsly. Hit me.

Trigger's been seeing it his whole life now, these piles of bodies moving. Sees them from the inside, though. Like he's under everyone, and the burden of their bones and marked flesh is too deep to climb out of. He tries reaching for light, but the bodies squirm and it keeps getting covered. Then black. Because that's what happens when the memory's not your own. You see it wrong.

23

Remember I heard nothing. He was in socks, no shoes. No sound of shoes coming my way's what I mean. So I didn't hear him coming.

I was in front the school. I'd go there to smoke, and clear my head. They had benches in front. So that's where I'd been. I didn't hear him coming, but then, there he was, on the sidewalk. First thing I said was, Where's your shoes? and he goes, Daddy! The kid, ten then, calling me Daddy. So I know something's wrong.

I got up, and walked quick. Up close could see he'd been crying. Or was crying, still. I hurt Eddie, he cried, hard, shaking. I hurt Eddie bad! I think he's dead!

It was night, November. The boy wasn't wearing no coat. I put my arms around him. Really. I did. Didn't gotta be told. He was blubbering against my shoulder.

You're fine, I said.

But Eddie—

Quiet, I said. It's fine.

I don't know what was happening, but I was holding him, I was, I know that much. And he was crying, and kept saying he killed Eddie, who's Harry's—who *was*

Harry and Sylvia's boy. I don't know what I was thinking, or what to do, so.

Remember the family tree? I think's what I said. You had to make that tree for Social Studies or what, so your mother made me sit you down at the table, and I showed you how people in our family's attached to other people in our family. And we talked about family lots, and how some don't got none. Some people aren't part of any tree. Either cause their family's dead, or've split, or them themselves've not had kids of their own. So some people are just broken branches pretty much, like limbs not attached to nothing. But not you. You're lucky. Remember. I showed you how lucky you are, to not be alone, but to be part of so many people. You'll always be one piece of a big big tree, Soccer.

I put my cigarette out on my buckle, and stood there on the sidewalk, and looked back at the bench. I tried to see how I'd appeared to him. Then looked down the street. Could see him still running. Far off now. A dot. The dot kept shrinking.

Half hour later my oldest ran by too. He stopped and stood where Soccer'd stopped and stood, but Carve wore shoes. He stared at me how Soccer'd just done. I got up. Started walking towards him. But he snapped back to it, whatever it was, and ran. So there was no time to've asked if it was true. Ask why Soccer'd been shoeless, calling me Daddy and that. Or ask if Eddie was fine. By the time I got to the sidewalk again, Carve was a dot too. Both my boys dots. Both them gone.

I struck a match with my thumb to pinch the flame, but felt nothing, turning opposite direction my boys'd gone, and headed back the way I came.

ACKNOWLEDGMENTS

Thank you:

Manners and Katos; Jennifer Duncan, Michael Helm, Catherine Bush, Sheila Heti and Russell Smith; the Toronto Arts Council; Greg and Siurong at Tailwinds; Max Bemis; MaHa, Bluddy, Hayja, Unagi Boy, B-Man, Jwa, Mr. Dumpling, Rawk-Steddy, Handsome Addie and all the Troublemakers in-between.

Goodly gratitude to Dylan Wagman.

Thanks from the most tender parts of my heart to Sara Flemington and little Cheesy.

Earlier versions of some chapters from *Most Perfect Things About People* previously appeared in: *Grain, EVENT, Ricepaper, Riddle Fence, Echolocation, Prairie Fire, The Dalhousie Review, The Antigonish Review, Little Fiction, untethered, The Impressment Gang, The Feathertale Review, PRISM international* and *The Fiddlehead*.

ABOUT THE AUTHOR

Mark Jordan Manner grew up in Aurora, Ontario, Canada. He holds an MFA in creative writing from the University of Guelph and a BA from York University. He lives in Toronto.